Of These Contented Hills

LETHA BOYER

*The Sequel to These Lonesome Hills
and Home in the Hills*

CAPPER, PRESS
Topeka, Kansas

◆

Published by Capper Press
616 Jefferson, Topeka, Kansas 66607

Cover Illustration and Calligraphy: *Catherine Seibel-Ledeker*
Production Manager: *Diana J. Edwardson Persell*
Editor: *Michele R. Webb*

◆

ISBN 0-941678-31-8

First printing, April 1992
Printed and bound in the United States of America

For more information about Capper Press titles
or to place an order, please call:
(Toll-free) 1-800-777-7171, extension 107, or (913) 295-1107.

Capper Fireside Library

Featuring
the most popular novels previously
published in *Capper's* magazine, as well as
original novels by favorite *Capper's* authors, the
Capper Fireside Library presents the best of fiction in
quality softcover editions for the family library. Born out of
the great popularity of *Capper's* serialized fiction, this
series is for readers of all ages who love a good
story. So curl up in a comfortable chair,
flip the page, and let the storyteller
whisk you away into the world
of this novel from the
*Capper Fireside
Library.*

Contents

Of These Contented Hills

CHAPTER ONE

Tension in the Air

*I*t was an early Saturday morning in mid-August so the weather was still quite warm, but as I stood before the open kitchen window of our log cabin, the breeze felt cool and fresh on my face. The sun shone brightly and in the nearby oak tree myriads of birds were chirping and singing. On the stove a pot of coffee was perking, sending its fragrance wafting past me.

I saw my husband approaching with his long swinging stride, a bucket of foaming milk carried in one hand. He wore faded blue jeans and a light blue work shirt that was frayed around the collar and sleeves, but that in no way detracted from his appearance. If anything, it added to it, I thought as I watched him.

He was a good-looking man, well-built, standing six feet two inches tall, slender but wide in the shoulders and with muscular arms. That came from all the wood he'd been sawing and chopping most of his life, I was sure. I knew the strength of those arms, but it was a strength well-leashed and controlled.

His hair was dark brown, his face bronzed from the summer sun. His jaw was square and his eyes were gray, and they could be as soft as a summer cloud or as sharp and cutting as steel. His lips were slightly full, and as he looked up and caught sight of me there at the window they parted over even white teeth with a smile of such sweetness that my heart stirred in my breast and my own lips began to smile.

1

"Hello, Handsome," I said as he came abreast of the window.

"Mornin', Beautiful," he returned in his soft drawl and passed on around the corner out of my sight.

I turned and watched for him to come through the door. I knew from experience exactly what he would do.

He was an early riser and often I did not hear him leave our bed, but I always woke soon after, perhaps subconsciously sensing his absence. I'd lie there a few minutes before I got up, knowing he'd be off to the barn to do the milking and feeding, and it would be at least a half hour before he returned.

He came in now and set the milk bucket on the counter, smiled at me and turned away to go through the door into the living room. I heard the sound of running water and knew he'd be washing his face and hands and shaving. Only then would he come to me and take me in his arms and kiss me.

I removed the coffee pot from the burner and took two cups down from the overhead cabinet. I poured two cups of coffee, took a jar from the refrigerator and added cream to my cup, then stood with my back to the counter as I sipped my cup of coffee. When he came back in clean-shaven and smelling slightly of after-shave, I indicated his cup of coffee with my free hand.

"I've poured your coffee for you," I said.

Instead of reaching for his cup he took mine from me, set it down and took me in his arms.

"I like a little sugar with my mornin' coffee," he said, and bent to kiss me.

After a short interval, he released me and reached for his coffee cup and stood sipping it. I took up my cup again.

"Hungry?" I asked him.

"Gettin' there."

"What would you like for breakfast?"

"Anything."

"Bacon and eggs? Or pancakes and sausage?"

"You decide. Either one sounds good to me."

"I think I'll fix scrambled eggs with sausage and pancakes, since it may be awhile before you'll be getting a full, leisurely breakfast again."

"Why's that?"

"Because, with school starting Monday, mornings may be a little hectic around here. You may have to get by with coffee and cold cereal."

I put my cup down and bent to take two heavy iron skillets out of the oven. He went over to the table and pulled out a chair and sat down.

"What have you got planned for today?" I asked him.

"Lewis won't be comin' this mornin'. He's got somethin' else he was wantin' to do, so I thought I might take Cal with me and saw up some of them slabs of wood we left layin' around."

"You will watch him, won't you, Davy?" I asked, feeling a little anxious. "He's not used to being around that big saw."

"He's gotta learn sometime, but I'll look out for him. Is he up?"

"Not yet. I thought I'd let him sleep awhile, since he won't have many more opportunities."

"What you doin' with yourself this mornin'? Want to come along with us?"

"Not this morning, Davy. I want to clean the house thoroughly, and then I hope I'll have time to do some baking. Will you be home for lunch?"

"I'll prob'ly bring Cal home then. Lewis is goin' to help me this afternoon."

"I'll have lunch ready right at twelve then."

A towheaded boy of twelve — still sleepy-eyed and

3

tousled — appeared in the doorway. It was Calvin, my husband's nephew, who had come to live with us just the week before. He was dressed in a rumpled short-sleeved shirt and blue jeans, and from their condition I guessed that he had slept in his clothes again. His feet were bare.

"Good morning, Calvin," I said. "Breakfast is almost ready. By the time you get your hands and face washed and your hair combed, I'll have breakfast on the table."

Obediently he disappeared from the doorway. Davy looked at me and grinned.

"Know how to handle him, don't you?"

"I hope so. I've had plenty of experience as a teacher. It shouldn't be too different as a mother."

I put breakfast on the table, and an hour later my husband and his nephew had gone off in the truck and I was left alone in the house, which suited me fine. I had plenty to do and I could get it done more quickly with no one else around.

About mid-morning, I heard a vehicle drive up and stop. Wondering if it was Davy and Calvin coming home early, I looked out the window and saw my mother and father getting out of their car. I hurried to the front door to greet them.

"What a nice surprise!" I exclaimed happily. I hugged Mama, reached up to give Daddy a kiss on the cheek, then stood aside for them to enter. "Come on in. This is wonderful. I was beginning to think you were never going to come to visit me."

I saw the look that passed between them and then I sensed tension in the air. Neither of them spoke.

"Is something wrong?" I asked, sobering.

"This is not a social visit," my father said, his voice cold and clipped. He followed Mama inside and stood rigid, his arms stiff at his sides, his eyes avoiding mine. I looked at Mama. Her eyes were downcast.

4

"What is it?" I asked, beginning to feel alarmed.

"Don't pretend you don't know, young lady," Daddy said.

"For heaven's sake, James," Mama said in exasperation. "Can't we even give our daughter a decent greeting before you start in?"

"I am in no mood for small talk," he snapped back.

"That at least is obvious."

My heart sank and all my happiness about this unexpected visit evaporated. I felt certain I knew why they had come.

"What is it, Mama?" I asked quietly.

"It's this marriage your sister is planning."

"I see. Well, come on in and sit down. Would you like a cup of coffee or perhaps a snack? You must have started fairly early to get here so — "

"Nothing for me," Daddy interrupted, his voice clipped. He seated himself at one end of the sofa, his eyes averted from me. I was hurt. A lump started to rise in my throat, but resolutely I swallowed it.

"Mama?"

"Coffee sounds good, Dear," she said.

She sat down at the other end of the sofa, as far away from my father as she could get. Both of them sat staring.

"It won't take a minute," I said. "Excuse me."

I went into the kitchen and made fresh coffee. Through the open door I heard the murmur of my mother's voice and the subdued but impatient reply of my father, but I couldn't hear what they were saying. I took a deep breath to calm myself before I joined them.

"Did you just hear about Liz and Jim's engagement then?" I asked, seating myself in one of the rockers.

"Liz came over and told us last night," Mama replied.

"I suppose you've known all along," Daddy said.

"I've known for a couple of weeks."

"And it never occurred to you that we might like to know what was going on?"

"I assumed you knew she was seeing Jim. Anyhow, it was her place to tell you, not mine."

"I might know you'd take that attitude, after the example you've set for her."

"What do you mean, Daddy?"

"Did you inform us of your plans when you decided to get married? Oh no, you call us up one Saturday and say you're getting married the following Saturday, come or don't come. You could've cared less."

"I didn't know myself before then, Daddy. We decided — rather suddenly."

"I'll say you did. You knew we wouldn't approve. That's why you rushed into it the way you did."

"That wasn't the reason."

"Did you let us know what you were planning, give us a chance to get acquainted with the man you were going to marry, give us a chance to talk it over with you, perhaps advise you? Oh no. What you did was none of our business. The way you rushed into it, what were we to think but that you <u>had</u> to get married?"

"Daddy!" I exclaimed, shocked and hurt.

He rose and began to pace around the room. Mama and I exchanged glances, but she said nothing.

"Why you had to come out here in the first place is beyond me," Daddy continued. "You had a good job, a respectable job. You had a good home and a decent man who wanted to marry you, but you had to throw it all away to come out here to this god-forsaken hole to teach a bunch of dirty, ignorant kids in a dingy little one-room school. Then, as if that's not bad enough, you disgrace us all by marrying an illiterate, backwoods hillbilly with no future who makes cabinets for a living."

"I haven't disgraced anyone," I exclaimed hotly, "and

6

Davy is not illiterate and what's wrong with making cabinets for a living? It's honest work and it takes skill. You couldn't make a cabinet if your life depended on it!"

I felt ashamed the moment I said that, but he didn't give me a chance to retract it.

"And what's the first thing your hillbilly husband does after he marries you? Foists his sister's illegitimate kid off on you."

"Davy didn't foist his nephew off on me! I was the one who wanted Calvin."

"Then more fool you."

"You're entitled to your opinion," I said, striving for calm. "I'll remind you, however, that you are in Davy's house now and I am his wife and I will not sit here and listen to you abuse him. Now if you — "

"Some house," Daddy snorted, interrupting me. He glanced rather contemptuously around the room. "A log cabin in the backwoods. Nobody who is anybody lives in a log cabin anymore."

"I don't happen to agree with you, but that's beside the point. You came here specifically to say something to me about Jim and Liz, I gather, not to make derogatory remarks about my husband and my home. What was it you wanted to say to me?"

"Just this. I want you to put a stop to this marriage your sister is planning."

"What makes you think I can do that?"

"You can do it because you're the one who got it all started in the first place. I saw your fine hand in this from the beginning. It's not enough that you've ruined your own life. Now you've got to ruin your sister's, too, by trying to get her tied to your husband's best friend. It's understandable that you, with your education, would find life out here among these yokels intolerable after the novelty wore off. We could have warned you of that if

7

you'd discussed it with us. As it is, you've made your bed, now you have to lie in it, but I see no reason why your sister should have to lie in any bed of your making."

"I'm going to ignore most of that, Daddy, because you don't know what you're talking about. I'm not unhappy with the decisions I've made and I certainly haven't made any decisions for Liz. Contrary to what you seem to think, I did not promote this marriage between her and Jim."

"You expect me to believe that, when you wrote that letter inviting her here to your open house and telling her there was a man out here who wanted to meet her? You knew just what to say to pique her interest, and don't tell me you hadn't told him all about your sister, either. Otherwise, why would he want to meet her?"

I found it impossible to reply immediately. The way he put it, it did sound as if I had deliberately plotted to get them together.

"Can you deny that she met him right here in your house? That you introduced them?" Daddy demanded.

"No. I don't deny that, but just because — "

"Don't make excuses. It's obvious what you've done, but I'm telling you right here and now, I won't have it, do you hear? Your mother and I — "

"Speak for yourself, James." My mother interrupted, speaking for the first time. "I'm as concerned about Liz as you are, but I don't blame Anne, just because she introduced them. Liz has been introduced to any number of men without becoming engaged to them. She's twenty years old, capable of making her own decisions. Just because Jim happened to take her fancy — "

"Capable!" my father burst out, turning on her. "You call it capable, getting herself engaged to an illiterate nobody with no background and no future?"

"Jim is not illiterate, any more than Davy is," I interjected. "You have to understand that out here — "

8

"I don't have to understand anything!" Daddy roared at me. "You're the one who has to understand. I will not have your sister throwing herself away as you have done! By heaven, he's even worse than the man you married! He's uneducated, with no background and no future, an errand boy in a lumber store, with one failed marriage behind him already. What kind of father would I be to allow my daughter to marry a man like that?"

"As Mama said," I said a little doggedly, "she's twenty. I'm afraid that's a decision she can legally make for herself."

Daddy shook his finger in my face. "You put a stop to it, do you hear me? I don't care how you do it, just do it." He turned to Mama. "Let's go," he said.

Mama rose to stand before him, her face set in lines of determination. "I'm not ready yet," she said. "I haven't had my coffee and I'd like a cup before we start back."

Daddy stood glaring at her, taken aback at the stand she had taken. Mama had always tried to be a submissive wife.

"You can wait in the car if you like," she continued. "I won't be long."

Daddy turned on his heel and marched to the door. His hand on the latch, he paused and turned back to me.

"If Liz marries that — that ignoramus, she's no daughter of mine." He pushed the screen open and paused again. "And neither are you!"

After he was gone, Mama and I stood silent and looked at each other.

"Well," I said then. "I guess now I know why you haven't come to visit me since my marriage." My voice broke on the last word and tears blurred my eyes. Mama came over and put her arm around me.

"I'm so sorry, Honey," she said.

"I think he hates me," I sobbed, wiping my eyes.

"He doesn't. He's just upset, and you know how he is when he gets upset."

"I knew, of course, that he wasn't too happy about my marriage, but I didn't know he felt that strongly about it. He didn't say anything when I visited you in the spring."

"This thing with Liz has really upset him. He doesn't like Jim. I'm afraid I — well, he didn't realize Liz was seeing Jim regularly and I didn't tell him."

"I really didn't promote their marriage, Mama," I said, drawing a deep breath. My emotions were under control again. "I know it must seem like it. I did write and tell her Jim wanted to meet her, but I never dreamed — "

"I'm afraid it happened at just the wrong time for Liz. She had been seeing another young man, thought she was desperately in love and was talking marriage, but something happened, I don't know what. Anyhow, they broke up and Liz took it hard. She was just ripe for something headstrong and foolish."

"I didn't know."

"No, I know you didn't. I just wish she wouldn't jump into this marriage so soon. It worries me."

"Rebound, you think?"

"I'm afraid so."

"Jim has an unhappy experience behind him, too, you know."

"Did you know his wife?"

"Yes. That is, I met her. I didn't really know her. Davy knew her fairly well, though."

"What was she like?"

"She was — not very friendly. At least, she never was to me. She was often jealous and she didn't like the country. Davy could tell you more than I can. I do know he felt she was more to blame for the failure of the marriage than Jim was. She married again soon after the divorce."

Mama sighed. "I like Jim. Who wouldn't? Except your father, of course. But I'll admit I'm concerned. I hope Liz is not making a terrible mistake that she'll regret the rest of her life. Well, I'd better not keep your father waiting. He's upset with me enough already."

"I'm afraid you're in for a very uncomfortable trip home."

"It can't possibly be any worse than the trip coming. I tried to get him to wait, to give himself time to cool off before he came, but you know your father. I wouldn't have come along except that I hoped my being here might help. I'm afraid it didn't, though."

"I'm glad you came anyhow. It's good to see you, even if it isn't under very pleasant circumstances."

"Anne, Honey, I know he's hurt you, but just remember, he always says more than he means when he's angry. He was hurt by your marriage, too, and the suddenness of it. That's been building up in him for a long time now."

"I'm sorry, Mama. I never meant to hurt either one of you. I'm afraid I didn't think that much about it. When Davy and I discovered we were in love there seemed no reason to wait. I guess we were selfish. I'm sorry."

"No need to apologize to me, Dear. You were of age and Davy is a fine person. I wasn't shocked when you called. I knew which way the wind was blowing when we visited here last fall. Unfortunately your father didn't. He hoped you'd marry Don Bradford."

"I was never in love with Don."

"I know, but Don wanted to marry you. He had talked about it to your father."

"I never gave him any encouragement to do that."

"I know. May I take just a quick peek through your house before I go, Anne?"

"Of course, Mama. I wish you could stay longer."

"Maybe next time."

"If there ever is a next time."

"There will be. I've gone along with your father so far because it was easier, and I thought he would soon become reconciled to your marriage. If he never does, well then, I might consider my own little private revolution. I don't intend to be permanently estranged from two of my daughters."

"I'm glad. I'll go pour you a cup of coffee while you look around. You can stay that much longer, at least."

I went into the kitchen and poured two cups of coffee and added cream. I had been baking cookies so I put a few on a plate and set them in the middle of the table. A minute later, Mama joined me.

"You've got the big country kitchen you've always wanted," she said with a smile. "Your house is delightful. I love it. You've made it into a real home."

"Thank you. We like it. Davy built it according to our own plans, you know. Sit down, Mama."

"Where is Davy, by the way?"

"He and Calvin are off somewhere cutting wood. We burn wood for heat here in the winter and it takes a lot. I'm glad he's not here. I'm not going to tell him how Daddy feels about him. It is wrong and unfair. Davy is a wonderful husband."

"Yes, Dear, I'm sure he is. Hopefully, your father will realize that someday. How is it working out with Calvin?"

"Very well. He's a sweet boy, and no trouble at all."

"Are you looking forward to the start of school?"

"Yes, I am. It starts Monday, you know, a couple of weeks earlier than the city schools. Daddy doesn't seem to understand why I came out here to teach. Do you, Mama?"

"I think so. You wanted adventure, something new and different."

"Not just that. There are plenty of good teachers in St. Louis, but out here they sometimes have a hard time finding good teachers because it's so isolated and it's more difficult to teach all eight grades. I know I'm a good teacher and I feel these children deserve just as much of a chance for an education as city children do. Even if they don't go beyond eighth grade, and the majority of them won't, I can give them a good basic education. Even if I never teach them more than just how to read and enjoy a good book, I've accomplished something. You don't know how many people out here can't even read, or at least can't read well. I'm doing something that I feel is worthwhile, something I enjoy. I'm just sorry Daddy seems to feel I've thrown my life away. I don't feel that I've thrown anything away and I certainly don't regret my decision to marry Davy."

There was the impatient honk of a horn. Mama and I both jumped.

"You'd better go," I said regretfully.

Mama shrugged. "I'll tell him I was trying to use a mother's influence," she said. She took a sip of coffee, then looked at me uncertainly. "There is just one question I'd like to ask before I go."

"What is it, Mama?"

"Remember when we were here before, when Davy's family had that get together and your father and Don and I came?"

"Yes."

"Remember before I left, I asked you about your relationship to Don and you said the reason you invited him was because you wanted it to appear as if you had a fellow waiting for you, and one of the reasons, if I remember correctly, was because a certain young married man was being attentive to you. Was that young man Jim Baker?"

13

My heart sank. I'd forgotten about that. It was going to be a difficult question to answer.

"Yes, it was, but I think maybe I blew that incident out of proportion. He was having problems in his marriage and just wanted to talk. Anyhow it only happened that once. I asked him not to come back and he didn't."

"Liz told me he thinks a lot of you."

"He and Davy have been friends for a long time and Jim and I are friends, too, that's all."

"That young man seems to fall in and out of love a little too often to suit me. I hope Liz knows what she is doing."

"Yes. I hope so, too. However, I am not going to deliberately try to break them up as Daddy wants me to."

"No, of course not. You don't have the right to do that."

The horn sounded again. Mama finished her coffee and got to her feet. I rose, too, and she came over and hugged me.

"I'm so sorry all this has happened," she said again. "Your father will be sorry, too. Unfortunately he's never learned how to say so. 'Bye, Dear. Tell Davy and Calvin hello for me, and give them my love. I'll write."

"Please do, Mama."

"Take care of yourself, and remember, Anne, water under the bridge."

"I'll try, Mama. 'Bye."

She hurried out and I watched from the doorway. Daddy started the car and Mama barely had her door closed before he drove off, staring straight ahead. Mama waved and I waved back, then I went and sat down in the rocker, my chin in my hand. As I stared into space, my thoughts were rather chaotic.

CHAPTER TWO

Not An Outsider Anymore

I was still sitting in the rocker when Davy and Calvin came in through the back door. I jumped to my feet and looked at the clock in consternation. I had been sitting there doing nothing for almost an hour.

"Is dinner ready?" Davy asked, frowning. He looked hot and tired and perhaps a little irritated. Calvin stood behind him and seemed to be trying to shrink out of sight. "We're runnin' late and I'm supposed to meet Lewis in half an hour," he added.

My feelings already bruised, I felt his words implied criticism. Quick tears sprang to my eyes, and I turned away so that he wouldn't see.

"I'm sorry," I managed to say. "I lost track of the time. I'll get dinner on while you wash up."

I was aware that he took a quick step toward me, but I brushed past him and hurried to the kitchen. Half blinded by tears, I went to the refrigerator and took out a piece of leftover roast beef. I put two plates on the table and two tall glasses, then took a loaf of bread from the bread box, and stood at the counter to make some sandwiches. Davy came up behind me and put his hands at my waist.

"Somethin' wrong?" he asked, and would have bent and kissed me on the cheek, but I turned away and put the plate of sandwiches on the table.

"You can start on the sandwiches while I get the rest of it ready," I said. "Do you want coffee or milk?"

"Milk," he answered, looking puzzled at me. Calvin

came in and they both sat down. "Ain't you eatin'?" he asked then, evidently noticing that I had set only two plates.

"I'm not hungry. I'll eat later."

I went to the refrigerator again and took out a bowl of cottage cheese and a jar of peaches. I put the peaches around the edge of the bowl and set it on the table, avoiding my husband's eyes. I sliced tomatoes and put them on the table, then poured milk into the two glasses.

"Will that be enough?" I asked them.

"That'll be fine," Davy said. "Are you sure you won't eat with us?"

"I'll eat later. Excuse me. I — I have something I need to do in the other room."

I went through the living room and into our bedroom and closed the door. I sat down on the side of the bed and fought with the tears that crowded up behind my eyes and the lump that seemed to obstruct my throat. When I felt I had them conquered, I went back to the kitchen.

Davy's glass was empty so I refilled it. I took some cookies out of the cookie jar, put them on a plate and put the plate on the table, then I drew a chair out and sat down.

"Well, how did it go this morning?" I asked, forcing my voice to lightness. "Did you get a lot of wood cut?"

I glanced at Calvin just then and saw the quick, wary glance he gave Davy.

"Some. Not a lot," Davy answered after a slight hesitation.

"I see. Would you like a cookie, Calvin?"

He took a cookie but couldn't seem to draw his eyes from Davy's face.

"If you're done, Cal, you can take your cookie out in the backyard," Davy said quietly and Calvin rose quickly and almost ran out.

"What happened?" I asked. "Did he get into some kind of trouble?"

"Jist about got himself killed with his daydreamin'. Durn near walked right into the saw."

"Oh!"

"Couldn't get anything done for havin' to watch him all the the time. Worse'n havin' a two-year-old underfoot. I'm leavin' him home with you this afternoon."

"Then I think, if you have no objection, I'll take him in to visit Granny Eldridge this afternoon. With school starting Monday, we may not have a chance to go again for awhile."

"Might be a good idea." He reached for a cookie, then looked directly at me, holding my eyes. "Want to tell me what's happened to upset you?"

I looked down at my hands lying on the table. For the first time, I didn't want to confide in my husband. I was hurt and I wanted to be alone so I could come to grips with this on my own.

"Was it somethin' I done?"

"Did," I corrected automatically.

"Did then. Was it something I did?"

"No."

"Are you gonna tell me why you been cryin'?"

I felt again the sting of tears behind my eyes. I bit my lower lip to stop its trembling. Davy's hand came over and covered mine.

"My mother and father were here this morning," I said finally, reluctantly.

"Your folks was here? Did they leave already then?"

I nodded.

"Is somethin' wrong?"

"They're upset about Liz and Jim, especially Daddy. He seems to think it's all my fault, that I planned and promoted their engagement."

17

"What makes him think that?"

"That letter I wrote inviting her here for our open house and telling her Jim wanted to meet her."

"You invited them out, too."

"I know, but — " I rose and began to clear the table, avoiding his eyes. "I really don't want to talk about it right now Davy, do you mind? It's time for you to meet Lewis and I have some things I need to get done, too, before I can take Calvin in to Granny's."

Davy rose and came and put his arms around me from behind. I leaned against him for a minute, fighting back tears, then I straightened and went to the sink and began filling it with water. I kept my back to him.

"I don't have to go back this afternoon if you want me to stay here," he said.

"I'm all right, Davy. Really. You go on to work," I said, willing him to go and wanting to be alone.

"You're sure?"

"I'm sure. I'll see you tonight. I'll be back in time to fix supper."

"Okay, Honey. I love you."

"I love you, too, Davy."

He put his arms around me from behind again and put his cheek against mine. "We'll talk tonight, okay?"

"Yes."

Davy left then. I felt anxious to be away and off somewhere where I could be alone. I stacked the rest of the dishes beside the sink, dried my hands, and went to the back door to call Calvin. He was sitting on the tire swing Davy had put up for him under the big oak tree.

"Calvin, I want you to come in now and get cleaned up," I said. "I'm going to take you in to Granny's. Hurry now. I want to leave in just a few minutes."

I went back inside and into my bedroom to change my clothes. When I was ready, I gathered up my purse, got my car keys ready, and went back into the living room. Calvin's door was closed.

"Are you ready, Calvin?" I called.

There was no answer, so I knocked lightly on the door and called again. Silence. I pushed the door open. He was not there.

He wasn't in the bathroom either. I stuck my head out the back door but he was nowhere in sight. I called again but there was no answer.

I went through the house and then through the backyard and around to the front, calling. Calvin was nowhere to be found. I was puzzled but not alarmed. Perhaps he was waiting in the car.

When I went to look, the car was empty. I put my purse on the front seat and the keys in the ignition and stood there with the car door open, looking around. There was no sign of him.

I closed the car door and went around the house again. I found no sign of him, but in the distance I saw my mother-in-law, Clemmy, hanging clothes on the line. I decided to see if she had seen Calvin. I walked the short distance to where she was.

"Clemmy, you haven't seen Calvin, have you?"

She paused, wiping her arm across her perspiring face. The August sun was hot and the clothesline was right out in the open. The clothes hung limp on the line, and there was not a stir of a breeze.

"I ain't seen him," she said with a tired sigh.

"This is really strange," I said, bewildered. "I called him in to get cleaned up because I was taking him in to town, and the next thing I know, he's disappeared. I can't find him anywhere."

"He's probably jist wandered off somewhere close by and got to daydreamin' an' forgot."

"Yes, he could have done that, of course." I smiled at

her. I was very fond of my mother-in-law. "Well, I'll find him sooner or later. Thank you, Clemmy."

I walked back home and did some more searching and calling with no results. I was becoming alarmed. Surely nothing bad could have happened to him in our own backyard.

I finally got in the car and drove to where I knew Davy was working. He and Lewis were sawing long slabs of wood into shorter pieces. When Davy saw me he turned the saw off and came to meet me.

"What's wrong?" he asked.

"The strangest thing. I called Calvin in to get ready, then he just disappeared. I've looked everywhere and I've called and called and he's nowhere. I thought there might be a chance he had come back here."

"No, he's not here."

"What on earth — "

"What did you say to him?"

"What did I say? Just that I wanted him to come in and clean up because I was taking him in to Granny's."

"You said it jist like that?"

"Yes. I think so. What difference does it make how I said it?"

"I chewed him out pretty good this mornin' for not lookin' where he was goin'. You can't afford to do that around a saw. Then you suddenly announce you're takin' him in to Granny's. You don't s'pose — "

"You think he thought I was taking him back to leave him with Granny?"

"Might've."

"Then he's run away?"

"Looks like it."

"But where could he be?"

"Could be anywhere. He knows these woods jist about as good as anyone. Well, looks like I ain't gonna get the rest of this wood cut today after all. Lewis, want to come help look for a runaway boy?"

Lewis came toward us, his face sober. He was a smaller man than Davy, quiet-spoken and mannerly. "Calvin?" he asked.

"Yep. Calvin."

I stood and waited while the men did some clearing up, feeling terrible about the way I had frightened Calvin. I had been so wrapped up in my own misery that I hadn't even thought how my words might sound to an insecure little boy. Davy was frowning when he came back to me, stripping off his gloves.

"Lewis'll take his team and drive to Granny's house to see if he's gone there. He'll drive by the school and keep his eyes open. I'll leave the truck here and go back with you. He might be hidin' out in the barn or somethin'."

We got into the car and drove silently back to the house. I went through the house and the yard again and Davy went to the barn. There was no sign of Calvin.

"Th' pup here?" Davy asked.

"He's here."

"Then I think it's safe to say he ain't far away. Mom hasn't seen him?"

"No."

"Dad not around?"

"I haven't seen him. Davy, you don't think — "

"Dad wouldn't do away with him, if that's what you're thinkin'. He's around somewhere, prob'ly in the woods."

"But what if it gets dark and we still haven't found him?"

"He's used to bein' on his own. He knows how to take care of himself."

"But he's only a little boy!"

"We'll find him. I'll go look in the woods back of the house. You better stay here. Lewis'll be comin' back soon with the wagon. He might have already found him."

I sat and waited. Lewis came soon afterward. He had not found Calvin. Davy came back empty-handed, too.

I was getting more and more upset, feeling responsible for Calvin's disappearance and worrying about where he might be and if we were going to be able to find him before dark. I left the men and went back out into the yard. I stood by the tire swing where I had last seen Calvin and rested my hand on it, feeling more like a failure than I had ever felt in my life.

I was so engulfed in my misery that I didn't immediately notice the stirring of the leaves above me. Then the movement came again, and surprised me because there was no breeze. I looked up. High above me I saw two dangling bare feet. I straightened and looked again and saw Calvin sitting on a large limb, almost hidden from sight among the greenery. I gasped.

"Calvin, you come down out of that tree this instant!" I cried, relief making me angry. "What do you mean, scaring us all half to death like that?"

He began a slow descent while I stood watching with my hands on my hips. Davy appeared in the back door.

"What is it?" he asked.

"He's here," I answered. "Up in the tree — and that's where he's been all along, I suppose."

Davy and Lewis came out and arrived at the tree just as Calvin dropped to the ground at my feet.

"I'm very angry with you, Calvin," I said severely. "Here we have been running around all over the place loooking for you, not knowing what had happened to you, and all the time you're right here. I must have passed under this tree at least a dozen times. Why didn't you answer me when I called you?"

He made no answer but stood looking up at me, his face wan and anxious and tear-streaked. My anger evaporated, and along with it the desire to grab him and shake him until his teeth rattled. I reached out and hugged him to me instead.

"I'm so sorry, Calvin," I said. "I didn't mean to scare you."

"I think this has been the most upsetting, exasperating day of my whole life," I told Davy that evening as we sat together in the living room. He sat in his rocker with the newspaper, and I sat at one end of the sofa with a book. Calvin was in bed and the house was quiet.

"First, Mama and Daddy come and I was so happy to see them, but they were no sooner in the door than Daddy started chewing me out about Jim and Liz and threatening to disown me. Then because I'm upset and feel I need to get away from it all for awhile, and also because I feel Calvin may be missing Granny, I fling that at him about taking him to her, not even thinking how it might sound to him after the morning he's had with you. Then that harrowing two hours searching for him when all the time he's right there in the tree in the backyard, and now this."

I thumped the book in my lap with disgust. Davy lowered his newspaper all the way and looked at me.

"What's this?" he asked mildly.

"This book," I answered. "I thought I'd review it to refresh my memory before school starts, and the very first thing I see is 'Never teach in the home school.' Funny, I don't remember reading that before."

Davy laid his newspaper on the floor beside his chair and came over to sit beside me. He put his arm around me and drew me against him, turning the book over to see the title. It was *Methods of Teaching in the Rural School*.

"Where'd you get this?" he asked.

"I found it in an old antique and junk store in St. Louis a couple of years ago. It's what got me interested in teaching in a one-room country school in the first place."

"Then bless that old antique and junk store," he said, nuzzling my cheek.

"But listen to this," I said. "It says, 'The old adage, familiarity breeds contempt, is never more true than in the teacher-pupil relationship. Where the student is used to hearing the teacher called by her first name, he is tempted to do likewise. This leads to further liberties and weakens the teacher's power to discipline and govern. There needs to be a kind of estrangement between student and teacher, for in this situation, the student is most suggestible. When the teacher is well known by the student outside the classroom, that student will be more likely to challenge the teacher's authority and credibility, and a parent should never be teacher to her own child. Here there is the danger that the parent will show partiality, thus creating an atmosphere of hostility among the rest of the students.'"

I looked up at Davy. "And here I was thinking my marriage to you would be an advantage in my teaching here, not a disadvantage."

"You taught half the year bein' married to me. Was it a disadvantage to you then?"

"No."

"Then why should it be this year?"

"I don't know, except that I am better known in the community and among the children now, and last year we didn't have Calvin."

"Says right here in the book 'Caution is here given to the young teacher who has grown up in the community not to teach in the home school.' You didn't grow up here and you ain't exactly what they're referrin' to as young, are you?"

"Well, I certainly don't consider myself old!"

"No, but you're twenty-five, and this was printed in 1917. Back then teachers was sometimes barely out of their teens, wasn't they? Seems to me I read about girls even bein' as young as seventeen or eighteen teachin' other kids not much younger'n them. I think this is referrin' to somethin' more along them lines, don't you?"

"Possibly."

"Besides, depends a lot on the teacher, whether or not she oughta teach in the home school, don't you think? The kids here like you and they know you're a good teacher and the parents do, too. Some of these old timers resent outsiders comin' in, tellin' them and their kids what to do. At least you're not an outsider anymore. I still think marryin' me is to your advantage in teachin' here."

"Maybe. I guess it's Calvin that's worrying me more than the other children. Not that I think I'll have any trouble being partial to him, but I didn't realize he was quite so sensitive. After what happened today, I'll be a little hesitant to correct him or discipline him, especially in front of others."

"Don't see why. He's jist gotta learn to speak up and say what he's feelin' instead of lettin' his imagination run away with him like that."

"Yes, I suppose. I'm glad we sat down and had that talk with him this afternoon. Hopefully it will prevent anything like that from happening again."

"You didn't get to go off by yourself to do your thinkin' like you wanted to, though."

"No, and I didn't get Calvin in to visit Granny. I'd half promised her I'd bring him in before school starts."

"Might be able to do it tomorrow."

"Possibly, though there's a lot I intended to do today that I didn't get done."

"You still upset about your Dad?"

"Not as much. Calvin's little escapade made it seem much less important somehow."

"Want to talk about it now?"

25

"Not particularly, Davy. I'd just as soon forget about it for now, though I'll probably have to deal with it later. Daddy more or less ordered me to put a stop to Liz and Jim's engagement, and as I have no intention of trying to do that, he'll just have to go ahead and disown me, I guess. I will do what I have to do, and he'll do what he feels he has to do. I won't attempt to live Liz's life for her and sooner or later he'll discover he can't either. If she wants to marry Jim, she'll marry Jim and neither of us will be able to stop her."

"What's he got against Jim?"

"Well, for one thing," I said evasively, "He doesn't like the fact that he's been married before."

"And —"

I shrugged. "He just doesn't care for Jim. He doesn't think he's right for Liz."

"Just like he don't think I'm right for you?"

"What my father thinks or doesn't think of you is beside the point," I said with an attempt at lightness. "I like you and that's all that matters. Besides," I hurried on before he could speak. "Mama likes you. She said to tell you hello and to give you her love. She would have liked to stay longer, but Daddy was in a hurry to get back. Let's go to bed, Davy. I'm tired and I don't want to talk about it anymore tonight, okay?"

CHAPTER THREE

Doubts

I didn't take Calvin in to visit his Granny the next afternoon, either, because my sister Liz arrived.

We were just finishing lunch when she drove up in her car. I went to open the door and she came in carrying a large white box with a red ribbon tied around it. She set the box on the floor, then straightened to hug me first, then Davy. She patted Calvin on the head.

"I've brought you a present," she said to him. She glanced from him to me and Davy. "I hope you don't mind."

"No, of course not. That was thoughtful of you, Liz," I said.

"Better wait 'til you see what it is before you say that. Go ahead and open it, Calvin."

Calvin knelt by the box and untied the ribbon. His face was eager, but a little uncertain. When he took the lid off the box, a small white rabbit with glowing pink eyes looked up at him. He gasped with pleasure and put his hand in to stroke its white fur. The rabbit sat quietly. Evidently it was very tame.

Liz sat on the other side of the box and stroked the rabbit, too. I stood and watched the two of them, thinking that my little sister was not so far removed from childhood herself. I glanced at Davy to see his eyes on them, too, warm and a little amused. I wondered if he was thinking the same thing I was. Liz looked up at us from her position on the floor.

"I went shopping yesterday and you know I can never pass up a pet store. They had these little rabbits and they were so darling, I couldn't resist buying one. But then my landlord said I couldn't keep a rabbit in my apartment, so I brought him to Calvin. I hope you don't mind."

"We don't mind, do we, Davy?"

"No. Cal likes animals."

"You'll have to make a cage for him," Liz told Davy. "I could have bought one, I suppose — "

"I'm glad you didn't. I got plenty of scrap lumber layin' around. Won't take long to make one," Davy answered.

"Can I take him out?" Calvin asked, raising shining eyes to me.

Davy knelt down beside the two of them. "There's a trick to liftin' them," he said. "Rabbits ain't as defenseless as they look. They got strong back legs and sharp claws. Even a little one like this can scratch th' dickens out of you if he thinks you're gonna hurt him. Always lift him like this."

Davy lifted the rabbit out of the box and put him on the floor. The rabbit began to hop around the floor and Calvin, delighted, crawled around the room after him. I went into the kitchen and got a carrot and gave it to Calvin. He held it out and the rabbit came over and began to nibble at it.

"What do you think you'll name him, Calvin?" Liz asked.

"Herman," Calvin replied promptly.

"Herman. I like it. He looks like a Herman somehow. Maybe you should put him back in the box soon. He isn't housebroken, you know."

She rose from the floor and we watched as Davy supervised Calvin as he lifted the rabbit and held it for a minute. He stroked its soft fur before putting it back in the box.

"That's a nice gift, Liz," I said. "You couldn't have given him anything he'd enjoy more."

"I thought about taking it to Jim, but then I decided Calvin might like to have it. I can always get myself another one, since it looks as if I'm going to be living in the country myself soon. I'm on my way to Jim's now. We're taking turns visiting each other, and this weekend is my turn. I wanted to stop by and give Calvin the rabbit, of course, but I also wanted to talk to you, Anne, if you have a few minutes."

"Of course, Liz. Have you had lunch?"

"Yes, and I'm running a little late. Jim is expecting me in half an hour. He's going to let me redo the inside of the house, so today we're going to decide what needs to be done. Then I'm going to cook an early dinner for him before I start back home, so I won't have time to stop back by here later."

"I think me and Cal better go out to the shop and see what we can find to make that cage out of," Davy said. "Come on, Cal. You can bring the rabbit." He looked at Liz. "Guess we'll be seein' you next time you come, then."

"Yes. I'll be here again in two weeks, and I may come on Saturday next time. Is it all right if I spend the night here with you?"

"Glad to have you." He touched her on the shoulder and followed Calvin, carrying the box, out the door.

"Mom asked me to come," Liz said when we were alone. "She was worried about you. She told me about their visit."

"I see. Tell her not to worry. I'm all right. Sit down, Liz. Would you like a cup of coffee or anything?"

"No thanks. I'm not much of a coffee drinker." She seated herself on the sofa and I sat down in one of the rockers. She looked soberly at me.

"Mom said Daddy blamed you for getting me involved with Jim. I'm sorry."

"There's no need to apologize. I suppose, in actual fact, he's right. I did invite you out and I did mention that Jim wanted to meet you. I wish now that I had just sent

29

the invitation without mentioning Jim at all. You would still have met him, but perhaps it would have been on more neutral ground."

"It wouldn't have made any difference how I met him."

"Perhaps not, but I doubt you'll get Daddy to believe that."

"Mama said he said some pretty hurtful things to you, about Davy and your house, and about your marriage to him."

"Yes, but that just proves one thing to me. He doesn't know Davy, and that was my mistake."

"What do you mean?"

"I mean, when Davy and I decided to get married, we saw no reason to wait. I realized, of course, that Daddy wouldn't be too pleased, but I didn't realize he'd feel as strongly about it as he evidently does. Looking back, I can see now that if I'd waited awhile, if I'd taken Davy to visit Mama and Daddy, let them get acquainted with him better, get to know the kind of person he is, Daddy might have been able to accept my marriage more easily."

"I doubt it. He thinks you married beneath you. He thinks because Davy is not well-educated and doesn't have a prestigious job, that he's a nobody, just as he thinks Jim is a nobody."

"Did he give you a pretty hard time when you told him about your engagement?"

"He blew his stack, but I didn't stay around to let him try to browbeat me. I just told him I was going to marry Jim and when he got upset, I just reminded him that I was of age and there was nothing he could do about it, then I left. I learned a long time ago that if I didn't stand up to Daddy, I'd never be able to have a life of my own. That's why I moved out and got my own apartment. I'm old enough to make my own decisions and I'm certainly not going to let him choose my husband for me any more than you let him choose yours."

"No, of course not, Liz, but I agree with Daddy about one thing. Marriage is a serious step. It's not something to be rushed into."

"You did."

"I know, and that's one of the reasons he was so upset with me. He said I set a bad example for you, and maybe he's right."

"Are you saying you're sorry you married Davy?"

"No, I'm not saying that at all. I've never regretted my marriage. What I am saying is perhaps I should have waited awhile. It wouldn't have hurt me, and it certainly would have been better as far as my relationship with Mama and Daddy are concerned."

"If you had waited, would you still have married Davy?"

I hesitated, and in my hesitation, felt a little stab of disloyalty to my husband. If I had waited, say until the end of the school year and gone back to St. Louis, would I still have married Davy? I didn't know the answer to that.

"I don't think anyone can say for sure what they would have done under different circumstances," I said slowly. "I hadn't thought too much about marriage until I met Davy. Teaching had always been my first love. I had big plans and if I'd gone back home — But one thing I can tell you for sure. If I hadn't married Davy, it would have been the biggest mistake of my life."

"I gather you're trying again to tell me I should wait to marry Jim, but suppose I do wait and I'm talked out of marrying him. Maybe that would turn out to be the biggest mistake of my life."

"The situation is not at all the same, Liz."

"Oh brother! Here we go again. Why do people always think their situation is different? I thought you were above that, Sis."

"Liz, everybody's situation is different. You think because you and Jim have known each other for almost the same length of time that Davy and I knew each other, that you're just as ready for marriage as we were. I say you're not, and for this reason. You and Jim see each other only on weekends. Davy and I saw each other almost every day. We ate a meal or two together almost every day. In the evenings, after his parents had gone to bed, we'd sit in the kitchen together. He'd read and I'd do homework. Sometimes we didn't talk much; other times we'd talk for hours. We saw each other in all kinds of situations, in good moods and bad, in all the ups and downs of everyday living. We got to be good friends. We learned to know and trust each other. Probably in that four months we got to know each other as well as the ordinary couple gets to know each other in a year. You think you and Jim know each other well. Perhaps you do, but not as well as Davy and I knew each other, and that's the reason I say you're not as ready for marriage as we were."

Liz sat silent, looking down at her hands, her expression thoughtful, but a little petulant. I thought again how young she looked.

"There's another way the situation is different," I continued gently. "No, there are two more ways. First, I was four years older than you are. Second, I had already lived here for four months and I knew what to expect and knew that I could face living here permanently. You told me you didn't like it out here, and while Jim says he'll move closer to town if you find you can't tolerate living here, if he's anything like Davy, and I think he is, he won't be happy anywhere else. If he's not happy, then neither of you will be happy."

"Maybe I've changed my mind about liking it out here," she said lightly.

"Have you?"

"Yes. I've seen more of it and I find it — restful. I think it could be almost like a refuge out here."

I felt fresh concern as I looked at her, remembering what Mama had told me. "Do you feel you need a refuge, Liz?" I asked.

She laughed. "Don't take everything so literally," she said. "I meant in a general sense, of course. Well, I really am late now," she said rising. "Jim will come looking for me if I don't get there soon. I'll tell Mom you're all right."

She rose and I rose with her. She did not directly meet my eyes, but I didn't feel there was anything else I could say to her.

"If you're coming back in two weeks, Liz, why don't you see if Mama will come with you? I'd love to have her spend the weekend here with us."

"I'll ask her."

"Thanks. Take care, Liz. Thanks for stopping and for the gift for Calvin."

"You're welcome. Tell Davy and Calvin 'bye for me. I'll probably see you in two weeks."

We hugged each other again and she ran out and got into her car and drove away. I stood thoughtful for a minute then decided to walk out to the shop where Calvin and Davy were.

The cage for the rabbit was almost done. Calvin was supposedly helping Davy with it, and I thought it was good to see them working together. I went over to scratch the rabbit behind his ears. His box was open but he was making no attempt to get out.

"Your sister gone?"

"Yes."

"Everything okay?"

"I guess so."

"Talk her out of it?"

"I didn't try. I did try to talk her into waiting, but I don't know how successful I was. She definitely has a mind of her own."

"You goin' in to Granny's?"

"No, I don't think so. I'm out of the mood, besides I have a lot to do before tomorrow. Perhaps next weekend will work out better."

Davy set the cage upright. It was finished. "Want to

put the rabbit in and see how he likes it?" he asked Calvin.

Calvin carefully lifted the rabbit and put him in the cage. Davy stood back and watched. Still feeling unsettled, I went to him, and he put his arm around me as I leaned against him for a minute, pondering again the question Liz had asked me. Would I have married Davy if I had waited and pondered the matter carefully and perhaps talked with my parents about it? I still didn't know the answer.

CHAPTER FOUR

First Day of School

"The students do not go to school the first day to study their lessons but to study their teacher. Therefore a teacher should be aware of the need to put her best foot forward. The first day can make or break a teacher or a school."

These words from the book I'd been reviewing on teaching in the rural elementary school were running through my mind as I dressed for school that first day. I had chosen a white blouse and a navy blue skirt, with navy blue low-heeled shoes. As I stepped in front of the full-length mirror to look at myself, further words from the book went through my mind.

"The teacher must be neatly and modestly dressed, in keeping with her position. She must be friendly, but not familiar, cheerful and busy, but not fussy, interested in her students, but not inquisitive, strong and masterful but not unreasonable or arbitrary."

The list went on and on and I was becoming less confident by the minute. I brushed my hair and wondered if it were too long. I probably should have gone to town and had it cut before school started, but Davy liked long hair and I had procrastinated about getting it done. Perhaps if I wore it up in a bun I would look more like a teacher should look. I tried it but my efforts were not too successful. I ended up brushing it back behind my ears and pinning it there. I put on lipstick then wiped most of it off. I tucked my blouse in, then pulled it out, then tucked it in again.

I must get a grip on myself. After all, it wasn't as if this was my first year here. The children all knew me and — as I liked to think — respected me. What judging they were going to do had likely already been done last year. So why was I so nervous?

My father's scornful evaluation of the school here and my own ability to help the children in any lasting way must have undermined my confidence more than I realized. Before he came, I had been looking forward to the new school year with no qualms.

I took a deep fortifying breath and went into the living room. Davy was just coming from the kitchen with a cup of coffee lifted to his lips. He lowered it and looked me over.

"You look like you mean business this mornin'," he said.

"Do I look the way you think an elementary school teacher should look, Davy?"

"Hm-m-m. I like a little more fluff myself."

"A teacher is not supposed to look fluffy," I retorted with a touch of irritation. I tapped on Calvin's door, glancing up at the clock. It was seven-thirty. "Are you about ready, Calvin?" I called.

His door opened and he came out and stood before me. His tow hair was plastered down with so much water that a little rivulet ran down his forehead, but he still had not succeeded in subduing the cowlick at the front of his head. Drops of water showed on the shoulders of his shirt. The jeans he wore fit well at the waist, but showed a good two inches of ankle above his bare feet.

"Are those the blue jeans your mother bought last spring and Granny put away because they were too big for you?" I asked in dismay.

He nodded.

"My goodness, I didn't realize you'd grown so tall. Do you have any other jeans you could wear?"

"Jist th' other pair like these."

36

"I see. Where are your shoes, Calvin?"

"They're gone."

"What do you mean, they're gone? I put them right there in your closet just a couple of days ago."

"They ain't there."

"Where are they?"

He shrugged his thin shoulders and gazed innocently up at me. I saw Davy hide a grin behind his coffee cup. I sighed.

"Very well, Calvin, but one day soon we're going shopping and those shoes had better turn up by then. Are you ready? I'd like to get there a little early."

He gathered up his pencils and tablet while I took the lunches I had prepared the night before out of the refrigerator and gathered up my own books.

"There's a sack lunch in the refrigerator for you, too, Davy," I said. "You won't forget to pick up Evelyn and Todd at three-thirty, will you?"

"I won't forget."

"Calvin and I will walk so you can drive my car. Bring them to the schoolhouse and they can walk from there."

I lifted my face for his kiss and turned to leave him, but he put his coffee cup down and took my books from me. My eyes widened slightly in surprise.

"I'll jist walk along with you this mornin', if you don't mind," he said.

We started out, Calvin running ahead, scuffing his bare feet through the dust, and periodically stopping to wait for us. It was going to be a hot day. I almost wished I could discard my own shoes.

As we came over the hill and saw the school buildings down below, I thought with a touch of pride how much better it looked this year than last. The new coat of paint we'd put on in the spring still looked bright and the schoolyard looked much neater because Davy had mowed it several times throughout the summer instead of letting the weeds and briars grow up as they usually did.

I took the key from my purse and unlocked the padlocked door and we went inside. The first thing I did was open all the windows so the air would be fresh when the children arrived.

There really wasn't much else to do. I had cleaned the room thoroughly a couple of weeks earlier and all it needed was a light dusting. The pictures I had hung last year were still there, the electric radio back on the shelf beside the world globe. The maps and blackboard were new. Everything was ready. There was nothing more to do but sit down at my desk and await the arrival of my students.

Davy sat down on the bench in front of me and watched me. Calvin had selected a book from one of the bookcases and was sitting at a desk reading. I took the long, flat ledger from the desk drawer and glanced over my notes on each of the students from the year before.

"Feel right at home behind that desk, don't you?" Davy said.

"It's been a nice summer, but I'm glad to be back," I admitted.

"Wonder if I oughta stay and see if you could learn me a few things about the proper way of talkin'."

"I can't <u>learn</u> you anything," I mocked. "I might teach you, but you'd have to do the learning yourself. Don't play ignorant with me, Davy Hilton. I happen to know you're not. If you'd put a little effort into it, you could use proper grammar as well as anyone."

"Think so?"

"Yes, I do think so."

The children began to arrive then. The first to come were the Johnson children, four of them. Nonie was the oldest this year since her brother Todd had started ninth grade. She was a seventh grader, and very much in charge of the younger ones.

Next came Tom and Ellen Hilton's four children, with Ruth, an eighth grader, leading her little sister, Charlie, by the hand. That was one of the things about this one-room, eight-grade school that I thought was an advantage over city schools: the little ones were not left on their own. Almost always there was an older brother or sister to look after them.

Lewis Proctor drove up with his wagon and mules and dropped off not only his two young daughters, but Jane Decker's boys, too. That was kind of him, I thought, since they no longer lived near the Deckers. Davy said goodbye to me then got into the wagon with Lewis since the two of them often worked together.

There were four Andersons this year, looking more ragged, neglected and dirty than ever. I thought the three Baxters were all boys until I discovered that the first grader was named Pearl. She was evidently wearing her brother's outgrown jeans and shirt and her hair was cropped close to her head. Perhaps her parents couldn't afford to buy girls' clothes for her.

There was Davy's sister Maggie's two children, his brother Brad's two little girls, and the four Lovettes, looking very much like the Andersons, but perhaps a little cleaner. There were also the two Sutton boys, and the two Miller girls, and Calvin. The number of children amounted to thirty-three, one more than last year.

As I stood at the door and greeted the children I felt my unease leave me and I was comfortable and happy again, doing what I loved and what I had been trained to do: teaching children.

CHAPTER FIVE

The Anderson Family

"**W**here are Evelyn and Todd?" I asked Davy as he arrived after school. "Surely Jim didn't forget to pick them up this morning?"

"No, he didn't forget, but Evelyn was nervous about bein' away from her Mama so long, so I took her on home. Dropped Todd off on the way."

"I see. How did it go, did they say?"

Davy came in and seated himself on the bench, his hat in his hand. I had dismissed school for the day and all the children had gone home. I was finishing a few last minute things and Calvin sat reading, waiting for me.

"Guess it was kinda big and scary for both of them," Davy said, answering my question, "but Mr. Hooper assigned a girl to help Evelyn and a boy to help Todd, so they made out okay."

"That was kind of Mr. Hooper. Was there any problem about getting to the bus this morning?"

"Didn't say nothin' if there was."

"Thank you for going to pick them up. I know it's inconvenient in the middle of the day like that, but maybe we can find someone willing to take turns with you."

"Might send Lewis in sometimes, if you don't mind him drivin' your car."

"I don't mind."

"How'd your day go here?"

"Fine. I had one little problem, but all in all, it went very well. The most exciting thing, Davy. Jimmie Decker can read!"

"Why is that excitin'?"

"Well, because he's never been to school before and also because Jane has never given me the impression that she reads to the boys much."

"Oh, he's the second one. I was thinkin' he was the oldest."

"No, that's Johnny. He's in third grade and he's a good reader, too. Perhaps Jimmie picked it up from him. It's exciting, Davy, because when I came out here last year to teach, so many of the children were such poor readers that it was difficult to teach them anything. I spent a good part of my time teaching them to read and to enjoy reading. I'll do that again this year, too, but to find two children like the Decker boys who are already excellent readers, well, it's rather like finding hidden treasure. Jimmie isn't just reading words either. Why he picked up that little first-grade reader and read it clear through for me from start to finish without missing a word. I wonder if Jane knows? Of course she does. I guess I'm just surprised because she told me he was a difficult child and I'd have my hands full with him. Well, I may at that, but not in the way she meant. He's not naughty, just eager to learn and above average in intelligence, if I'm not mistaken. I'll have to go out and talk to Jane about him."

"You love teachin', don't you?"

"Yes, Davy, I do."

"You'd have a awful hard time givin' it up, wouldn't you?"

I didn't answer immediately, my eyes on the papers before me, aware that my husband was observing me closely. I had rediscovered all the old joy and satisfaction in my chosen profession and his question was not easy to answer.

"I don't think I ever could," I admitted finally. "I might not mind taking some time off from it now and then, but I don't think I'd ever want to give it up totally."

"You said once a while back that you'd be willin' to

give it up for me. Have you changed your mind?"

"If I had to choose between you and teaching, I'd choose you, of course," I said a little too readily. I glanced up and met his eyes steady on mine. I bit my lip. "That is, I <u>think</u> I would," I added truthfully. "I'm hoping I'll never have to make a choice like that."

"I won't make you make it," he said easily. "Ain't ever' backwoods hillbilly farmer that can talk a good-lookin' teacher like you into bein' his wife. If I made you quit teachin' I couldn't go around braggin' about it no more."

"If you <u>made</u> me quit teaching?" I challenged, my chin lifted.

"If I <u>tried</u> to make you quit teachin'," he amended with a little grin.

"That's better."

"Missed you today."

"Did you?"

"Yep. You miss me?"

"I thought about you, but I can't really say I missed you. I didn't have time."

"They always do say one loves more'n the other one," he said mournfully.

"Not true," I retorted. "Our circumstances are different, that's all. You're alone a good part of the time. If you'd been surrounded by thirty-three kids all day, as I have been, you wouldn't have had time to miss me either."

"Think not?"

"I know it."

"You said you had a problem today. Anything I can help with?"

"No, I don't think so, but thanks. I had to send the youngest Anderson boy home this afternoon. I'm afraid he just isn't ready for school yet."

"Can you tell that in jist one day? Could be he's jist bashful. The Andersons don't mix much with other people, you know."

"This isn't a case of shyness. If it was, I could handle that. The fact is, Frankie Anderson just isn't, for want of a better expression, properly housebroken."

"Housebroken?"

"I used that term because he's like a puppy. If he has to go, he just goes, and it doesn't seem to matter where or when."

"Oh."

"I make allowances for first graders. If they don't have an older brother or sister here, I arrange for one of the older students to take him or her to the toilet at regular intervals. Still, sometimes there will be an accident because the child has to go and is too shy to ask. I always make sure I have a change of clothes on hand at the beginning of the year for just such emergencies, but Frankie wet his pants not a half hour after he got here. I had his sister take him in the cloakroom and change him into dry clothes. An hour or so later, he did it again. Then just shortly before last recess, he did more than just wet his pants, so I had Mattie take him home and tell her mother I'd come by and talk to her after school today. I have enough to do, training their minds. I just don't have the time to train them as far as their bodily functions are concerned, too."

"So you're goin' to the Andersons?"

"Yes. I'll have to explain to his parents."

"I ain't so sure I shouldn't go along with you."

"Why?"

"'Cause you don't know what you're gettin' into. Remember the Simpsons?"

"The family with the little identical twin girls?"

"Yes. You went to their house once, too, remember?"

"Will it be that bad?"

"Jist about."

"I was afraid of that. Those children are terribly neglected. Last year I had a problem with Frankie's brother. Several times at the beginning of the year, he'd

43

just go behind a tree and pull his pants down and go. He didn't want to bother going all the way to the toilet until I made him. But at least he went outside and he did pull his pants down. Frankie didn't bother to do either and he's five years old. There is no excuse for a child of that age not to be toilet trained. Do you know the parents very well?"

"I know 'em, not well, but well enough to know I don't want you goin' inside if ol' man Anderson happens to be there by himself."

"No, I won't. Davy, please don't call him old man Anderson. He can't be that much older than you, after all. You should call him Mr. Anderson."

"Betcha you won't be callin' him Mister anymore once you meet him and see their place up close," he retorted with a little grin, rising. "Sure you don't want me to go along?"

"No. This is a school matter and it's best if I handle it alone. Is the car outside?"

"Yep. You go ahead and take it. Me an' Cal'll walk home."

"All right. I shouldn't be too long."

"You won't go inside 'less she's there, will you?"

"No, I won't. Calvin, don't forget to take your spelling book home and we'll go over those spelling words together later. See you both in about an hour."

Soon after they left, I got in my car and drove to the Anderson home. I was not looking forward to this visit. I had driven past the home many times because it was on the road that led to town. It was the most dilapidated place I had ever seen. I had met the mother but not the father. However, I had heard a lot about him, and none of it good. The children always came to school ragged, dirty and smelly. None of the other children wanted to sit by them. It was a sad situation, and one I didn't know quite how to deal with. So far I had avoided a confrontation with the parents, but that ended now.

When I pulled up into the yard and stopped, two mangy mongrel dogs ran out barking. I sat for a moment, looking at the dismal scene. Several of the children were out in the yard and they stopped what they were doing to stare at me. Dingy clothes hung limp on the line. The yard was cluttered with debris: an old car, old crates, brush and boards, and a big pile of tin cans and bottles that was not far from the back door.

The house needed repair. Paint was peeling, windows were broken out, the steps were rotted and broken-down, the screen door hung on one hinge, and the corner of the screen was torn out. Just looking at the place was depressing. I couldn't imagine how it would feel to live like that.

I opened the car door and cautiously put one foot out, wondering if I was going to be bitten by the dogs. No one made an attempt to call them off or come out of the house to greet me.

After a few more barks, the dogs lost interest and went away. I got out of the car and went up the path to the back door. The pile of cans was swarming with flies. As I neared the house the stench was strong. A child was crying inside the house. I paused just outside the back door and knocked.

The oldest girl came to the door with a child of about a year on her hip. The baby wore only a soiled diaper and she was very dirty. Behind Mattie, the child who was crying hung onto her dress with a dirty hand, while with the other hand she knuckled her eyes. She was perhaps three years old and was also clad only in a filthy diaper.

"Hello, Mattie," I said. "Is your mother here?"

"Mom!" Mattie opened her mouth and yelled. "Teacher's here!"

She stepped back and I was left standing there, waiting for her mother. The child continued to cry until I heard the sound of a sharp slap and a barked order to "shut your mouth, Clarie."

45

Mrs. Anderson appeared in the doorway, looking tired and harassed and none too happy to see me. She was somewhat cleaner than her children, but her faded and worn dress hung without shape on her. I wondered if she was expecting another child. She had an air of utter defeat and hopelessness about her, and I couldn't help but feel sympathetic.

"Come on in," she said ungraciously.

I forced myself to step inside. The stench here was even worse. The smell of urine and alcohol was strong, and the room was in wild disorder. Another child, a boy, looked to be about the same age as the little girl. He was dressed in a ragged pair of jeans that he had wet in. He stood beside an old coffee table, dipping his hand into an open can of peaches and bringing a piece, dripping on the table and the floor and down his bare chest, to his mouth. Filth and flies were everywhere. Then I noticed the man who lay prone on the sofa, his eyes closed and his mouth open. He was dirty and unshaven and an empty whiskey bottle lay on the floor near one limp hand.

I began to feel queasy and wished I hadn't accepted her invitation to come inside. The place was appalling.

"I'm sorry," I said, almost with a gasp. The acrid smell made my nostrils feel pinched and almost took my breath away. "I didn't know your husband was asleep. Perhaps we should step outside to talk so we won't disturb him."

"Don't nothin' bother him when he's like that," she said with open contempt. "You want to set down?"

"No thanks," I said, fearful of picking up some kind of vermin if I sat in the broken-down, overstuffed chair she indicated. "I just have a minute. I wanted to stop by and talk to you about Frankie."

She turned and yelled at the little boy who had overturned the can of peaches, but she made no move to clean up the mess. With the baby still on her hip and the toddler clinging to her skirt, Mattie stood in the background looking at us.

"I'm afraid Frankie won't be able to come back to school until he's fully toilet trained," I said as kindly as I could.

"I can't do ever'thing," she muttered, her voice sulky. "He was toilet trained 'til jist a few weeks ago, then he started messin' in his pants again. I can't watch him ever' minute. I got these three other young'uns to look after, too."

"Yes, I can see you have your hands full. I didn't know you had three other little ones at home. Are the little boy and girl twins?"

"No. Jackie there's 'bout a year older."

"I see. So you have seven children under ten. It must be very difficult to — to get everything done." I ended lamely.

"I don't get nothin' done. I don't even try no more. It don't do no good. If I get 'em all fed an' keep 'em from killin' each other an' keep him," with a contemptuous gesture toward the man on the sofa, "from killin' one of them, I'm a doin' good."

I didn't know what to say. I felt sorry for her, but surely she could do better than this. I had adjusted to the smell, but it seemed impossible that anyone could live in such squalor.

"About Frankie," I said. "Perhaps he just needs a little more time. He's not quite six yet. If he has to wait until next year to start school, it won't hurt him."

"I was wantin' him to go this year," she said, sounding sullen again.

"I'm sorry. He can't go to school until he's fully toilet trained."

The little boy, Jackie, had wandered over by the sofa. I kept glancing apprehensively at him because he had picked up the whiskey bottle and was examining it. A moment later he lifted it to his lips. Without thought, I rushed over and snatched it out of his hands. He looked up at me, surprised, then began to cry.

"I'm sorry," I said again, "but he shouldn't drink whiskey."

"Wasn't nothin' in it," she said, stiff with resentment. She took the bottle from me and tossed it through the open door onto the pile of tin cans.

"Even a small amount of whiskey can be fatal to a child," I said.

She didn't reply. I felt there should be something I could say or do to help her, but I didn't know what. I had overstayed my welcome and besides, my stomach was beginning to roll. I turned to the door.

"Goodbye, Mrs. Anderson. 'Bye Mattie. I'll see you tomorrow."

I went out to my car and quickly got in and drove away. Once out of sight of the house, I stopped to open all the windows, gratefully breathing in the fresh air. I felt hopeless and heartsick for the family and I wished I hadn't gone there. Now that I knew the situation firsthand, I couldn't ignore it any longer, but what to do? I hadn't a clue.

"Well, how did it go?" Davy asked when I arrived home.

"Don't ask or come near me until I've had a bath."

"Bad, huh?"

"Horrible. Indescribable. I've never seen anything so pathetic. Seven children under the age of ten living in utter squalor and another one on the way, if I'm not mistaken."

"Make the acquaintance of Mister Anderson?"

I looked at him from under lowered brows and he grinned.

"Dead drunk on the sofa," I said. "I felt so sorry for her. I think she's just given up, well, I know she has because she said so. I wish I knew of some way to help her."

"You could offer to help her clean house," he replied, tongue-in-cheek.

"The only way I'd try to clean that place up would be to burn it to the ground," I replied, going into the bathroom to start my bath.

Before the week was over, I knew something had to be done about the Anderson children. None of the other children wanted to sit near them and I didn't blame them.

Last year it had been a problem and I had handled it by classroom discussion. This year the problem had worsened, even though Frankie hadn't come back to school, and I wasn't going to be able to wait on classroom discussion. The room was not big enough to seat the three children off to themselves.

I decided against another visit to the home. I would put it directly to the children, and if that didn't work, I would make an appeal to their mother, although I hadn't much hope of that producing any satisfying results.

On Thursday, I gave Davy a shopping list, since he was going into town to deliver some cabinets to his brother. On Friday, I asked the Anderson children to stay for a few minutes after I dismissed school for the day.

They stood before my desk with wide-eyed apprehension. The girl and two boys were dirty, unkempt and strongly odorous. When all the other children were gone, I turned to Calvin, who waited by his desk, and told him to go on home and tell Davy I would be late. I was going out to visit with Jane Decker for a few minutes after I had talked with the Anderson children. Silently, he gathered up his books and went out. I turned back to the children who waited and smiled. I was hoping to make this as inoffensive as possible for all of us.

"I won't keep you long," I said. "You are not being punished for anything, but I wanted to ask you to do something for me, please. You have a big family, seven children, and that makes a lot of work for your mother. Now Mattie, I saw when I was at your house Monday that you're a big help to your mother and that's good. I hope

49

you boys are being helpful, too. I want to ask the three of you to do as much as you can for yourselves to take the burden off your mother. Every Sunday afternoon or evening, I want each of you to take a bath and wash your hair and make sure you have a clean change of clothes to put on when you get ready for school Monday morning. Then every morning before you come to school, you must wash your face and hands, comb your hair, and brush your teeth. In this sack is a bar of soap, a bottle of shampoo for your hair, a comb and brush, a tube of toothpaste, and a toothbrush for each of you. I want you to take them home with you and use them. Mattie, since you're the oldest, I'm going to depend on you to remind the boys. You might help your mother bathe the little ones, too. Being clean makes you feel good about yourself and it helps you stay healthy, too.

"You may go now and I'll see you Monday morning. Have a nice weekend."

I gave the sack to Mattie and dismissed them with a smile and gathered up the things I wanted to take home. Since the sky was cloudless I left all the windows partially open at the top. If it clouded up over the weekend I could always come back and close them.

Davy had driven the truck in to pick up Evelyn and Todd, so I had the car waiting for me. I got in it and drove to Jane Decker's home. She met me at the door. The four boys were playing in the yard.

"How are you, Jane?" I asked when she had invited me inside and indicated a chair.

"Fair to middlin'," she replied. "My boys been givin' you trouble?"

"Oh no. In fact, just the opposite. I had to come out and tell you how well they're both doing. You can really be proud of them, Jane."

She blinked in surprise. "Jimmie ain't been drivin' you up th' walls?"

"Not at all. Actually, at this point, I'd say he's my most

promising student. He is so eager to learn, so interested in everything. Who taught him how to read, Jane?"

"Oh that. He learned when his daddy was helpin' Johnny when he was in first grade."

"I wondered if he didn't learn with Johnny. It's wonderful how well he reads, and with such feeling. He read *Three Billy Goats Gruff* to the whole school today and did a wonderful job," I said.

"Their daddy used to read to them all th' time, most ever' night. That was always Jimmie's favor-rite story. Jesse'd read it over an' over to him an' you'd a thought he was practicin' to be in one of them movie pictures or somethin', way he'd carry on. Likely Jimmie's recitin' it from memory, more'n he's readin' it."

"Oh, do you think so? He never missed a word, but whether he was reading it or reciting it, he did a fantastic job. I thought you'd like to know."

She nodded, but said nothing. I was disappointed that she didn't show more interest.

"Jimmie is very intelligent," I said. "So is Johnny, of course, but Jimmie is so enthusiastic about learning, so eager to know why things are the way they are."

"Likely that's why he took th' only clock we got apart last night then," she said dryly. "Only thing is, he couldn't get it back together again."

"It is curiosity, Jane, not naughtiness. I'm sure he didn't mean to ruin the clock."

"Course he didn't, but that don't make no difference in th' long run. He took it apart without askin' an' now we ain't got no clock, so if them boys start showin' up late for school, you'll know why. Ain't likely I'll be gettin' a new clock right away, either," she said.

"He needs more to do, challenging things. Do you have any books around for him to read, or puzzles, or anything like that?"

"Ain't got much. Th' four of them got to share, an' bein' boys, things don't hold up long around here."

51

"Maybe I can send a book home with him from time to time — perhaps something he can read to his little brothers. Do you do much reading to them, Jane?"

"Ain't got th' time or th' inclination. Jesse always done that while I got on with th' work."

"I see. Well, perhaps Johnny and Jimmie can take turns reading to the whole family in the evenings. It would be very good for Jerry and Josh. It would help prepare them for school later on. Being a good reader is so vital to getting a good education. Well, I suppose I'd better get home and start supper. How are things going for you now, Jane?"

"Good as can be expected, I reckon. Them commodities sure do help, though a body does get a might tired of cheese an' macaroni an' beans an' rice. I ain't complainin' though, I'm real glad to be gettin' them. Ain't started on my canned goods yet. I'm savin' them for winter in case them commodities don't hold out. You an' your man an' that young'un you took in doin' okay?"

"We're doing just fine. Is there anything you need?"

"Not that I can think of. Gotta go out an' find me some more firewood 'fore long, but it sure don't feel much like winter comin' on yet, does it?"

"No, it's been unusually warm, and will be for a month or so yet, I suppose. Well, goodbye, Jane. Take care."

I drove away feeling slightly deflated. The excitement I felt over Jimmie's reading ability was evidently not shared by his mother. Perhaps that was because of the example set by her husband, who was about as worthless as a man could get, I thought. However, I did have to admire the effort he had put into teaching his boys a love for reading.

When I got home, Calvin was in the backyard with his hand in the rabbit cage. I went inside the house, put my books away, and went into the kitchen to make a cup of coffee. Davy came up behind me and put his arms around me. I leaned back against him with a sigh, and then turned to smile up at him.

"It's been a long week," he said.

"And a busy one," I agreed. "I'm glad it's over, too, Davy. I love teaching but — "

I caught sight of Calvin in the doorway and drew away from my husband.

"Hello, Calvin." I said. "Are you hungry?"

"No, but Herman is. Can I have a carrot for him?" He glanced quickly at Davy and I.

"Yes, of course."

He got the carrot out of the refrigerator and went out again. I looked at Davy and had to smile at the disgruntled look on his face.

"What's wrong?" I asked him.

"Does that kid have to appear out of the blue ever' time I come near you?" he complained.

"Why Davy!"

"Seems like I ain't hardly had a minute alone with you all week."

"We've had the evenings and the nights."

"Yeah, sure. And what happened last night, after you asked me about my day? Right in the middle of what I was sayin', you started snorin'."

"I did not! I don't snore!"

"You did, too, and here I was thinkin' I was makin' my story real interestin', too."

"I'm sorry. I guess I was more tired than I realized. I'll make it up to you."

"I intend to see that you do. Well, how'd it go with the Anderson kids?"

"We'll see on Monday morning, I guess. I gave them the shampoo and the other things and told them as kindly as I knew how just what I expected of them. I hope it works."

"And if it don't?"

"Then I guess I'll have to go talk to Mrs. Anderson

again, poor thing. Would you like a cup of coffee?"

I poured us each a cup and we sat down at the table. Davy reached for my free hand and held it.

"So what was it you were trying to tell me last night when I fell asleep?" I asked.

"I was tryin' to tell you 'bout the experience I had in town buyin' the stuff to make our heatin' stove out of."

"Tell me about it now."

"Don't seem interestin' enough to tell you anymore," he said mournfully.

"I'm sorry."

"Jist kiddin'. Wasn't anything special."

"So you're getting ready to make the stove now?"

"Started on it today. Should have it done in a couple weeks. I'm makin' it with a flat top so you can do a little cookin' on it, if you have to, in case the 'lectricity goes off."

"That's a good idea. You're very clever, Davy. You think of everything."

"Ain't so much bein' clever as havin' experience. I seen the time when the 'lectricity goes off in a ice storm and don't get fixed for a good week or two."

"It sounds cozy, an ice storm outside and sitting around a wood fire with a pot of stew simmering on top of the stove."

"You're forgettin' there'd be wood to carry in and animals to feed and ice to chop on the pond so the animals could drink."

"But you'd be doing all that while I waited all cozy by the fire."

"You and Calvin," he said a little dryly.

"Davy, are you jealous of Calvin?" I chided.

"Guess maybe I am a little. Seems like when you're here, ever' time I turn around I step on him."

"You're exaggerating. He isn't underfoot right now."

"No, but give him a few more minutes and he will be."

"He'll relax and get more independent as he gets used to being with us."

The screen door slammed and Davy looked at me with raised eyebrows.

"See what I mean?" he said.

"It's time I started supper anyhow. Is there anything special you'd like me to fix?"

"Mom sent over a extry chicken she killed and cleaned today. It's there in the refrigerator. She sent over some green beans and tomatoes from the garden, too, and a extry pound of butter she had."

I wanted to correct him. "Don't say extry, say extra," I wanted to say, "and don't always be dropping your g's like that, and don't say was instead of were, and done instead of did." I didn't say it, though. I didn't want him to think I was criticizing him, but somehow, someday, I would see if I couldn't get my husband to start using better grammar. I was sure his poor grammar was more habit than anything else. He was capable of speaking properly. If he put his mind to it.

"That was nice of your mother," I said. "I'll have to see what I can do to pay her back a little for all she does for us. If I invited them over for a meal one of these days, do you think they'd come?"

"Don't know. Wouldn't hurt to ask, I guess."

"Then I think I will, perhaps sometime this weekend."

Calvin entered the kitchen then and Davy rose from the table and went out to start on the evening chores while I prepared supper.

CHAPTER SIX

Concern for Clemmy

I knew when Davy left the bed that next morning, but I snuggled down under the sheet and went back to sleep. The next time I opened my eyes, sunlight was streaming in around the blinds and I knew it was late. I stretched lazily but did not get up immediately.

"She's awake now," I heard Calvin say in a hushed voice, and a few minutes later, he and Davy came into the bedroom. Davy carried a tray and Calvin carefully balanced a cup of coffee on a saucer.

"Rise and shine, Sleepyhead," Davy told me.

I sat up and arranged the pillows behind me. "Breakfast in bed. What luxury!" I took the cup and saucer from Calvin and Davy set the tray on my lap. It contained a bowl of sliced bananas with milk and sugar, a thick slice of bread piled high with apple butter, and a hard-boiled egg. "Thank you." I said. "It looks delicious. Have the two of you eaten?"

"Long time ago." Davy answered.

"What time is it?"

"Nearly ten o'clock."

"Goodness, I should have been up hours ago. I have the laundry to do."

"It'll wait." He leaned down and kissed me on the forehead. "I'll be out at the shop if you need me."

"All right. Thanks for breakfast and for letting me sleep in."

I ate my breakfast in leisure, then got up and dressed in

a plain cotton housedress. When I went into the living room Calvin was sitting at the corner of the sofa and was busily writing on a tablet on his knee. I touched his head as I passed him but he was engrossed and didn't look up.

I washed the few dishes in the sink, then filled the washer and tubs on the side porch with water. While the clothes washed, I did other small jobs around the house. By noon, the laundry was washed and ready to be hung out. I had fixed a light lunch for Calvin and Davy since I was not hungry myself, and left them to eat it while I went outside to hang out the clothes.

It was a warm, breezy day so the clothes would dry quickly. I enjoyed hanging them out amidst the quiet and solitude. It was wonderful to have some time alone.

After that, I decided to make a big pot of vegetable soup, so there would be enough left over for Davy to warm up for his lunch for a day or two. I put on some navy beans to precook, then decided to walk to my mother-in law's house to invite them to have supper with us the next day. Calvin was back in his corner of the sofa writing.

"Calvin," I said. "I'm going to walk down to Clemmy's for a few minutes, I've put some beans on. If I'm not back in a half hour or so, will you turn the stove off, please?"

He looked up, his gaze abstracted, and nodded, then went back to his writing. I had to smile, glad to see him so engrossed. To my knowledge he hadn't done any writing since he had come to live with us.

I walked to the home of Davy's parents. Through the screen door I could see Clemmy pouring water from the teakettle into the dishpan.

"Knock, knock," I said before I opened the door and went inside. "Why Clemmy, what's wrong with your hand? Did you burn yourself?"

"Don't know what I done," she answered, replacing the kettle on the stove. "It started crampin' up on me yesterday evenin' an' it's hurtin' me so bad, can't hardly use it at all."

I took her hand in mine and gently unwound the bandage. Her skin looked red and puffy and felt hot to the touch.

"Is it your wrist, Clemmy? Have you sprained it?"

"It's mostly in my thumb. Funny how you don't even notice you got a thumb 'til somethin' like this happens. Can't open a jar, or lift a skillet, or sweep th' floor, or hardly do anything. It's right in th' joint there."

"I can see it's swollen. Have you taken anything for the pain?"

"No. Rubbed a little linament on it."

"I'd take a couple of aspirin if I were you. Do you have any?"

"Right up on that shelf there, if you'd care to reach them down for me."

I got the bottle, opened it and gave her two aspirin, and poured her a glass of water.

"You sit down, Clemmy," I said. "I'll do those dishes for you. You can't very well do them with one hand."

"Hate to make a fuss. Seems awful triflin', lettin' jist a little ol' thumb put me clear outta commission, but I ain't had nothin' hurt me so bad long as I can remember. Jist makes a body wanna cry when it gets to crampin' up."

"You go ahead and make a fuss, Clemmy. You do everything for everyone else. Maybe it's time you sat back and let others do for you. You probably need to rest that hand completely for a few days. I'll do these dishes and sweep the floor now, then I'll come back this evening and strain the milk for you and wash the milk bucket. I'm making a big pot of vegetable soup for supper and I'll bring some over for you and Mr. Hilton. Is he here?"

"He's about somewheres."

"Does he know about your hand?"

"He knows it's been hurtin' some."

"Well, if he comes in and wants you to do something, I

think you just ought to tell him you can't. Matter of fact, I think you ought to go in and lie down for awhile. You look tired."

"Didn't get much sleep last night 'cause of th' hurtin'.'"

"Do you want to go to the doctor? I'll take you, if you'd like."

"Reckon it ain't nothin' doctorin' will help. Maybe if I jist rest it, it'll be better. Likely I got a touch of rheumatism in it."

"I'll tell you what I think has caused it. All that scrubbing you do on that washboard. I noticed you had the lines full a couple of times this week."

"Figgered it was time I got all th' beddin' washed an' aired out 'fore it comes winter."

I lifted the dishpan and carried it to the back door and threw the water out into the yard. Then I wiped the pan out and hung it on its nail behind the stove. I took up the dishcloth and dried the dishes, putting them away in the cupboard.

"Clemmy," I said. "I want you to start doing your laundry at my house in my washing machine."

"I ain't never used no washin' machine."

"It's easy. Once I show you how, you won't have a bit of trouble. I did my whole wash this morning in just a couple of hours, with no aching back from bending over a washboard and no knuckles skinned raw and bleeding. The clothes are just as clean, too, I promise you."

I put the last dish away and hung the dishcloth on a nail and turned back to Clemmy.

"There's so much you've done for me and so little I can do for you. Please Clemmy, consider it at least. Now that school has started, I'll only be using the washer on Saturday, so you could come over any time during the week and wash to your heart's content. Why don't you come over, say tomorrow afternoon, and I'll show you how it works? With your hand hurting like that you're not going to be able to use the washboard very well for awhile." I looked at her with hopeful eyes.

"Reckon I could come over and take a look at it at least."

"Good. Tomorrow afternoon then. Has the pain in your hand eased a little?"

"B'lieve it is jist a mite easier."

"Why don't you go lie down and take a little nap? I'll sweep the floor for you before I go home. Is there anything else you need done?"

"Don't reckon so."

"Well, if there is I'll do it when I come back later this afternoon. Sleep well, Clemmy."

I helped her to her feet and she went off to the bedroom. I swept the floor then went to the shop to find Davy. He was bent over his workbench.

"Jist can't stay away from me, can you?" he teased with a grin when he saw me.

"You're totally irresistible, of course, but actually I was looking for your father. Do you know where he is?"

"Ain't seen him today."

"Your mother has hurt her hand. She's in a lot of pain so I sent her off to bed, since she obviously didn't get much sleep last night."

"You sent her off to bed?"

"Well, I suggested it, at least, and she didn't argue, which proves she's not herself."

"What'd she do?"

"Nothing that she knows of. I think it's probably all that washing she did this week. I told her I want her to start using my washing machine."

"Think she will?"

"I don't know, but she might now, with that hand hurting as bad as it is. Anyhow, she said she'd come over tomorrow and let me show her how it works. If I can get her to use it just once, maybe she'll see how easy it is so that she'll never want to go back to that washboard again. At least I'm hoping it will work that way."

Davy put an arm around my shoulders and kissed me on the cheek. "Wisht my sisters was as concerned about Mom as you are."

"I don't think it's so much that they're not concerned. It's just that they're not as close to her as we are, and perhaps they don't realize she's getting older. She really looks her age today."

"I'll have to go in and see her."

"Not now. She needs sleep right now more than she needs anything. I've told her I'll bring supper for them tonight. Maybe you can go then."

"Okay."

"I don't suppose it would work for Calvin to go along and all of us have supper together?"

"Don't think I'd push it."

I sighed. "No, perhaps not, especially with your mother not feeling well. She might not be up to one of your father's outbursts right now."

"You gotta let Dad come around in his way and time. At least he ain't made a fuss about Calvin livin' right next door to them."

"He'd just better not make a fuss. Calvin is a sweet, innocent little boy and his own grandson. To forbid him to enter his house because of a mistake his parents made is pretty narrow-minded, if you ask me."

"Maybe. That why you're lookin' for him, to tell him that?"

"No," I said, subsiding. "I just wanted to tell him I'll fix their supper tonight so he won't bring home any rabbits or squirrels, expecting your mother to cook for him. She can't use that hand at all, Davy. If you see him, will you tell him?"

"Okay. Want to take a look at the stove I'm makin'?"

I spent a few more minutes in the shop, then I left and walked down the gently sloping hill to our log cabin, admiring the picture it made, nestled there in the trees. Suddenly I saw a thin stream of smoke drifting out the kitchen window. Alarmed, I ran toward the house. The stench of burning beans greeted my nostrils as I rushed into the kitchen. Smoke was pouring from the pan on the stove. I turned off the burner, grabbed a pot holder and lifted the pan from the stove and carried it outside. When I took the lid off, the beans were black and the pan was ruined. I left the pan on the grass and went back inside. Calvin was standing in the kitchen doorway, his eyes wide and apprehensive. I ignored him until I had switched on the exhaust fan above the stove and opened both the windows. Then I turned to him, hands on my hips.

"Didn't you hear me tell you to turn the stove off if I wasn't back in a half hour, Calvin?" I asked.

"I forgot," he gulped.

"The house might have burned down if I hadn't come home when I did. Didn't you smell the beans burning or see the smoke?"

He shook his head, his eyes looking too big for his face.

"Calvin, you can't let yourself get so engrossed in your writing or reading that you're oblivious to what's going on around you. That could be very dangerous. Remember that you nearly walked into the saw when you were helping Davy cut wood the other day?"

He nodded.

"What were you doing then, thinking of a story?"

He nodded again.

"Well, they say that's a sign of true genius, if the roof can fall in on you and you don't even notice, but Calvin, I want you to start training yourself to be more aware of what's going on around you. The ability to write is a wonderful gift, but it's not going to be of much value to you if you get yourself killed in the process. Promise me you'll start working on that."

"Okay," he said in a choked voice.

I relented and walked over to him and drew him gently against me. "All right, Calvin, we'll leave it at that then. May I ask what you're writing?"

"It's a story."

"Yes, I realize it's a story, but what is it about?"

"Some dogs."

"I see."

I thought about the experience he'd had with the wild dogs during the summer and wondered if he was writing about that. I had been concerned that he'd had no obvious aftereffects from the experience, although I believed he had suffered a severe trauma. It would be very good for him to write about his feelings.

I put on a fresh pot of beans and Calvin went back to his story.

"Mom said for me to tell you her hand's some better and she won't be troublin' you to fix their dinner," Davy said as he came in the door.

I was mixing up a chocolate cake. I paused and looked at Davy. "You mean they're not coming?"

"Guess not. Dad went huntin' early this mornin' and brought back a couple rabbits. Mom's fixin' them."

"Is it because your father doesn't like my cooking or just because he doesn't want to come over here and eat?"

Davy shrugged. "Dunno," he said.

"That makes me mad. There was nothing wrong with the soup and sandwiches I took over last night. I notice he ate enough, even if he did turn up his nose at first."

"Guess he ain't used to eatin' anything but what Mom has cooked."

"It wouldn't hurt him to stop thinking about himself and start thinking about your mother for a change. She shouldn't have to be cooking with her hand bothering her so much."

"They're used to doin' for theirselves."

"They're used to her doing for him, you mean," I said. "Well, I'll get this cake baked, then I'll go over and see if I can help her and if your father doesn't like it, well that's just too bad."

When the cake was out of the oven and cooling, I walked over to Clemmy's house. She was in the kitchen flouring pieces of the rabbit and putting them in the skillet on the stove. Her left hand was unbandaged, but it hung useless at her side. A pan of unpeeled potatoes sat on the table and Clemmy's kitchen was more cluttered than usual.

"How is your hand?" I asked.

"Thought it was better, but when I was cuttin' up th' rabbit it started crampin' up on me again," she replied in a flat, weary voice.

"You shouldn't have had to cut up the rabbit at all," I said shortly. "If Mr. Hilton insists you fix lunch, he should at least have stayed around to help you. You sit down, Clemmy. I'll do that."

"If you've a mind to help, you could peel them taters for me. Reckon I can finish this up with jist one hand."

I poured a couple of dippers of water from the bucket on the washstand over the potatoes and sat down in a chair, taking the pan on my lap. We didn't talk as I peeled potatoes and Clemmy put the rest of the rabbit into the skillets to fry. I was angry at my father-in-law for expecting so much of his wife, and half exasperated with her for allowing him to do it. She was evidently feeling guilty about turning down my invitation to lunch.

"It's right nice of you to be helpin' out like this," she said after a while.

"I'm glad to do it. You do much more for me than I've ever done for you, Clemmy," I replied. "But I really feel you're going to have to rest that hand as much as possible if it's ever going to get better. Hasn't Mr. Hilton ever had to fix a meal for himself?"

"Don't reckon he'd know th' first thing about cookin'."

"He could learn. You spoil him, Clemmy. What would he ever do if you really got sick?"

"I ain't never been 'lowed to be too sick to cook, 'cept when I had th' babies. Then a neighbor woman come in to do th' cookin'."

I got up and rinsed the potatoes and put them in a pan, added water and a lid and put them on the stove. I poured the potato peelings into the slop bucket behind the stove, rinsed the pan and hung it on its nail.

"I think it's time you went on strike," I told my mother-in-law. "You've got enough food here for two meals. Let him eat leftovers tonight."

"He don't mind cold rabbit but I'll have to make th' cornbread an' if there's enough taters left over, I can make tater cakes. They ain't much work."

"Well, if I were you, I'd let him make his own cornbread and potato cakes. What else can I do, Clemmy?"

"Would you mind goin' out to th' garden an' gettin' a few ears of corn an' a few tomatoes an' an onion or two?"

"No, I don't mind. I think I'll get some corn and tomatoes for our supper, too, while I'm out there."

"There's a plenty."

I took a basket and went out to the garden, being careful where I stepped. I would never forget how Davy's dog Brownie had been bitten by a snake there at the edge of the garden last fall. This year Davy had made sure the grass was mowed regularly and not allowed to grow up so that a snake might be hidden in it. I was grateful as I walked gingerly to the rows I needed.

I picked the tomatoes and the corn and pulled a few onions. When I got back to the house, I spread newspaper on the table and removed the shucks and the silk from the corn and cut off the ends with Clemmy's big butcher knife. I put five ears aside for my family, washed the other five, put them in a pan, covered them with water, and put them on the stove. After that was done I washed four of the big tomatoes and put them in the center of the table whole, knowing that Clemmy didn't like them sliced because if they were not eaten they would soon spoil.

"Shall I peel an onion?" I asked.

"Peel one an' cut it into fourths an' put it in a bowl.

Dad was feelin' like he might be comin' down with a cold this mornin'."

I did as she instructed. The onion was hot and tears were rolling down my cheeks before I finished. I washed my hands and splashed water over my eyes to get rid of the burning.

I took down two of the heavy plates and set them on the table along with two tall glasses. I took the water bucket and went out and pumped it full of fresh water and brought it in.

"Anything else I can do?"

"No. You'd best be gettin' back to your place to fix your own dinner, but it was right nice of you to come over an' help me out."

"I was glad to do it. Don't try to do the dishes. I'll come back and do them for you later."

I went home and fixed lunch for myself, Davy and Calvin. When lunch was over and I had cleaned up my kitchen I went over to help Clemmy. I took along with me two pieces of cake, covered with waxed paper.

Clemmy was standing before the stove with her left hand in a pan of water. There were tears of pain on her cheeks.

"Is it worse?" I asked in quick sympathy.

She nodded and wiped the tears away on the sleeve of her right arm. "Worse'n ever," she said. "Thought puttin' it in hot water might ease it some. Hurts all th' way up my arm."

"Have you taken any more aspirin?"

"Didn't think about it."

"I'll get them for you."

She took the two aspirin I gave her with the glass of water. I stood by helplessly and looked at her, wishing there was something more I could do.

"If it's not better tomorrow, I think you should go to the doctor. I'm sure Davy will take you."

"Seems like if I could jist wrap somethin' tight around

it it might stop crampin' up so bad," she said. "There's a piece of old sheet in that drawer over there, if you'd want to get it for me an' tear off a strip of it."

I got the sheet and tore the strip off. Clemmy took her hand from the water and I handed her the towel to dry it. I could tell by the way she winced that it hurt just to move the hand. She carefully rubbed some linament on the swollen area of the joint of her thumb, then I wrapped the strip of sheet around it, pulling it tighter at her direction, and pinned it with a safety pin. Then I filled a hot water bottle and placed it on the arm of her rocker. She sat down, resting her hand on the water bottle, her face weary.

The remains of the meal were still on the table and I saw that there were three used plates instead of the two I had set earlier. I began to clear the table, seething inside. It wasn't enough that Mr. Hilton had insisted she fix a big meal for him — he had brought one of his cronies home for the meal, too. As much food as she had fixed, there was very little left over. Now she'd probably have to cook supper, too.

I covered the leftovers and washed the dishes and put them away while Clemmy sat in her chair, nursing her sore hand. Then I picked up the pan of dishwater, carried it to the door, pushed the screen open with my shoulder, and tossed the water out into the yard, as I'd seen Clemmy do so many times before.

Too late I saw Mr. Hilton come around the corner of the house. The warm sudsy water splashed in his face and he stepped back sputtering. I gasped and almost dropped the pan.

"Oh, Mr. Hilton!" I cried. "I'm so sorry. I didn't see you."

He was wiping his face with his sleeve, and his head and shoulders were drenched. He shook his head like a wet dog and looked up at me out of reddened eyes. I put the pan down and grabbed the towel that hung there by the door and stepped outside, holding it out to him. He took it without a word and went to the pump and began pumping with one hand while with the other he splashed water over his face and head. I stood and watched, my heart pounding, not knowing what to expect. He straightened and passed the towel over his face and hair.

"I'm sorry," I said again. "I had no idea you were going to be coming around that corner."

Without a word he walked past me into the house. I stood a moment looking after him.

"Serves you right, for being so inconsiderate of Clemmy," I thought with a strange, exultant kind of satisfaction.

"I just threw dishwater all over your husband," I told her in a subdued voice as I picked up the pan. I wiped it out and hung it up, then stood there, uncertain what to do. Clemmy just looked at me and said nothing, even though I thought I detected a small gleam of amusement in her eyes.

"I think I'd better go home," I said then, and turned and went out the door.

CHAPTER SEVEN

Wedding Plans

"*I*'ve made some extra macaroni and cheese and some fruit salad," I told Davy when he came in later that afternoon. "Will you take it over to your Mom and Dad?"

"You can't take it over?"

"I'm afraid I might get thrown out."

"What you been up to, young lady? Finally get up enough nerve to tell Dad off?"

"No. I threw dishwater in his face."

"You <u>what</u>?"

"Well, I didn't do it on purpose," I said defensively. "He was coming around the corner of the house just as I threw the dishwater out, and I didn't see him in time."

"Are you sure?"

"Yes, I'm sure," I retorted. "Not that I'm denying I wouldn't have been tempted to do it, if I'd thought of it, but I didn't. It was an accident."

"Was he mad?"

"I don't know. He didn't say anything, but your mother didn't come over so I could show her about the washing machine, and I don't know if it's because she didn't feel well enough or whether he wouldn't let her. I'm afraid to go over and find out."

"So now I gotta go?"

"Yes, please. Your mother was in a lot of pain. She shouldn't be using that hand at all. There was some rabbit left over from lunch and I'm hoping that and the macaroni and salad will be enough for their supper. Will you please take it over there now before she starts cooking?"

He sighed, but took the two plastic bowls I handed him.

"You might see if there's anything she needs done while you're there," I added as he went out the door.

It was quite awhile before he came back, looking troubled. My heart sank, hoping I had not created another problem for him with his family.

"What happened?"

"Ain't seen Mom hurtin' like that, long as I can remember," he said. "She ain't able to use that hand at all."

"And she was trying to cook a big supper?"

"Wasn't doin' nothin', just settin' there, holdin' her sore hand."

"I hope she won't try to cook."

"I put the things you sent on the table and got out some plates and cups and told her to let it go at that. She didn't argue, so she's gotta be hurtin' pretty bad. Told her I'd take her in to the doctor tomorrow, if she ain't better."

"I think that's a good idea. She may even have broken something. Was your father there?"

"Nope, didn't see him."

"Did she say anything about my throwing dishwater on him?"

"No. Didn't mention it."

"So I still don't know if I'm in his black book or not. Are you ready to eat?"

"Starvin'."

"It's ready, if you'll go call Calvin. He's in the backyard, I think."

After we had eaten and I had cleaned up the kitchen, I was worried about Clemmy and had just about decided to go over and check on her, whatever the consequences, but about that time Jim Baker drove up in his small red truck. He got out and came rather jauntily up the path.

"Anybody home?" he called through the screen door.

"Come on in, Jim," I said.

"Howdy, Sis. How you doin'?" he asked as he stepped inside.

"Sis, is it?" I asked with raised brows.

"Jist as good as. Davy around?"

"He's out doing the chores. He should be in soon. Have you been to St. Louis this weekend?"

"Jist come from there. I'm on my way home, but Liz wanted me to stop by an' give you a message."

"Sit down, Jim. Would you like a cup of coffee? There's some cake left, too."

"Sounds good."

He followed me into the kitchen and pulled a chair out from the table and sat down. I put the cake and coffee before him and sat down across from him.

"So what is the message?" I asked him.

"First of all, much as she'd like to, your mom can't come an' spend next weekend with you. She says she's a little afraid to rock th' boat right now, but she'll be comin' one of these days an' she may not jist spend th' weekend, she may spend th' whole week."

"I'm sorry she can't come but I don't think I really expected her to. Was there something else? You said there was a message from Liz."

"Me an' her went over last night an' had a long talk with your folks."

"How did it go?"

"Ain't too sure. Your daddy don't like me much, that's for sure. Don't seem to like Davy much better, though."

"No, but I'd just as soon Davy didn't know too much about that, Jim."

He nodded. "Liz said she didn't think you'd told him too much about th' things your daddy said when he was here a couple of weeks ago."

"No. I don't think it's necessary. Daddy doesn't mean all he says when he's angry. Was he — how did he treat you?"

"Not exactly like a long lost friend," Jim admitted dryly. "We didn't tell him we was comin'. Liz was afraid he'd take off if he knew so we jist walked in. He wasn't welcomin', but at least he didn't show me the door."

"What happened?"

"Well, Liz talked right up to him, and wasn't a bit scared of him. She told him decidin' to marry me wasn't any of your doin', that you'd tried to talk her out of it, an' it wasn't fair for him to blame you. Then I told him it was my idea to invite Liz out that time an' I was th' one who told you to write that part about me wantin' to meet her. I told him I thought you was jist about th' prettiest, sweetest littlest thing I ever did meet, up to that time, a course, an' if you had a sister, I wanted to meet her. Told him he sure had reason to be proud of his pretty girls, hopin' to soften him up a little, you know. Told him how much ever'one out here admires you an' looks up to you."

"Thank you, Jim," I said a little dryly. "And was he softened up?"

"Dunno. Didn't kick me out, at least. Then Liz told him she was gonna marry me an' couldn't no one stop her. She said she's of age, but since you'd asked her to wait awhile an' not rush into it, we wouldn't be gettin' married right away. Said she wanted him an' your mom to get to know me better."

"I see. Are you angry with me for doing that?"

"Reckon you got your reasons. Anyway, we ain't waitin' long. We set th' date for th' last Saturday in October. Course we ain't tellin' him that yet. That cake is mighty good. Can I have another piece?"

I got up and cut him another piece of cake and refilled his coffee cup, wondering what was keeping Davy. Perhaps he had gone to see how his mother was after he finished his chores.

"Liz an' me been talkin' 'bout th' weddin'," Jim said. "Don't neither one of us want a big weddin'. We'd rather save our money for a nice honeymoon."

He paused and took another bite of cake, and I had a moment to remember that Liz had always dreamed of an elaborate wedding with all the trimmings. Well, perhaps she had changed her mind.

"She was tellin' me about yours an' Davy's weddin' at them friends of yours in town."

"The Carters," I said.

"Yes. Well, she said it was real simple, you didn't even have anyone stand up with you, it was jist you an' Davy an' th' preacher an' about a dozen people. She was thinkin' maybe she'd like to have our weddin' there, too, since your families know each other so good, but th' thing is, I don't know them an' they don't know me. So I was wonderin', would you an' Davy mind if we have it here?"

"Have the wedding at our house?"

"If you don't mind. Course if you'd rather not, 'cause of th' way your daddy feels, it's all right an' no hard feelin's. I jist thought since you're Liz's sister an' Davy's my best friend, an' since we're goin' to be livin' out here, I'd rather have it here. Liz said why didn't I just mention it to you an' you can be thinkin' about it. Don't have to decide right now."

"I'll talk to Davy about it and we'll let you know."

He pushed his plate back with a sigh. "That sure hit th' spot," he said.

"So you and Liz have definitely decided to live out here?"

"For th' winter, anyway. She wants me to get 'lectricity put in so I'm goin' ahead an' get that done. Shouldn't be any trouble, runnin' the line out from th' Proctor's. Ain't that far. How's school goin'?"

"It's going well, so far. How is it working out for you, taking Evelyn and Todd in to meet the bus?"

"No trouble at all. Todd walks to Evelyn's house, I drive not more'n half a mile out of my way an' they're standin' there waitin'. I stop an' they pile in an' we're on our way."

"I really do appreciate it, Jim. I'm determined for all these children out here to get the chance to go to high school."

"How's it workin' out for Davy, goin' in to get them?"

"It's inconvenient for him, but he doesn't complain."

"Still willin' to do anything for you, huh? That means th' glamour ain't wore off yet," he said with a grin. He rose and pushed his chair back under the table. "Better get on home. Been gone all weekend. Tell Davy howdy. I won't stick around to see him this time."

"I'll tell him. Thanks for stopping, Jim."

He bent and kissed me on the cheek, said 'bye and went out. I sat down at the piano. I hadn't had time to touch it all week, but now I found it relaxing to play through some of the old familiar pieces.

I sent Calvin to bed at nine o'clock, and when Davy came in a short time later, he told me he had been visiting with his mother. He thought he'd have to take her in to the doctor because she wasn't feeling any better. I told Davy about Jim's visit and we sat and talked awhile about the possibility of having the wedding at our house.

CHAPTER EIGHT

A Little Boy's Sobs

 O n Monday the three Anderson children came to school combed and brushed and reasonably clean, and Jimmie Decker came to school sporting a very black and swollen eye.

I made a point of telling the Anderson children individually how nice they looked. I asked Jimmie what happened, but he ducked his head and didn't answer. His brother, Johnny, volunteered the information that Jimmie had been hit in the eye with a doorknob.

Jimmie's eye bothered him that day. He kept blinking and putting his hand up to touch it. He was quiet during recitation period and stood off by himself during recess and didn't join in the games of the other children. Once I saw Johnny go to him and try to put his arm around his shoulder, but Jimmie shrugged it off and turned away.

Toward the end of the day I happened to look in Jimmie's direction and saw him wiping tears away with the back of his hand. As soon as I could, without drawing special attention to him, I walked down the aisle by the first graders and stopped beside him. I had a word or two with the children around him, then put my hand on his shoulder.

"Jimmie," I said gently. "Is your eye bothering you?"

He nodded, then put his head down on his desk and cried, gulping and sobbing and shaking. I knelt beside him and put my arm around him until he had quieted some, then I rose.

"Ruth, will you go up to my desk, please, and be in

charge while I take Jimmie out to the pump and wash his eye? It's bothering him quite a bit. Perhaps some cold water will soothe it."

Ruth rose immediately and went to sit behind my desk. I helped Jimmie to his feet and led him outside, stopping on the way to take a clean handkerchief from my purse. I pumped the water until it was cold, then wet the handkerchief and gently washed Jimmie's face. The tears had stopped, but a rough hiccuping sob racked his small body every few seconds. I wet the handkerchief again and folded it and held it over the black, swollen eye, studying his downcast, woebegone face.

I remembered that Jane had told me once that this was the tough one of her sons. She'd said you could whip him all day long and he wouldn't cry, but he certainly had cried hard enough just now. The conviction had been growing on me all day that there was more here than appeared on the surface. I didn't think Jimmie would cry that hard over a black eye, painful though it undoubtedly was. There had been heartbreak in those sobs.

I wet the handkerchief again and replaced it over his eye. The hiccuping sobs had lessened but not the woebegone expression.

"Is it feeling a little better?" I asked him, and he nodded.

"Let's go sit on the steps a minute, shall we? Can you hold the handkerchief in place?"

He put his hand up and held the handkerchief over his eye while I led him over to the steps with my hand on his shoulder. We sat down, side by side.

"Do you want to tell me what happened, Jimmie?" I asked gently, after a short silence.

He didn't answer, just hunched over, his head down, his elbows on his knees.

"Did you run into the doorknob, or did someone open a door when you weren't expecting it and hit you in the eye?"

Still no answer. I sat observing him for a minute, wondering if perhaps I should walk home with him and Johnny after school and talk to his mother.

I waited a minute longer until I was sure he wasn't going to confide in me, then I took the handkerchief from him, wet it again and handed it back to him.

"Do you feel like going back inside now, Jimmie?" I asked.

He nodded and rose and we went back inside. He went to his desk and sat down, holding the wet handkerchief over his eye until I dismissed school some twenty minutes later.

Just as the children were leaving, I saw Lewis Proctor drive by with his wagon and team of mules. Evelyn Horton and Todd Johnson were with him. I hurried outside, anxious to see Evelyn and Todd. I hadn't had a chance to talk to either of them since they had started high school.

"Hello, Lewis," I called. "Evelyn, how are you? And you, Todd?"

I hardly gave them time to answer but put an arm around Evelyn when she jumped down from the wagon, and put a restraining hand on Todd's arm.

"Lewis, are you going on home now?" I asked.

"Davy gave me the rest of the day off. He had to take his Mom in to the doctor," he answered.

"Would you mind very much taking Johnny and Jimmie Decker home? Jimmie has injured his eye and it's bothering him. I'd feel better if he didn't have to walk all the way."

"Sure. I'll take them."

"Thank you. Come on, boys, get in the wagon. Mr. Proctor will take you home."

They climbed in behind Lewis' two daughters and crouched down in the back of the wagon. When they were settled, I went toward the front of the wagon and looked up at Lewis.

"Will you stop long enough to tell Jane that I asked you to take them home and that Jimmie's eye is bothering him? And will you see — well, how things are going for her and if she needs anything?"

"I'll do it."

"Thanks, Lewis. Tell Sue hello and kiss little David for me. Jimmie, if you keep a cold, wet cloth over that eye, perhaps it will be better tomorrow."

They drove off and I turned my attention back to Todd and Evelyn.

"So how are the two of you?" I asked again. "And how is school?"

"It's hard," Evelyn said.

"Rough," Todd replied.

"It's bound to be a little difficult right at first," I said. "But you'll soon get used to it and you'll do fine. Are you finding your way around more easily now?"

"I couldn't get my locker open this mornin' an' I was late for first class, but they didn't say nothin'," Evelyn said.

"I went to girls gym class today 'stead of boys," Todd admitted with a wry grin.

I laughed. "Everyone has a few problems at the beginning of school. They make allowances. I'm proud of you both and I want you to stick with it, okay?"

They agreed and Todd went off after his brothers and sisters. Evelyn lingered a few minutes longer.

"How is your mother?" I asked her.

"Okay, I guess," she said, but there was a small troubled frown on her face. "Daddy ain't in such a good mood, though. He's havin' to come back to th' house a lot more an' check on Mama durin' th' day. He's worried about her bein' alone so much."

"Is there anyone you know of who might check in on her once a day, or something like that?"

"I don't know of anyone."

"Let me think about it for a few days. Maybe I can

arrange for someone to help your mother."

"Daddy don't like bein' beholdin' to no one."

"Well, let me think about it anyhow. You must finish high school if it's at all possible, Evelyn."

"I got to go. Mama'll be worryin'."

"All right. It's good to see you. Stop in again when you can."

She hurried off. Calvin was on one of the swings so I went back inside to straighten up and leave the school presentable for the next day.

CHAPTER NINE

Through the Wringer

"Calvin," I said as we walked down the hill toward home. "Do you think you might like to do a little extra work in school this year so that you could go into sixth grade next year and skip fifth? That way you could make up one of the years you lost."

He looked inquiringly up at me but didn't answer.

"Perhaps with extra homework and combining some of your classes at school, you could do it. I'll be there to help you in the evenings if you have questions or don't understand everything perfectly. Would you like to try it?"

"I guess so."

"You're doing quite well so far this year. If you really apply yourself, I think you could manage without too much trouble. If you'd like, we can start this evening."

"Okay."

When we got home Davy was not there, but I knew he was back from town because both the truck and the car were there. I set the cookie jar on the table and poured Calvin a glass of milk, then walked to Clemmy's house to see how she was feeling and what the doctor had told her.

Davy was there building up the fire in the kitchen stove. Clemmy was one-handedly clearing the table of used dishes and putting them in the dishpan. I touched my husband on the arm by way of greeting and turned to my mother-in-law.

"How is your hand, Clemmy? What did the doctor tell you today?"

"He says I got arthur-itis in that hand," she answered

in her slow drawl. "He give me some pills an' they're a helpin' already, but he says I gotta rest it awhile, 'til it quits crampin' up on me."

"Then you'd better follow his advice. Why don't you and Mr. Hilton come over to our house for supper tonight?"

"Reckon we won't be troublin' you. Davy's gonna slice a piece of that ham hangin' in th' smokehouse for our supper so I won't have to be cuttin' no meat up. Got them green beans an' taters left over from dinner an' I can stir up a batch of cornbread all right. Like I said, my hand's feelin' some better, but I'm thankin' you for askin'."

"All right, Clemmy, but let me do those dishes for you."

"Ain't got no hot water yet. Davy'll be fetchin' some in directly."

She let me finish clearing the table and went to sit in her rocker. She was still favoring her left hand but her face was not longer puckered with pain. She began to rock gently to and fro.

"Davy, get a extry slice of that ham for your own supper," she told him when he came in with the bucket of fresh water.

He dipped some of the water into the teakettle that was always on the back of the stove and replaced it to heat the water for the dishes. Then he picked up a large butcher knife and a pan and went out again.

"How's th' boy doin' there with you?"

My head lifted in surprise. It was the first time she had asked me about Calvin.

"He's doing quite well," I answered. "He's still very quiet, but with time I'm sure he'll open up and talk more. He spends quite a lot of time with the dog and with the rabbit my sister gave him. I hear him talking to them some. He seems to relate better to animals than to people. That experience he had during the summer with the wild dogs didn't seem to leave any permanent scars. He wrote

81

a story about it, where he was the hero and made a pet of the big German shepherd."

I glanced over at her. Her face was placid and her eyes had a far away dreaming look. I wondered if she was thinking of Calvin's mother.

"The other day when I couldn't find him, he had climbed up in the big oak tree in our backyard. I'd told him I was taking him to Granny's, and he evidently thought I was returning him to her rather than just going for a visit, so he hid from me. From that, I assume he's happy with us and doesn't want to leave."

The water was warm now, so I poured water from the teakettle into the dishpan, added soap, and began washing the dishes. Davy came back with the ham and set the pan, along with the butcher knife, on the table.

"Wash your hands and grab a dishtowel," I told him.

He did as he was told, but twisted the towel into a tight rope and swatted me across the backside before he took the wet plate I handed him.

"Set the table as you go," I said. "Ow! That hurts!" I exclaimed as he swatted me again. "Clemmy, make him stop."

"Mom don't never interfere between husband an' wife, do you Mom?" he said, doing it again.

"You're going to get a cup of soap suds in the face if you do it again," I warned.

He grinned and leaned over to give me a peck on the cheek as he took another plate.

"Okay. I know you'd do it, even if you did make a mess in Mom's kitchen, so I'll stop."

"Davy, don't you think your mother has probably hurt her hand by doing all that scrubbing on her washboard?"

"Could be."

"You wouldn't be saying 'could be' if you'd tried it a few times yourself. I tried it and I know it's murder on hands."

"The doctor said he figgered she musta bruised that

hand up pretty bad at some time or other."

"There, you see Clemmy? From now on, I think you should do your wash at my house, with my machine."

There was no comment. I looked around at Davy. "Don't you think so?" I asked him.

"Don't see why not. It's jist settin' there all week. Somebody jist as well be usin' it."

"I think you should, Clemmy. If the doctor said not to use that hand for awhile, then you shouldn't. Wait until Saturday to do your wash, them come to my house right after breakfast and I'll show you how to use the washing machine. You'll be surprised at how much easier and quicker it is. Then after you learn how to use it, you can come over any time during the week and do your wash. Say you will, Clemmy. You want your hand to get better, don't you?"

"Ain't no good for nothin' one-handed, an' I ain't used to no one doin' for me, just don't seem right, but won't you be doin' your own washin' on Saturday?"

"Yes, but I can do it later. There'll be plenty of time. I'm going to hold you to it now, and if Mr. Hilton objects, then just offer to let him do your wash on the washboard himself because you're not allowed. Doctor's orders."

"Likely his britches 'ud be standin' up by their self 'fore he'd be a washin' 'em," she said dryly, "but I ain't used to machines much. Reckon I could do it?"

"Of course you can. It's easy. You'll see."

I washed the last dish then squeezed the water from the dishcloth and draped it across the plastic line Clemmy had strung between nails behind the stove.

"If you'll empty the dishwater, Davy, I'll put the ham in a skillet for your mother. Is there anything else you need for me to do before I go?"

"Reckon not."

Davy emptied the dishwater by tossing it into the backyard. Then he refilled the teakettle and went out for a fresh bucket of water. When we left to go to our own house, the pan of green beans and potatoes was on the back of the stove, the ham was sizzling in the skillet, the dishes were done and the table set. All that was left for Clemmy to do was make the cornbread. We left her sitting there with time on her hands, which was very rare for Davy's mother.

"Good morning, Clemmy," I said cheerfully as she and Davy appeared around the corner of the cabin early the next Saturday morning. Davy was carrying two bushel baskets of clothes, one stacked on top of the other, and Clemmy was carrying a bucket containing some of her lye soap. Davy deposited his load on the porch and left while Clemmy stepped up on the porch beside me and eyed the washer and tubs rather warily.

"How is your hand this morning?" I asked.

"Better. Don't hurt me none now, 'less I bump it."

"Good. Well, I've already filled the washer and tubs for you. Come closer and I'll show you how it works."

I went through the procedure carefully, step by step, then stayed with her until the first load was washed.

"Now you have to be a little careful with the wringer," I said. "The garment has to be fed in flat, otherwise if it gets bunched up, it will trip the wringer. I'll show you what to do if that happens. Also, you have to watch the smaller pieces, sometimes they'll stick to the wringer and start going around and around. Feeding one garment in over the other without a break will help prevent that. You'll have to really watch the buckles on Mr. Hilton's overalls. If they go in the wringer any way but flat, they'll get bent all out of shape and he won't like that." As I talked, I demonstrated how the wringer worked, then I stepped back to let her take my place. "You go ahead and do the rest, Clemmy. Don't get your fingers too close to the wringer. If something should get tangled up, just hit the release bar here and the top roller will pop up so you can get it untangled."

I watched until the last of the first load of clothes was in the clothesbasket and Clemmy, with a sigh of relief, turned the wringer off.

"There, now wasn't that easy?" I asked.

"I ain't so sure it is," she said. "I feel plumb wore out."

"Why, Clemmy, you have a dozen things washed there in the time it would have taken you to wash only one or two things by hand. You're just nervous because all this is new to you. You'll soon get used to it."

"Maybe. What'll I do next?"

"I think I'd do the sheets and then the towels next. Any time you want to change the water you can."

When the sheets were washed and the towels in the washer, Clemmy was becoming more confident and I was able to relax my vigilance. Nevertheless, I didn't feel comfortable leaving her completely on her own yet, so I went inside and got my sewing box and a pair of Davy's jeans that needed mending and took them back to the porch. While Clemmy dealt with the rest of her laundry, I sat on the bench and did my mending.

It was a warm summer day with a slight breeze blowing. Birds were singing in the nearby trees and Calvin was swinging on the tire under the big oak. It was relaxing and peaceful sitting there, occasionally chatting with my mother-in-law. I loved teaching, but this was a pleasant change from my normal routine.

Something made me glance up. One of Clemmy's long braids had fallen down and was feeding itself into the wringer. Clemmy's eyes were wide and hypnotized, her hands limp at her sides.

I gasped and jumped up from the bench, sending the sewing box to the floor with a crash. I flew to the washer and hit the release bar with the ball of my hand. Clemmy slowly straightened, her eyes still wide and staring, the braid intact.

"Clemmy, are you all right?" I cried.

"I'm awright," she said with a little gulp.

"Did it hurt your scalp? Let me see. There's no blood, at least."

"I'm awright," she repeated in a more normal tone of voice. "Didn't hurt me none. Jist scart me half to death."

There was a moment of silence. I could see that she really was all right, the skin at the base of the braid wasn't even reddened. I had looked up in time so that no damage was done. Suddenly the whole thing struck me as funny. I began to laugh, and once started, I couldn't seem to stop.

"Oh Clemmy, I'm sorry," I gasped, "but you looked so f-funny. Now I know what it means when someone says 'their eyes were as big as saucers.' Yours certainly were."

The scissors I had brought out with my sewing were lying on the bench where I had been sitting. Clemmy snatched them up and grimly sawed through the offending braid. I was instantly sobered.

"Clemmy!" I cried.

"Durn braid's been botherin' me all my life," she said. "Always gettin' in my way, fallin' down an' gettin' into things. I'm tard of it."

She took the pins out of her hair and unwound the other braid from around her head and cut it off, too. Then she just stood there looking at the two braids in one hand and the scissors in the other. Her expression was hard to define.

"Oh Clemmy! What will Mr. Hilton say?"

"Ain't his hair," she said a bit defiantly.

"But you've always worn braids. I'm afraid he'll be terribly upset."

Just then Davy came around the corner and stopped short. I had taken the scissors from Clemmy in order to put them back on the bench. Clemmy still stood, holding the braids. Davy's eyes left his mother and came back to me with an accusing glare.

"What have you done?" he demanded, sounding shocked.

"I didn't do it!" I cried defensively.

"I done it myself," his mother said. She walked over to the wastebasket I kept on the porch and dropped the braids in, then lifted her chin a little as she looked at Davy. I felt the laughter well up in me again, and collapsed onto the bench.

"What happened?" Davy asked, looking from his mother to me.

"One of her braids fell down and got in the wringer," I managed to say. "I hit the release bar before it did any damage, then she grabbed up the scissors and cut the braid off before I even knew what was happening. Then she cut the other one off. I've never seen anything so funny in my whole life."

"I don't see anythin' so funny," Davy said shortly. "Mom's had them braids long as I can remember. Stop laughin', will you?"

"I'm sorry, Clemmy," I managed to say again.

"Wasn't none of your doin'."

"Your son seems to think it was. Probably your husband will think so, too, but I don't care. If you're tired of braids and they're always getting in your way, then you shouldn't have to have braids. Besides, long hair can be hazardous. Think what might have happened if I hadn't been here. We'll finish your washing, then we'll see what we can do with your hair. I'm not much good at cutting hair, but maybe I can even it up a little. Go away, Davy. This is woman's work and your presence is not needed."

As I lifted my head, I met his eyes. Davy shook his head and turned away.

"Ellen's pretty good at hair cuttin'," Clemmy said slowly.

"Is she? Then maybe we should ask her to do it. Davy, wait a minute."

He turned back. "First it's go away, then it's come back," he grumbled. "Well, what is it?"

"You wouldn't happen to be going out toward Tom and Ellen's any time today, would you?"

"Wasn't plannin' on it. Why?"

"I thought maybe you could ask Ellen to come and trim your mother's hair. I don't think I'd better try it, considering the unjust accusation that has already been made against me."

He looked at me under lowered brows. "I'll go. You want her to come now?"

"The sooner the better. Before your father gets home, if possible."

He nodded and turned away and a minute later, we heard the truck start up. I turned back to my mother-in-law.

"I'm afraid I'm a bad influence on you, Clemmy," I said with mock sorrow.

Clemmy had just finished her laundry when Davy came back with Ellen and all five of her children. It was ten-thirty and I had intended to get at my own laundry while Clemmy hung hers out, but when everyone piled out of the truck, I decided to wait. I really liked Ellen and her children, particularly her oldest daughter Ruth, but it wasn't often I had a chance to visit with them. Clemmy and I stood on the porch and waited for them.

"Tom's workin' at th' sawmill today, so Davy said it'd be okay to bring th' kids," Ellen said a little apologetically after we had exchanged greetings.

"Of course," I said. "I'm glad you did. Shall we go inside?"

"Might be better to do th' hair cuttin' out here on th' porch so we don't get hairs all over your house. Mornin' Miz Hilton," she said to Clemmy with a glint of amusement in her eyes. "Thought I was th' only one that cut hair around here."

"I oughten to a done it," Clemmy said. "Jist got so mad I grabbed up them scissors an' cut it off before I give myself time to think."

"It was my fault, I'm afraid," I admitted slowly. "I

laughed, not because she got her braid in the wringer, but because of the expression on her face. I hope Mr. Hilton won't be too upset."

"Likely he won't even notice for days on end," she said a bit dryly. "You kids go on an' play. Ruthie, you keep a eye on th' two little ones."

"Calvin's there in the backyard somewhere," I said. "What do you need, Ellen?"

"I got ever'thing I need, 'cept maybe a chair, if you don't mind bringin' one out."

I brought the chair and Ellen seated Clemmy in it and draped a sheet around her. She unbraided what was left of the braids and combed the hair out. The ends were jagged and uneven, one side considerably shorter than the other. I looked at her with dismay. Clemmy's hair was thin and fine. It looked awful. I looked at Ellen, but she was concentrating on what she was doing.

"Shall I go hang these clothes out for you so they'll be sure and get dry, Clemmy?" I asked, since there was nothing I could do there.

"Hate to be askin' you to do that."

"I don't mind."

"Tell Ruthie to help you," Ellen said. "Think I could cut this hair better if it was wet. You got a pan we could use an' some shampoo?"

"Why don't you use the kitchen sink? I'll get the shampoo and some towels. There's plenty of water. Don't be afraid to use it."

I laid out what was needed then went back out to the porch and took up one of the baskets of clothes. Ruth came and took the other one and we carried them to Clemmy's house and hung them on her clothesline.

Ruth wanted to talk to me about high school. She was an eighth grader and this would be her last year of school here. She told me she wanted to go through high school and then on to nursing school. I answered her questions and listened to her plans for the future. If she attained her goals, she would be one of the ones who would leave the hills and probably never return. So few of the younger generation chose to stay.

The younger children and Calvin were running and shouting around the house, evidently playing Indians or something equally noisy. I wondered how Clemmy and Ellen were making out. I was beginning to feel terribly guilty about Clemmy's hair.

After the clothes were on the lines, Ruth went to join the other children and Ellen was just removing the sheet she had draped around Clemmy's shoulders. I stood and looked at her handiwork.

Clemmy's hair, with the waves from the braids washed out, was about as straight as it could possibly be. Ellen was trying in vain to push a wave into the side of it. It was cut evenly now, but it was too fine and thin to have any body. It just hung there, limp and straight. Clemy didn't look like herself.

"You need a home permanent, Clemmy," I said.

She looked at me, her expression a little anxious. "You don't think it's a sin to put curl where God didn't put no curl?" she asked.

"If it is, then I've been sinning regularly since I was fifteen. I don't see anything wrong with it, Clemmy, if it makes you look and feel better. Do you, Ellen?"

"I give myself home permanents all th' time, an' I'm gettin' ready to give Ruthie one, too, soon as I can get around to it."

"Your hair is very fine," I said. "A gentle permanent would give it body so that it would be much easier to manage. It wouldn't have to be anything extreme."

"Well, my folks always held to th' notion that for a woman to cut her hair off is a sin anyway, so don't reckon it'll make much difference one way or th' other now. You got a mirror handy?"

I brought a hand mirror to her. She gazed into it for a long time then let it drop into her lap with a sigh.

"Reckon I'll have to hide out 'til it grows out again," she said. "I'm apt to scare some poor soul half to death if I go around lookin' like this."

"Is Mr. Hilton coming home for lunch today?" I asked.

"He won't be back 'til evenin'."

"Good. That gives us a little time. I'm going to get my curlers and curl your hair. It won't take long to dry out here and then you'll be able to see what it looks like, so you can decide whether to go ahead with the permanent or not. If you don't like it, you can wash it right out before Mr. Hilton sees you and no harm done. All right?"

"I reckon."

"Ellen, will you and the children stay and have lunch with us?"

She looked uncertain. She was still guarded with me. I liked her and hoped to eventually break down the barriers between us.

"Please," I said. "It won't be much, just sandwiches, and I have some ice cream in the freezer that the children will enjoy."

"I hate to put you out," she said, still hesitant.

"You won't be. I want you to stay. Clemmy, you'll stay, too, won't you? We'll have a kind of party. It will be a nice change for all of us."

"If you're sure it ain't too much bother."

"It isn't. Tell you what. If you'll put the curlers in Clemmy's hair, I'll go bake some cookies to go with the ice cream. It won't take much more than a half hour or so."

When Ellen came into the kitchen a short while later, I was putting the first batch of cookies in the oven.

"Can I do anything?" she asked. "I brushed myself off good an' washed up at th' pump."

"You can start making the sandwiches," I said. "There's some leftover roast in the refrigerator, but I'm not sure there's enough. Do you think the children would mind peanut butter and jelly?"

"It's their favor-rite."

"Good. We'd better make plenty. The way they're running and shouting out there, they're using up a lot of energy. I'm glad you came, Ellen, and brought the children. Calvin needs someone to play with. He does too much sitting around when he's here alone. Where's Clemmy?"

"She took th' chair out in th' yard an' is settin' out there dryin' her hair."

"I'm going to emancipate Clemmy, Ellen," I said, as I set the sandwich makings on the table before her. "I mean, I'm going to free her. She works too hard and has too little pleasure in her life. After today, I hope I've convinced her to do her wash over here. Then after she gets used to that, I'm going to show her how easy it is to use my iron, instead of those heavy irons she has to heat on top of the stove. I wish someone could convince Mr. Hilton to run the electric line on up to their house so she wouldn't have to stand over that hot stove so much in the summer, and go all the way down to the creek to cool her milk and butter. I'm going to work on him so that maybe by next summer — but then I haven't really seen him since I threw the dishwater on him. He may not be speaking to me, and after he sees Clemmy's hair — "

"You throwed dishwater on him?" Ellen asked, aghast. She was making the sandwiches and I was taking the first batch of cookies out of the oven. The kitchen was filled with the delicious smell of melting chocolate chips.

"Not on purpose," I explained. "It was an accident. I expected him to be furious, but he didn't say anything, and as I said, I haven't seen him since. Do you have electricity, Ellen?"

"No, but Tom says we can maybe get it put in in th' next year or two. Is it awful expensive?"

"No, not really. It's well worth the expense, I think, but Mr. Hilton doesn't approve of new-fangled things, or so I've been told. Are you — do you know him very well, Ellen?"

"Me?" she exclaimed. "I don't hardly know him at all. I don't think nobody does. He's more at home out in th' woods with th' wild animals than he is with people."

"Yes, I have noticed that. I'm glad Davy isn't like that."

"Davy's good," she said simply.

"Yes, Davy is good. He's a wonderful husband."

"So is Tom."

"I'm glad, and I'm glad things are working out so well for you, Ellen."

"Them cookies sure do smell good," she said after a short silence. "They won't last long with my bunch around."

"That's what they're for. Well, they're done. I wonder how Clemmy is making out."

I glanced out the window and cried with dismay. "Those little rascals have Clemmy all tied up and it looks as if they're intending to scalp her!"

I rushed outside with Ellen right behind me. Clemmy was sitting there with a rope wound around her and the chair, while the six children, including Ruth, were dancing and whooping in a circle around her, brandishing sticks. Calvin and his cousin Tommy each held aloft a long braid.

Ellen and I stopped short of the scene, seeing that Clemmy was sitting there placid and unharmed. We both started laughing, and seeing they had an audience, the children whooped and danced all the harder.

"I wonder what Mr. Hilton would think if he came home right now," I said. I raised my voice. "All right, you young Indians. That's enough now. The war party is over. Go wash up and get ready for lunch. Clemmy, are you all right?"

"At least them kids got some fun outta them braids of mine," she said as we untied her. "Ain't all been for nothin'." Her face was flushed and cherubic, with the pink curlers adorning her head.

"You must be hot, sitting out here in the sun so long.

Maybe Ellen can comb your hair while I get the rest of lunch on. I'll bring you a glass of cool water."

I made a big pitcher of Kool-aid for the children, adding a generous amount of ice, since the children out here almost never had ice in the summertime. The cookies were on the counter. I made a fresh pot of coffee and set out the paper plates, cups, and napkins that I kept at the back of the cabinet for just such an occasion. Then I took out a big bag of potato chips that I had hidden away and poured the chips out into a big bowl and put it in the middle of the table.

Ellen and Clemmy came in and I stared at a transformed Clemmy. Soft curls framed her face, taking years off her age. Her cheeks were still flushed with heat.

"Why Clemmy, you're beautiful!" I exclaimed.

"Don't she look nice?" Ellen said with a soft touch of pride and affection.

"She certainly does. Clemmy, you should have chopped those braids off years ago. Have you seen yourself? Go look in the bathroom mirror there."

Bemused, she did so. It was several minutes before she came back.

"Do you like it?" I asked.

"Didn't hardly recognize myself," she admitted. "An' it feels so light an' free. Feels like maybe I won't be havin' all them headaches I been havin' for years either."

"It's just possible you won't and I won't have to worry about you getting your braids in the wringer again either. Come sit here, Clemmy. Lunch is ready. I'll call the children. I wonder where Davy is. Ah, here he is. I wonder how he'll like your hair now."

Davy stood regarding his mother for a long minute while she gazed back at him, her head lifted a little as if she challenged him.

"It looks real good, Mom," he said then. "I like it."

"I wonder how Mr. Hilton will like it. If you'll sit here across from your mother, Davy, and Ellen, you sit there on the other side of him, I'll sit over here in case I have to get anything from the kitchen."

I seated the children, then before I could sit down myself, Ellen's oldest boy, Chad, stood up and reached across the table to the bowl of chips. That seemed to be the signal for his brother and Calvin to do the same, evidently afraid they wouldn't get their fair share. Chips were a rarity for these children. One of the children knocked over a glass of Kool-aid, which began to spread in a red pool across the table.

I grabbed the dishtowel to stem the tide, and at the same time removed the bowl of chips from the table with my other hand. Ellen looked mortified.

"Boys, sit," I ordered. They obeyed immediately. "It's all right, Ellen. No harm done. I should have known better than to put the chips in a bowl in the middle of the table. I should have just put some on each plate. There. Now we can eat."

The children ate like young wolves. Ellen was nervous and I could see she was afraid her family's table manners wouldn't be up to my standards. I strove to put her at ease and eventually she began to relax and enjoy herself. But it was Clemmy who was having the best time. She had a new confidence in herself and she was enjoying the free give and take of her grandchildren. Mealtime had never been like this at her house.

While I was serving the ice cream and cookies, a car drove up and I glanced out the window to see Jim and Liz getting out of her car. I would have to make more sandwiches. I hoped they wouldn't mind peanut butter and jelly.

I introduced my sister to Ellen and her family, then suggested the children take their ice cream and cookies into the backyard to make more room at the table. Liz and Jim seated themselves at the table without a second invitation.

"An' who might th' young lady settin' there at th' end

of th' table be?" Jim quipped. "Ain't you gonna introduce her, too?"

"Don't you go tryin' none of your sweet talk on me, Jim Baker," Clemmy retorted. "I knowed you since you was a little bitty thing, an' I ain't fallin' for it."

"Why, if it ain't Miz Hilton! I swear I didn't rec'onize you. Thought it must be your kid sister come to visit, or somethin'. What you gone an' done to yourself? Or maybe I oughta ask, what's Teacher gone an' done to you?"

"I didn't do it, but I don't mind being credited with it. I think she looks terrific, don't you?"

"I sure do. Ain't never seen you without braids before, an' it takes some gettin' used to, but I like it. Ain't never seen you lookin' so good."

"It's very attractive," Liz murmured. "I'll bet it's a relief not to have to bother with those long braids."

"It is that. Well, that was a real nice dinner, Anne. S'pect I better be gettin' on home, if you don't need me to help clean up here."

"No, Clemmy, there's very little to do, with the paper plates and cups, but thanks anyhow, and thank you for staying for lunch. We enjoyed having you."

"You have a choice of peanut butter and jelly or grilled cheese sandwiches," I told Jim and Liz when she was gone.

"Make mine peanut butter and jelly, an' I'll have some of that Kool-aid, too. Ain't had any Kool-aid for a long time an' it sure looks good."

"Liz?"

"I'll have the same."

"'Fraid I got some awful bad news for you two ladies," Jim said mournfully. "You're both gonna be jist heartbroken."

Ellen and I exchanged puzzled glances. "What is it, Jim?" I asked.

"Hate to be the one to have to break it to you."

"Just tell us, Jim."

"Hear tell Goldie Sutton's done moved into town an' got herself a job an' a apartment. 'Fraid you won't be seein' much of her around here no more."

Ellen and I looked at each other and Ellen blushed. I had to smile. Across the table, Davy hid a grin behind his coffee cup.

"Know how terrible both of you'll miss her," Jim added blandly.

"Of course," I agreed just as blandly, setting his sandwich before him, "but as long as she's happy, we'll manage, won't we, Ellen?"

Ellen laughed nervously but said nothing.

"Who is Goldie Sutton?" Liz asked, puzzled.

"You met her when you were here for our housewarming party last spring," I said. "She was here when you arrived, the blonde in the tight blue dress? I introduced you, remember?"

"Oh yes, but I didn't know she was a particular friend of yours."

"She isn't."

"Then why will you — Oh."

"Precisely," I said dryly. "Jim is indulging in his weird sense of humor again."

"Weird! Well, I like that! You gonna set there an' let your wife insult me like that?"

"Think maybe I better stay out of it," Davy said.

"I'll have some of them cookies an' some of that ice cream now, Teacher, if you got any left."

I rose to get the cookies and ice cream. I set a bowl before Liz, too. "Are the two of you off to town?" I asked.

"Yes. We're going to look at wallpaper. I've talked him into letting me paper the living room and the bedroom."

"Jim and Liz are engaged to be married," I explained to Ellen, in case she hadn't heard. I turned back to Liz. "You're going to spend the night here with us then?"

"Yes, if it's all right."

"It's fine. You can have Calvin's room."

"Oh no, really Anne, I'd rather just sleep on the sofa. It may be late when we get back, so if you'll just leave a pillow and a light blanket out for me, I'll be fine."

"If you're sure."

"I'm sure."

"That was a real good dinner, Teacher," Jim said rising. "S'pose we better be goin'. If I don't see you tonight, I'll prob'ly see you in th' mornin'. Biscuits an' gravy an' ham an' eggs will be all right for my breakfast."

I made a face at him and he grinned at me and reached over and flicked my cheek with a careless finger.

Ellen left soon after they did, it was nap time for her four-year-old. Calvin decided to ride along with them, so the six children climbed into the back of Davy's truck, Ellen got in the front with him, and waving, they drove away. I went back to the house and out to the back porch to belatedly do my own wash for the week.

CHAPTER TEN

Changing Habits

I had no opportunity to talk to Liz alone that weekend. We'd gone to bed long before she came in, and Jim was there in the morning very soon after we got up. I did make one attempt to get her alone, but she was evasive, so I gave it up. Her decision was made and she evidently wanted no interference from me.

After breakfast, the four of us sat around the table and talked. We decided that the wedding would be at our house, very simple. Davy and I would stand up with them. Only a few guests would be invited to the wedding, but whether Daddy would come, none of us knew. Liz had not talked to him again but she had talked to Mama, and Mama promised to be there, no matter what.

When they had gone, I did some housecleaning and the week's ironing and set Calvin to some extra homework, thinking half-heartedly that I ought to take him in to visit Granny. She would be wondering what had become of us.

My mother-in-law came right after lunch. All the curl was gone from her hair and it hung straight and lank around her face.

"I come to tell you maybe I better have that permanent wave you was talkin' about," she said. "When I got up this mornin' all th' curl was gone an' it was stickin' out ever' which way. Can't do nothin' with it."

"All right, Clemmy. I don't have a home permanent kit right now, but maybe Davy can go into town soon and then either I or Ellen can give it to you. Why don't you sit down here and I'll put the curlers in again. Then it will look nice for the rest of the day, at least."

"If you got th' time. Pert near scart myself to death when I looked in th' mirror this mornin'," she said with wry humor, seating herself in the chair I had indicated.

"What did Mr. Hilton say?" I asked, as I wound her hair around the pink rollers.

"Didn't say much yesterday, jist stared at me then asked me what in th' world I thought I was up to, but this mornin' he asked me where was my broomstick. I did look mighty like a witch."

"We'll show him, Clemmy. After you get your permanent, the curl won't come out at night and you'll look beautiful. You have the prettiest complexion I've ever seen, hardly a wrinkle in sight. Is there some magic secret?"

"Well, I'll tell you, if you won't laugh. My folks never did hold with a woman wearin' them cosmetics, though all my daughters come to it sooner or later, but my mama said ain't nothin' wrong in usin' th' natural things God give us. She told me if I wanted to keep my skin lookin' nice, ever' night I should take a slice of raw tater an' run it over my face an' neck, an' that's what I done all these years. Wasn't nothin' I could do to stop my hair goin' gray, but at least I ain't been troubled much with wrinkles, like most women my age."

"There's nothing wrong with gray hair, Clemmy. Yours is quite pretty when it's curled. If you'll come back in about an hour, I'll take the curlers out and comb it for you."

I stepped back and she stood up and prepared to leave. I looked after her with a smile of amused affection. It looked slightly incongruous, seeing her in pink curlers.

I went on with my work and an hour later Clemmy was back, with a scarf wrapped around her head. I removed the curlers and combed her hair, waving it back from her face. I used hair spray to keep it in place, then stood back to view my handiwork, realizing she must have been a very pretty young woman.

"There you are, Clemmy," I said with satisfaction. "You're beautiful again. I've added just a little hair spray to make the curl stay in longer. It may feel a little stiff, but that will come out when you comb it."

She stepped into the bathroom and took a long look at herself in the mirror. "Have to admit, I ain't lookin' so bad to myself," she said. "Wouldn't think an ol' woman like me could be so vain, would you?"

"You aren't vain. Everyone likes to look their best. We always feel better when we know we look nice. Not that you haven't always looked well, but the different hair style makes you look ten years younger, so go ahead and enjoy your good looks, Clemmy. After all, God loved beauty, too. Look at all the beautiful things He's made."

"Bless you, Child. I ain't beautiful, but I ain't so bad lookin' either. What's done is done an' I ain't goin' around feelin' guilty about it no more. If you'll have Davy buy that home permanent for me, I'll be gettin' it in, soon as you or Ellen can do it."

"Good for you, Clemmy. I'll tell Davy."

I walked partway home with her and stopped off at the shop, where Davy was. He was bent over his work bench with a pencil and a ruler in his hand. When I entered he straightened and looked around.

"Somethin' wrong?" he asked.

"No. I just thought I'd walk down and see what you were doing."

"Jist finishin' up some cabinets for John."

"Is it a rush job?"

"Not 'specially. Why?"

"I just wondered. I should take Calvin in to see Granny. I wondered if you'd like to go along?"

"Er, come to think of it, I did more or less promise John I'd finish them up this week," he said with a grin.

I sighed. "I'm not looking forward to it either."

"Why don't you wait 'til next Saturday, then maybe we can all go in and make a day of it. I'll take these cabinets on in to John while you and Calvin visit with Granny, then I'll come back to pick you up and we'll go on in to town and do some shoppin', maybe go to a picture show or somethin'. You was sayin' Cal needs new clothes, wasn't you?"

"Yes, definitely he does, and I'll need a new dress if I'm going to be Liz's matron of honor. All right, I'll put it off one more week, though I'll hear from Granny when I do get him there."

"Was there somethin' else you was wantin' to talk about?"

"No, not particularly, it's just that — "

"Jist what?"

"Nothing. It's been a hectic weekend, so much company, so much going on. We haven't really had much of a chance to talk, that's all."

He came to me and put his hands at my waist. "I know it," he said. "Seems like I ain't hardly seen you all week."

I put my head on his chest and he drew me close. "I guess I hadn't quite realized how much more there would be to do, with a husband and a child and a home to care for, besides teaching school."

"Don't forget in-laws and a sister and a best friend, besides a weddin' comin' up soon."

"Everything seems to be happening at once, doesn't it?"

"Sure does. Maybe you an' me oughta try to get away by ourselves one of these weekends. I know a special place where I'd sure like to take you."

"I don't see how we could right now, Davy. Besides, what would we do with Calvin?"

"Leave him with Granny."

"I don't think that's a good idea, so soon after he's come to us. He's still pretty insecure."

"Never thought I'd be jealous of a twelve-year-old boy," he said, half humorously.

"You have no reason to be jealous. He'll settle down and be less dependent on us as time goes on, but I don't think we ought to leave him yet."

He sighed and released me. "Okay, whatever you say."

"I'd better get back to the house. I still have a lot to do. I'll see you at supper."

I kept busy the rest of the afternoon but I didn't have time to get any of my schoolwork done, so after Calvin was in bed I sat on the sofa with my papers spread out before me on the coffee table. Davy sat in his rocker reading the newspaper. The house was silent. I looked at my husband, an idea growing in my mind. When he laid the paper aside I spoke.

"Davy, would you mind helping me grade some of these papers?"

He looked surprised. "You want me to help you grade school papers?"

"Yes. Why not?"

He came over to sit beside me. I gathered up several papers and handed them to him, along with a pencil.

"Where's the answer sheet?"

"There is no answer sheet. I made that test up myself."

I was aware that he cast a sidelong glance at me, but I pretended not to notice. I busily sorted out some more papers. I had given him test papers to grade that I had given to the three upper grades the Friday before in language class. It was a multiple choice in grammar.

I graded some arithmetic papers and looked over a couple of compositions. When Davy handed the papers back to me, I gave him another handful, this time on spelling. While he graded them, I glanced through the papers he had already checked. Then I sat for a moment and looked at him.

"Did I get them all wrong?" he asked, glancing up.

"No," I said. "You got them all right, which proves to me something I've suspected for some time."

103

"What?"

"That you do know the basics of good grammar as well as anyone."

"I do?"

"Yes. I thought you probably did. After all, you went through ninth grade, and most of the rules of grammar are taught in elementary school. So why don't you use it, Davy?"

"Habit, I guess," he said ruefully.

"Habits can be changed," I said.

"I keep forgettin'. When you've talked a certain way all your life and when you're around other people that talk that way — "

"I know it's hard. I have the same problem with my students. I can teach them good grammar all day long and in class they'll do it perfectly, but then as soon as they go outside at recess, it's 'I done this,' or 'you done that.' It's frustrating for a teacher."

"I s'pose it's more frustratin' for the teacher not to be able to get her own husband to use good grammar, huh?"

"It is a little. I'd really like it if you'd at least try, Davy."

"Thought you was — were gonna give me lessons."

"You don't need lessons, just practice. You can do it if you really want to."

He was silent for a minute, looking down at the papers in his hands while I sat and looked at him. "I been thinkin'," he said. "Maybe I ought to take one of them — one of those correspondent courses, go ahead and get my high school diploma. What do you think?"

"I think that would be wonderful, but do it because it's what <u>you</u> want to do, Davy, not because you think it's what I'd like."

"I been thinkin' about it for several years, jist haven't done anything about it yet. Think maybe I will this winter. Well, what better time than now, with a teacher right here in the house to help me?"

"I'll help you all I can, but I doubt if you'll need much help. You're actually a very well-educated man in most ways."

"Jist not in the way I talk, huh?"

"Just try being a little more conscious of it, will you, Davy? Don't try to do it all at once, but gradually you can train yourself to use good grammar. It really isn't that hard."

"I'll try."

"Thank you." I leaned over and kissed him. "I love you, you know that don't you?"

"I love you, too."

CHAPTER ELEVEN

Classroom Chaos

Monday turned out to be an eventful day. The Anderson children were already at school when Calvin and I arrived, and Frankie, the first grader I had sent home on the first day, was with them. They were all just as dirty and unkempt as they had been before my little talk with them about the importance of cleanliness. I felt dismayed and at a loss as to what to do. Mattie, the oldest, came and stood before my desk.

"Mama said tell you Frankie's got to go to school," she said, half belligerent, half fearful. "She says you ain't got no right to keep him out."

"I'm afraid I do have that right, Mattie," I said as kindly as I could. "Any child who is not toilet trained is not ready for school."

"Mama says he's gotta go," she repeated doggedly.

"Why has he got to go?"

Her face puckered, tears filled her eyes and rolled down her cheeks. "Daddy's been drinkin', all day yesterday an' all night last night. He hit Mama, then he started hittin' us kids, too. Mama said she'll have a hard enough time keepin' th' little ones outta his hair today, let alone havin' Frankie there, too, so he's gotta go to school. Don't make him go back home, Miz Hilton. I'm afraid of what Daddy'll do."

I put my hand on her shoulder. "All right, Mattie," I said gently. "I won't send him back home today, but I want you to watch over him. Take him to the toilet before school starts, and be sure he goes at every recess, and any other time you think he has to go. You don't have to ask permission today, just take him."

"But I can't take him to the boys' toilet," she said aghast, her tears arrested.

"No, I suppose not. All right then, Phillip can take him, but you must help keep an eye on him, too. Do you think your mother needs help?"

"I'm scairt, Miz Hilton. Daddy ain't never been this bad before."

"All right, Mattie, I'll see what can be done. Now you don't worry about it anymore, okay? Didn't you bring your lunches?"

"Mama said we couldn't wait for no lunches. We been settin' out there at th' edge of th' woods for pert near a hour, waitin' for you to come."

"I see. Did you have breakfast?"

"Jist a cold biscuit."

"You must be hungry then." I reached for mine and Calvin's lunches and gave them to her. "You and your brothers go out and wash your hands and faces at the pump, then go sit on the grass somewhere and eat what's in the sacks. Then all of you go to the toilet and wash your hands again before you come in, and don't worry. We'll get some help for your mother and the little ones."

They obeyed. I looked at my watch. It was still early.

"Calvin."

He looked up from the book he was reading, his expression far away. I doubted he had heard a word of the conversation between me and Mattie. He could lose himself completely in a story.

"Calvin, I need your help," I said. "I want you to run home and find Davy. Tell him I want him to come here, and right away. I need him. If you can't find him and Lewis is there, tell Lewis to come. Have you got that?"

He nodded, rising.

"Hurry now, but don't exhaust yourself. Tell Davy to bring the car and you come back with him."

He left the room, and a minute later I saw him running down the hill, swift as a deer. He would be home in a matter of minutes. I just hoped Davy hadn't left yet.

The other children began to arrive and I greeted them as usual, although I was tense and worried whether I was doing the right thing in sending for Davy. He would know better than I what to do, but I didn't want him involved in a brawl with a drunken man.

About twenty minutes later I saw the car appear over the hill. With a sigh of relief, I saw that Lewis was with Davy. Calvin's head showed between them, sticking up over the back of the seat. I went outside to await their arrival. They all came quickly to me.

"What's wrong?" Davy asked rather sharply.

I smiled at the Johnson children, who were just arriving. "Good morning," I said. "You may go on inside. I'll be there in just a moment. You may go, too, Calvin." Then I turned back to Lewis and Davy. "Let's step over here to the car," I said.

"I'm sorry to send for you, but I didn't know what else to do. Thank you for coming, too, Lewis. It's Mrs. Anderson. She sent the children off early without any breakfast or lunch because their father is drinking and she was afraid he was going to hurt one of them. She's there at home with him with the three little ones, and Mattie is afraid. She says she's never seen him so bad. I didn't know what to do, so I sent for you."

Davy took his hat off and scratched his head. "Won't be the first time he's got drunk and roughed her up. Don't much like to step in between a man and his wife."

"I don't either, but what if he really hurts one of them or even — "

"You think it's that bad?"

"I don't know a thing about it. All I know is what Mattie told me and that she's frightened. You know them better than I. What do you think?"

He and Lewis exchanged glances. I waited.

"I'll go over," Davy said then.

"I'll go with you," Lewis said.

"It might be better if there was a woman with you. Unfortunately I can't go. Do you think your mother — "

Davy nodded. "She'll have to stay in the car, but we'll take her with us for the look of it."

"Thank you. Don't wait too long though."

"We'll go now."

"Be careful and let me know, will you, so I can reassure the children. Oh and Davy, if you have time later, could you bring something for our lunches, Calvin's and mine and the Anderson children? I gave them our lunches for their breakfast. Some apples and cookies will probably be enough."

"Okay."

The two men got into the car and drove away and I went inside to begin the day's classes.

In spite of my anxiety over the Andersons and Davy and Lewis, I couldn't help but notice that Jimmie Decker was withdrawn and uncommunicative again, almost sullen. He sat in his seat and stared straight ahead, and when I called the first grade up to the bench, he just sat there and had to be called again before he came. Even then he didn't participate. His attitude was so different from the beginning of school that I was seriously disturbed. On the other hand, his brother Johnny seemed nervous and too anxious to please. Something was wrong. I resolved that I must find the time to go out and visit with Jane soon and see if I could find out what the problem was.

Just before first recess, Nonie Johnson surged up from her seat, and with both hands brought her spelling book down hard on Lonnie Baxter's head. The dull thud was loud in the room. All eyes turned toward Nonie as she stood there, the book still held threateningly in both hands, her eyes flashing fire. Lonnie's head was bowed, his face brick red, and he had an abashed, rather silly grin on his face.

"Nonie!" I said. "What is the meaning of this?"

"I ain't settin' in front of him no more," she said hotly. "Even if you whip me for it, I ain't goin' to, Miz Hilton."

I walked over to them, observing her angry face and his evident embarrassment. I had an idea what this was about and couldn't help feeling sorry for both of them.

"All right, Nonie, but hitting people over the head with books is not the way to solve problems."

"He deserved it!"

"Do you think you deserved it, Lonnie?"

He hung his head and didn't answer.

"Nellie, I would like for you to exchange seats with Lonnie, please. You may sit back down, Nonie, and get on with your work."

She obeyed, sliding down in her seat, the spelling book held open before her face, her cheeks red. I let my hand rest for a moment on her shoulder. Both Lonnie and Nellie were taking their belongings out of their desks. Nellie came back to Lonnie's seat and he went up to hers. This put him at the front of the row where he would be more conscious of my watchful eye. I walked back up to the front of the room.

"Nonie and Lonnie, you will stay in your seats, please," I said. "The rest of you are dismissed for recess."

Quietly the rest of the children rose while Nonie and Lonnie remained seated. I waited until the other children were outside, then closed the inside door.

"All right, Nonie," I said then. "Do you want to tell me why you hit Lonnie?"

She didn't reply for a long minute, obviously embarrassed, though her eyes were still angry. "He was bein' nasty," she said then.

"Well, Lonnie, what do you have to say for yourself?"

"Nothin'."

"Do you think you deserved to be hit over the head?"

He shrugged. "Didn't hurt me none."

"You're fortunate she didn't use her geography book. All right, Nonie. You may go outside."

She rose and went out. I stood and looked at Lonnie. He tried to meet my eyes and failed. His hands twisted themselves together on the desk.

"It's hard growing up, isn't it?"

His eyes flew up in surprise, then fell again. His face grew redder. I sat at a desk across from him and waited a moment before I went on.

"Every boy your age experiences the same problem you do, Lonnie, learning how to handle the new feelings, the new emotions. I'm not going to embarrass you by talking about it, but I am going to tell you this. You have a good mind, but you're not using it for the right things right now. Your grades are suffering and you're not very happy with yourself, if I'm not mistaken. I'm going to make some suggestions and I'd like to see you follow through on them. No, I'm going to expect you to follow through on them, at least here at school. At recess, instead of sitting around watching the girls and talking with the other boys about who knows what, I want to see you playing basketball, baseball, running and jumping and using up some of that excess energy in the right way. I guarantee you'll feel better and be able to concentrate more on your lessons. I'm going to be keeping an eye on you so watch yourself. Any questions?"

He shook his head, still lowered.

"All right, Lonnie, you may go outside for a few minutes. Recess is almost over."

He ambled outside and I hoped the problem was solved, though I doubted it would be that easy.

Davy came back a short time later and walked quietly into the schoolroom. He had a sack in his hand and put it on my desk.

"She's okay," he said in a low voice. "He'd passed out, time we got there. She says he'll be out most of the day, and when he wakes up, he'll be too sick to do much. She says they'll be okay."

"Good. Thank you for going, Davy, I appreciate it."

"S'okay. Mom made some sandwiches and I put in the cookies and apples, like you said."

"Thank you."

"Anything else you need?"

"No, I don't think so. I'm sorry I sent you on a wild goose chase."

"S'all right. Well, I'll be goin'. See you this evenin'."

I found the opportunity to quietly tell Mattie that her family was all right. She looked tired and had dark circles under her eyes. The next two or three hours were uneventful, then right after last recess, Chad Hilton raised his hand. There had been some whispering going on there at the back of the room, but as long as it didn't become disruptive, I made it a practice to ignore it.

"Yes, Chad?" I said.

"Aunt Annie," he said in a rather loud voice. "Can I get me a drink?"

I fixed him with a stern eye. "I beg your pardon. What did you say?"

"I said, Aunt Annie, can I get me a drink?"

There were a few surpresed giggles, and from across the aisle Ruth hissed a warning at her brother.

112

"No," I said sternly. "You may not get a drink. That's what recess is for, and I am <u>not</u> your Aunt Annie. In this classroom, I'm not even your Aunt Anne. You may call me either Mrs. Hilton, or Teacher, if you prefer, but not Aunt. Is that clear?"

"Yes ma'am." And then, barely audible, "Aunt Annie."

I ignored it. That's what came of getting too chummy with my husband's relatives. Chad wasn't a bad boy, but he did like to show off. However, this was something that had to be nipped in the bud if I wanted to continue being an effective teacher.

Chad had his hand up again a few minutes later but I ignored it, not willing to put it to the test. At the end of the day, Frankie Anderson had made a puddle under his seat, but otherwise he had done pretty well, and Mattie had fallen asleep with her head on her desk. Evidently the boys had not suffered a sleepless night as she had. I almost hated to see them start for home.

"Chad, you will stay in at first recess tomorrow," I said as I dismissed the children for the day. He looked at me skeptically.

Chad would have to be disciplined. He had called me Aunt Annie again when he came up to the bench for arithmetic class.

The next morning as I sat at my desk doing a few preliminary things and watching the children arrive, I heard the jingling harness of a team being driven up. I rose and looked out the window and saw Davy's brother Tom with his children, getting down from his wagon. My heart dropped, but I went back to my seat and sat down, determined not to let him intimidate me. He came in alone.

"Good morning, Tom," I said with what I hoped was a casual, friendly smile.

113

"Mornin'." he returned soberly. His eyes, so like Davy's, deliberately held mine. "My boy tells me you're keepin' him in at recess."

"Yes, I am. Ideally, I should have kept him in after school yesterday, but I didn't want to do that and make him have to walk home alone."

"He says you told him you ain't his aunt."

I rose and stood to face him. Sitting, I felt at a disadvantage. "I told him that, in the schoolroom, I'm not his aunt," I explained. "Chad was deliberately creating a disturbance yesterday. He kept holding his hand up for trivial things, then when I called on him, he would call me 'Aunt Annie', making some of the other children laugh. It's a small matter, I'll admit, but I can't let him go unpunished. Family relationships cannot be a factor in the schoolroom, Tom. If I allowed him to call me aunt, it wouldn't be long before some of the other children would be doing it, too, and it would split this schoolroom right down the middle, since so many of the children are Davy's nieces and nephews. If the relationship was constantly emphasized, the other children would perhaps begin to feel they were being discriminated against. I can't let that happen. I'm here for all the children and they will all be treated the same, family connections not withstanding. That's why I told Chad that here at school, he's to call me only Mrs. Hilton, or Teacher, as the rest of the children do. Since he defied me and continued to call me Aunt Annie, he will be punished, as any other child would be punished."

Tom had listened quietly, his keen gray eyes never leaving mine. I hoped I sounded more poised and assured than I felt.

"An' would th' same thing go for Calvin if he was to call you Aunt? Or maybe Mama?"

"Most certainly. Here in the classroom, I'm nobody's

aunt and no one's mother. Calvin calls me Teacher."

"An' would you make him stay in at recess, too, if he done somethin' you didn't like?"

"I don't keep any of the children in just because they might happen to do something I don't like. It's when they deliberately do something wrong and that they know is wrong that I punish them. What Chad did yesterday was deliberate, and it was disruptive, and it was repeated several times. Therefore he will be punished."

He stood there looking at me a minute longer, then he nodded, turned, and walked out. I let my breath out in a small sigh of relief and sat back down.

His children came in then, Ruth eyeing me a little uneasily. I smiled and said good morning as I usually did. Frankie was with the Anderson children again. When they were seated and just before time to ring the bell I went over to speak to them privately, feeling less critical now that I better understood their situation.

"Mattie, how is your mother?" I asked.

"She's awright."

"Good," I replied, not wanting to probe. Their faces were washed and their hair combed, but their clothes were frankly filthy. I turned to the youngest one.

"Hello, Frankie. How are you today?"

No reply.

"You did quite well yesterday," I continued. "You must try very hard to do as well today. If you have to go to the toilet, be sure and tell Phillip and he will take you. Be sure he goes at every recess, Phillip. Did you take him this morning before you came inside?"

Phillip shook his head.

"Then take him now, but hurry. It's almost time for the bell. If you're a few minutes late, don't worry about it." I left them and walked back down the aisle and stopped beside Johnny and Jimmie Decker.

"Hello, boys," I said. "How are you this morning?"

"Fine," Johnny said.

"And you, Jimmie?"

He looked up at me, his eyes wide and sober, but the sullen look of yesterday seemed to be gone. He did not smile but he said, "I'm okay."

"Good." I put my hand briefly on his shoulder. "I'm looking forward to the story we're reading today, aren't you?"

He nodded and I passed on, pausing to speak to the other children. I tried to personally greet each student and have just a few words with them individually. I made no exception of Chad, just because he was to be disciplined. He acted smug.

The first half of the morning went smoothly. When I dismissed them for first recess, Chad rose with the rest of the children, evidently thinking his father had fixed it with me.

"Chad, you will return to your seat, please," I said.

"But Daddy said — "

"Return to your seat, please."

He turned and stomped back to his seat and flung himself down in it, his expression belligerent.

I waited until all the children were outside, then went and sat in a seat across from him and gave him basically the same explanation I'd told his father. I kept my voice pleasant and friendly in spite of his sullen look, but I was firm about it.

"Daddy said I can call you Aunt Annie any time I want to, 'cause you are my aunt," he said when I had finished.

"You may call me Aunt Annie outside the classroom if you'd like, though I'd much prefer Aunt Anne, but not here at school, Chad. And I would like to remind you that here at school, I am in charge, not your father." I rose and stood a moment beside him. "Now I want you to get your spelling book out and write the assigned words ten times each. At the end of the day I'm going to give them to you again and I want you to be letter perfect. You missed close to half of them this morning."

I turned away, but familiar with the ways of young boys, turned back again. He jerked upright and put his tongue back in his mouth. I stood with my eyes holding his for a long moment before he ducked his head and pulled his speller out of his desk. He took out paper and pencil and got to work. I went back to my desk and sat down.

"Will you bring your paper up now so I can check it?" I asked toward the end of recess. Panic filled his face. He crumpled the paper into a ball with both hands.

"Bring it up, Chad," I ordered firmly.

Reluctantly he rose, and with dragging steps, came forward. I took the crumpled ball from him and smoothed it out on my desk while he stood beside me, his eyes wide and frightened. He had written each of the ten words as instructed but the margins of the paper were decorated with pictures of witches on broomsticks and big-mouthed, frowning and ugly faces of women. Under each picture he had written "teacher." I studied the paper carefully, drawing the moment out longer than necessary.

"You are quite a good artist," I said then. "The pictures express your feelings quite clearly. Perhaps you should consider taking a few drawing lessons."

I opened the wide flat drawer before me and placed the paper inside. "All right, Chad. You may go outside now and get yourself a drink and go to the toilet."

He shot out the door so fast that I found myself laughing.

I went out on the porch and rang the five-minute warning bell, causing a flurry of last minute activity out in the schoolyard.

117

Chad was a model student the rest of the day. I called him up and gave him the spelling words just before the end of the day and he spelled every one of them correctly. I commended him and sent him back to his seat, then shortly afterward, dismissed the children for the day. As I gathered up the things I wanted to take home, I decided on an impulse to take Chad's paper with the drawings. They really were quite good and I thought I'd like to show them to Davy and perhaps Clemmy, too.

Davy came into the house shortly after Calvin and I got home. We were in the kitchen having a snack when he came in to join us.

"I was always hungry as a kid when I got home from school," he said after he had greeted us. "Never thought about the teacher bein' hungry, too."

"I'm starved. I didn't see you after school. Did you pick up Todd and Evelyn today?"

"Jist Todd. Evelyn ain't been to school yet this week. Her mama took a bad turn over the weekend and she's havin' to stay with her."

"Oh. That's too bad. I hope it isn't serious and that Evelyn doesn't have to miss too much school."

"I went in early and went on in to town. Mom was frettin' about her hair so I got that home permanent like you ordered, then I went out and got Ellen and she's givin' it to her now."

"Ellen's up at the house?"

"Yeah. What's so funny about that?"

"Let me show you something." I went and got the paper with Chad's spelling words and the drawings on it and gave it to Davy.

"Who done this?" he asked, after he had studied it for a minute.

"I beg your pardon?" I asked, cocking an eyebrow at him.

"Huh? Oh. I mean, who <u>did</u> this?"

"Your nephew Chad."

"Oh, oh. What'd you do to him, whip him?"

"I didn't do anything to him for that. I'd kept him in at recess so he was naturally upset, but since he'd copied his spelling words ten times as I'd told him to, I didn't feel punishment was called for. I think he was expecting me to swoop down on him at any moment, though. He was as good as gold the rest of the day."

"Why'd you keep him in at recess?"

"Because yesterday he kept calling me Aunt Annie. Your brother came to see me about it this morning."

"Tom?"

"Yes. He seemed to think Chad could call me Aunt Annie if he wanted to."

"What happened?"

"Nothing. I explained it to him and he seemed to accept it. At least he went away without saying anything more about it."

"I thought Ellen seemed quieter than usual."

"Was she? Maybe I ought to walk over and talk to her. I wonder if I should show her this?"

"I wouldn't if I was you."

"Oh? Why not? It's quite good, don't you think? And quite amusing."

"It may be to you, but it might not be to Ellen. She takes things pretty serious, wants her kids to grow up respectin' their elders and all. You didn't whip Chad, but she might, and that would maybe make him resent you and it might cause problems with Tom, too. It seems like you got the upper hand, handlin' it the way you did. If I was you, I'd leave it at that."

"You may be right. Nevertheless, I'm going to keep this to add to my teaching memorabilia. I'll enjoy looking back and laughing at it when I'm old and gray. I'd never noticed it before, but I think he has an artistic flair. I'll have to see what we can do to develop it."

"You're not mad at him for drawin' pictures like that?"

"No. There are many more harmful ways of letting off steam. Besides, perhaps it does a teacher good to see herself occasionally as her students see her."

Davy shook his head. "If I'd done somethin' like that when I was in school, I wouldn't of been able to set down for a week."

"I'm a great believer in a teacher not taking herself too seriously. Her work yes, but not herself."

I returned the picture to the folder I had taken it from, then I smiled up at my husband. "Well, what else have you been doing with yourself today?"

CHAPTER TWELVE

Goin' to Granny's

On the third day that Lewis Proctor drove up after school with only Todd with him, I went out and detained Todd for a few minutes.

"I'm going to write a note to Mr. Hooper asking him to send some homework for Evelyn, if she doesn't get to go to school tomorrow," I told him. "I'd like for you to give it to him first thing. Then, if you don't mind, he can send it home by you and if you'll drop it off here after school, I'll take it on out to her. Will you do that for me, Todd?"

"Sure," he said easily, and I thought with a certain amount of pride that he was growing into a fine young man.

I wrote the note, explaining briefly about Mrs. Horton's condition and asking Mr. Hooper to send what information Evelyn would need to keep up with the rest of the class. Then I gave the note to Todd and he placed it carefully in his notebook and sprinted off to catch up with his brothers and sisters. The next morning I drove my car to school, in case I should have to drive out to the Horton's. Todd was alone again that afternoon. He brought a stack of books in and deposited them on my desk. I sent Calvin home, then put the books and papers in the front seat beside me and drove to the Horton's. Evelyn opened the door for me.

"Hello, Evelyn. How are you?" I greeted her with a smile.

"Fine."

"I've brought some homework for you."

121

"Thanks. Todd said you was — were goin' to," she said in her shy way, taking the books from me.

"How is your mother?"

"She's gettin' a little stronger, but she still has to stay in bed. She's sleepin' right now."

"Then we won't disturb her. Was it a bad attack?"

"Pretty bad. Daddy was mad. He thinks it happened 'cause she was tryin' to do too much."

I reached out and touched her arm. "I'm sorry, Evelyn. Is there anything I can do?"

She shook her head, but her face brightened. "Ruthie's mama was here today. She's goin' to stay with Mama tomorrow so I can go to school. Daddy won't like it, 'cause he don't like to be beholdin' to no one, but Mama said if he don't like it, he can jist lump it. Daddy'll give in to her, 'cause she can't get upset or excited, but it'll make him awful mad."

"Perhaps not," I said. "Perhaps he'll realize it will be good for your mother to have another woman around to talk to. She doesn't have too much opportunity for visiting, does she?"

"No. She likes to read, but she ain't even been able to do much of that this week. I been readin' to her a lot."

"You're a good daughter, Evelyn, but you might be surprised at how much your mother will enjoy a little company. Ellen's a very nice person. You and Ruth are pretty good friends, aren't you?"

"Yes. We been friends all our life an' Mama likes Miz Hilton. Ruthie's mama, I mean. They never done much visitin' back an' forth, but they get along good."

"That's fine then. Well, Evelyn, I suppose I should go and let you get at that homework. Looks like there's a lot of it. Tell your mother hello for me and if there's any way I can help, let me know."

As I was leaving, I impulsively decided to drive over

to Tom and Ellen's for a few minutes. It was only a short distance out of my way and I wanted to thank Ellen for her kindness to Evelyn.

The four younger children were out in the yard playing when I drove up. They stopped and stared at me, then the three younger ones came running over to the car, along with their three dogs. Only Chad stood aloof, his expression wary.

"Hello again," I said to the two that were my students, then bent and greeted the youngest, a little girl. She was shy and hid her face against her sister. "Is your mother home?" I asked Tommy.

"She's in th' house," he replied.

I started up to the house, escorted by the children and the dogs. I saw Chad disappear around the corner of the house as I drew nearer and realized that he thought I had come to tell his parents about the pictures he had drawn. Since he had disappeared, there was no way I could reassure him.

The children were all for me going right in, but I stopped and knocked at the open door. Through the screen I saw Ruth and her mother in the kitchen. When Ellen looked up and saw me, an odd look crossed her face, but she immediately invited me in.

"Thank you. Actually, I only have a minute," I said as I stepped inside. "I have to get home and start supper, too."

She pulled up a rocker and indicated that I should sit down. She sat opposite me, the dishtowel she had used to dry her hands clasped rather tightly in her lap. Ruth came to the doorway and stood leaning there. I smiled at her.

"I was just over at the Horton's," I explained to Ellen. "I took some homework over to Evelyn and she told me you had been by and were going to spend tomorrow with her mother so she can go to school."

She nodded. "Ruthie told me you was worried about Evelyn missin' so much. I didn't know 'til then her mama had had another bad turn. Mr. Horton's proud an' don't mix much with th' neighbors."

"Yes, so I've heard. I just wanted to tell you I appreciate what you're doing, and if there's a problem with taking little Angela along with you tomorrow, I was going to suggest that Ruth bring her to school with her. She'll be starting first grade next year and it won't hurt her to learn a little about school routine before she starts. I'm sure she would be good."

Out of the corner of my eye, I saw Chad peek around the door from the kitchen. When he saw that I had seen him, he ducked back out of sight again.

"She'll be all right with me," Ellen said. "She's th' quietest one of them all. When she's by herself, she'll set an' play with her doll or a couple little cars for hours at a time, an' she still takes a nap after dinner. She won't be no trouble. Later on though, I might send her to school for maybe half a day, if that's all right with you. That way, she can see what school is like before she has to start."

"I think that's a good idea." I rose and smiled at Ellen. "Well, I suppose I should be getting on home. Thanks again for helping Evelyn."

She rose, too, and looked at me rather blankly. "Was that all you come for?" she asked.

"Why yes. Was there something else you wanted to talk to me about?"

She shook her head. "I just thought — No. There wasn't nothin'."

I paused at the door. "By the way, Clemmy's hair looks good since you gave her that permanent. It has just enough curl to make it look soft and natural."

"That's good. I ain't seen her since I give it to her, but I was worried it wouldn't take or that it might be frizzy."

"It looks great. Clemmy loves it. What does Tom think? Has he said?"

"Don't think he's seen it yet. What does Davy think?"

"He hasn't said, but he keeps looking at his mother as if he hardly knows her," I said with a little laugh. "Well, I'll see all of you later. Thanks again, Ellen."

Still smiling, I got in my car and drove away.

Evelyn stopped in after school on Friday to ask me about some of her homework. They had started something new in math class when she was absent and she didn't understand it. I spent about a half hour with her, then closed the school for the weekend. It had been a long week and I was looking forward to our trip into town the next day.

We were planning on staying in town the entire day. I wanted to buy school clothes for Calvin, besides the suit I wanted to outfit him in for my sister's wedding. Davy needed a new shirt, and I had to look for a suitable dress to wear as matron of honor. We also planned to have lunch at a nice restaurant and then go to an afternoon movie, but first we had to stop and visit Granny Eldridge. Fortunately, it was not out of the way. We would pass right by her daughter's house as we entered town.

We got an early start, about eight in the morning. Somehow, the hated shoes had turned up and Calvin had them on now. Calvin sat in the truck between Davy and me. Calvin's small face was eager. His trips into town had been few and far between. He and I had been to a movie when I took him with me to St. Louis earlier in the year, his very first. He couldn't wait to go again. I looked at him with affection and amusement. I rarely saw his expression so animated.

"I wonder how many of the other children out here have ever been to a movie," I mused aloud.

"Prob'ly not many," Davy said.

"I wonder if it would be feasible for me to take them to one sometime. They have afternoon matinees in the summer. I wonder if they have them here during the school year."

"Dunno. You could ask, I guess."

"I think I will. It would be such a treat for the children."

"How would you get them all in to town?"

"You, dear husband," I said. "Why do you think I married you anyhow? You could take them in in this truck. They could ride in the back, if you drove carefully."

"So that's the reason you married me."

"What else? Don't forget we have to stop at Granny's."

"I'll drop you and Cal off, then I'll take these cabinets on in to John. Shouldn't take much more'n an hour. That be long enough to get your visit out with Granny?"

"Plenty long."

He drew up before the house and stopped the truck, then he waited until Calvin and I were invited in before he drove away with a wave of his hand and a sly grin.

"'Bout time you was comin' in to visit me," was Granny's clipped greeting as her daughter ushered us in. She was seated in an overstuffed chair and made no effort to rise, though she did lean forward and hold out her hands to Calvin, her sharp eyes greedily devouring him. I felt a pang of remorse. After all, she had raised him from the time he was a baby. She naturally would have missed him.

"Come on over here an' let me have a look at you," she commanded him. He seemed to be holding back so I gave him a slight push forward with my hand.

"I'm sorry it's been so long, Granny," I said, "but we've been so busy with school starting and all."

126

"Humph," she snorted. "School started all of three weeks ago." She pulled Calvin to her and enfolded him in a smothering embrace. Calvin did not hug her back, but then he was not a demonstrative child.

"Growin' like a weed," Granny said, holding him away from her and studying him with her piercing eyes. "Seems to me you're lookin' kinda seedy though. Skinny an' a little peaked." Her eyes darted to me. "You ain't so busy you're forgettin' to feed him regular, are you?" she demanded.

"No, Granny," I said, holding on to my temper with difficulty, thinking that in that department, at least, he fared a lot better with Davy and me than he had with her. "He eats well, three meals a day, plus a snack after school, but as you see, he's having a growth spurt, up, not out. Those are the jeans that were too long for him when his mother bought them for him last spring."

"Humph," she said again, as if she doubted the truth of my statement. "They treatin' you right?" she asked Calvin. "You happy with them?"

Calvin nodded solemnly and she released him.

"Well, go ahead an' set down," she said a bit ungraciously to me. I didn't blame her for being upset with me. I had promised to bring Calvin in sooner. I seated myself on the sofa across from her and Calvin came and sat down beside me, close but not quite touching. Granny's eyes observed us closely.

"I apologize for not bringing him sooner," I said. "I've intended to but there's been so much going on, I just haven't had the time."

"An' what's been goin' on that's so all-fired important, 'sides school startin' three weeks ago?" she inquired with a peevish snap. "You ain't havin' school on weekends now, are you?"

"No, but my parents came the weekend before school

127

started," I answered, hurrying on before she could question me about their visit. "I had planned on bringing him in then but it didn't work out." I was tempted to tell her of the little incident that happened when Calvin thought I was taking him in to her to leave him, but of course I couldn't do that.

"Then," I continued, "the next weekend, Clemmy hurt her hand and couldn't use it and I had to help her. Then my sister came to visit. It's just been one thing after another, but I should have found the time to bring him in sooner. I'm sorry." She mellowed then and began to ask me questions about this family and that. I brought her up to date on everything that had been happening at home, steering a careful course between news and gossip. Calvin sat quietly by my side and listened but contributed nothing to the conversation.

"Where's that man of yours?" Granny suddenly asked.

"He took some cabinets he'd made in to his brother John. He'll be back for us soon, then we're going in to town for the day."

"You can leave th' boy here with me then an' pick him up on your way back home."

Calvin sat up straight and turned pleading eyes on me. His hand crept into mine.

"I'm sorry, Granny," I said. "I'm afraid we can't do that this time. One of the reasons we're going in today is to get Calvin some new clothes. He's outgrowing everything. I'll have to have him with me to make sure of the size, but next time I go in to town, I'll leave him with you. Will that be all right?"

"That'd be good, long as that ain't too long from now. You been by that house of mine lately?"

"No, I haven't."

"Gotta get shed of all that stuff I left out there. Guess I'll get my nephew to go out an' load it up in his truck an' take it to the sale barn one of these Fridays. Then I'm hopin' to rent th' house out. Don't know of anybody wantin' to rent a house, do you?"

"No, Granny, I'm sorry, I don't."

"'Spect I'll have to leave th' furniture. Can't very well haul all that off to th' sale barn, least not all at once. I ain't wantin' to sell th' house. It was built by Grandpa Eldridge an' it's been passed down to th' oldest Eldridge boy ever since. Woulda went to my boy, Ben, had he a lived, so I'm aimin' to pass it on to Calvin here when I'm gone. Sticks in my craw that he ain't named Eldridge like he shoulda been. Guess th' name'll die out when I'm gone."

"Well, Granny, perhaps you'll be pleased to know that Calvin refuses to be called by the name Hilton. He says his name is Eldridge and that's the way he writes it on his school papers and at the end of his stories. Davy and I have decided not to make an issue of it and if, when he's of age, he wants to get it legally changed, we won't object."

"I'm glad to hear th' boy's got some idea of what's fittin'," she said with satisfaction.

Davy came soon after that and we left. I thought Calvin was as relieved to go as I was.

We spent the morning shopping and by lunch time I was exhausted. We'd found the clothes I wanted for Calvin and the shirt and a new tie for Davy, but I decided that for me to shop for a dress accompanied by two male companions was not a good idea. I gave it up and we went to a nice restaurant for lunch. I'd have to do my dress shopping another time.

When we left the restaurant, Calvin had shed his shoes and I let him carry them while we walked the two blocks to the movie theater. We arrived half an hour early so I had time to make inquiries about matinees during the school year. I was directed to the manager, a young man not much older than myself. He was very helpful.

"At the end of the school year," he told me, "many of the teachers make arrangements to bring their students here to the theater. There is a matinee scheduled every Friday afternoon at one o'clock during the month of May. At which school do you teach, Mrs. Hilton, and which grade? You must be new to the district. I'm familiar with the schools here and most of the teachers, but I don't believe I've met you."

"I don't teach here in town," I told him. "I'm a teacher in the hills and I teach all eight grades. It's called Willow Creek Elementary School."

"Ah yes, I see. I believe Mr. Hooper did mention you at our last board meeting and what a fine job you're doing. You married one of the local men out there, didn't you?"

"Yes. That's my husband sitting over there and that's his nephew Calvin, who lives with us."

"I see. You're staying for the movie this afternoon?"

"Yes, we are. I'm glad it's a Lassie show. I know Calvin will love it."

"We always do try to schedule something appropriate for the kiddies at the matinee, and of course that carries through for the matinees we schedule in May. What we usually do is send out a program to each of the schools that request them, listing the movies and when they are scheduled. Then you check your first and second choice and the number of students you expect to bring. We make the reservation for you and send back a confirmation. Shall I put you on our mailing list, Mrs. Hilton?"

"Yes, please do."

"I'll need your mailing address, please."

I gave it to him and he wrote it down and assured me I would get the information in plenty of time to make all the arrangements. I went back to join Davy and Calvin and we went in to the movie together.

CHAPTER THIRTEEN

Jane

Something was definitely wrong as far as the Decker boys were concerned. Jimmie was withdrawn and uncooperative, his attitude almost sullen. He refused to leave his seat Monday morning when I called the first grade up to recite, and he refused to answer when I spoke to him. On the other hand, Johnny was jumpy and nervous and too anxious to please. When I dismissed the children for first recess, I kept Jimmie inside.

"Jimmie," I said, seating myself at one of the desks beside him. "Do you want to tell me what's bothering you?"

He stared straight ahead and made no answer. I studied his small face, so closed off and remote and cold.

"When school first started," I said, "you were so eager to learn, so willing to participate. I thought you were going to be my star pupil. Now you seem to have lost all interest. Can you tell me why? Has something happened here at school that I don't know about? Have any of the kids been picking on you or teasing you or anything like that?"

Still no answer.

"How about at home? Is everything all right at home?"

His eyelids flickered, he looked down at his desk, but he still didn't speak. I watched him closely.

"How is your mother? Is she feeling all right now?"

Still no answer. I rose and stood beside him, uncertain how to proceed. I would have to go out and have a talk with his mother, and I probably should do it today. I put my hand on his shoulder and felt him flinch.

I stood still while a wave of shock went through me. Beneath the thin material of his shirt, I could feel the welts under my fingers. I removed my hand and knelt beside him.

"Jimmie, I want to look at your back," I said gently.

"We won't take your shirt off. I'll just unbutton the two top buttons — "

His hand went up to the neck of his shirt and held it. For the first time he looked directly at me, his eyes wide and apprehensive.

"It's all right, Jimmie. I just want to help. I won't tell anyone."

After a moment, his hand dropped. I unbuttoned the two top buttons so that I could lift the shirt up and away from his back and shoulders. What I saw was even worse than I expected. His whole upper back and shoulders were ridged with angry red welts. I let the shirt fall and rebuttoned the front, then just squatted there beside him for a minute, not knowing what to say.

"I'm sorry," I said then. "I can see why you don't feel like participating in class. You can just sit at your desk and color or read for the rest of the day, if you'd like. Do you want to go outside for the rest of recess?"

He shook his head.

"I know this is very difficult, but do you want to talk about it? Do you want to tell me what happened?"

Another more vigorous shake of the head.

"All right, I understand."

I rose and went back up to my desk and a few minutes later, rang the bell to call the other children inside. Jimmie began to thaw a little as the day went on. At noon I was able to persuade him to go outside with me and we ate our lunch together, sitting on the grass under one of the large oak trees. He still had nothing to say, but he seemed to listen with interest when I told him about the background of the story I was reading aloud to them at the end of each school day. I noticed that Calvin, who generally ate his lunch with me, sat alone on the front steps. He was looking glum. Probably he was jealous, I thought with an inward sigh. I'd have to talk to him later this evening.

The afternoon passed without incident. Just as school was dismissed for the day, I saw Lewis drive up in my car with Evelyn and Todd. Quietly, I asked Johnny and Jimmie to wait while I went over to speak to Lewis.

"Lewis, are you through for the day?" I asked him, after I had exchanged a few words with Evelyn and Todd.

"Yes. I thought I'd walk my girls home for a change. Was there something you needed?"

"Just my car. I'm going to drive Johnny and Jimmie home and visit with Jane a little. Tell Sue hello for me. How is she? And the baby, too, of course?"

"They're fine. Why don't you and Davy come out and visit us one of these days?"

"I'd love to, Lewis, I really would, but there's so much going on right now. Perhaps soon. 'Bye, girls. See you tomorrow."

I turned to Calvin, who stood waiting. "Calvin, you run along home now. I'm going to take Jimmie and Johnny home. Tell Davy I may be awhile, but I'll be home as soon as I can. Okay?"

He was still looking glum, but I didn't have time to deal with that at the moment. I opened the door to the back seat and ushered the Decker boys in, then drove away, aware that Calvin stood looking after us for some time before he started down the hill toward home. The Decker boys and I didn't have anything to say to one another on that drive. I knew by their expressions that they were apprehensive, but I didn't know how to reassure them. I was aware that I might be rushing in where angels fear to tread, but in an isolated country school such as this one, the teacher handled whatever problems arose on her own. Besides, Jane and I were friends. Surely we could discuss this rationally.

When we drove up into the yard, I got out and opened the door for the boys. The house was quiet, only the dog came out to greet us. I walked up to the door and knocked while the boys hung back, watching me.

"Hello, Jane," I said when she came to the door, forcing myself to smile and appear at ease. "I brought the boys home and I thought you and I might have time for a little visit."

She seemed to hesitate, peering out at the boys. She didn't look well, her clothes were rumpled, as if she might have been lying down, her eyes were heavy.

"I ain't feelin' so good today," she said. "An' th' house is awful hot."

"I'm sorry you're not feeling well, but I do need to talk to you. I won't stay long."

Her eyes met mine, then looked away. She pushed the screen open. "Come on in then," she said a bit ungraciously. "Have a seat."

I seated myself in the rocker she indicated, and she sat at one end of the sofa and tried to tidy her hair by pushing it back with a rather unsteady hand. She really did look ill. I felt concerned.

"What is it, Jane? Are you ill?"

"No, jist ain't been feelin' too good with this young'un I'm a carryin'. Thought I was over th' sick feelin'. Don't have it so much in th' mornin' no more, but it jist comes on me off an' on when I ain't expectin' it. Likely it's th' heat gettin' to me."

"It is unusually hot. I wish it would rain. We need it. How are the younger boys?"

"Fine. Sleepin' right now. I should get them up soon or they won't be wantin' to go to bed tonight. What was it you was wantin' to talk to me about? My boys givin' you trouble?"

"No, not exactly," I said, not sure how to begin. It was a ticklish business, accusing a parent of mistreating her child. "But I'm afraid we do have a problem. When school first started, I was very impressed with Jimmie's attitude, his cooperation, and eagerness to learn. That lasted about two weeks, then one Monday he came to school with a very black eye. Johnny said he hit it on a doorknob."

I paused. She said nothing but sat waiting.

"Jimmie was upset all that day, more upset than a painful black eye warranted. He cried very hard later in the day, as if his heart was broken."

I paused again, but she still didn't speak. I took a deep breath and continued.

"After that he seemed to perk up and be interested again, then last week he seemed to lose all interest again. Today he was totally withdrawn, wouldn't talk, wouldn't participate in class. Do you have any idea why?"

She shrugged her thin shoulders. "Likely th' newness jist wore off," she said.

"I'm afraid it's more than that, Jane. Today I happened to put my hand on his back and I felt the welts there. I saw them. Someone whipped him hard just recently, this morning probably, and with a belt, too, I'd guess. I think that was why he was withdrawn and uncooperative. I think he was hurting, not just physically but emotionally, too. I think he's a very disturbed little boy because he's being punished severely for something he doesn't understand."

"He understands all right," she said grimly. "Sure I whipped him this mornin'. I ain't takin' no lip off'n no seven-year-old kid. He's been mouthin' off ever since he started in to school. Seems to think he knows more'n anyone. If I let him get by with it now, what'll he be doin' time he gets older? An' if I let him get by with it, pretty soon th' others'll start in, an' where would I be then?"

"Were you angry when you whipped him?"

"Sure I was. Made me madder'n a ol' wet hen. You'd be mad too if he talked to you, way he talked to me."

"Jane, it isn't at all unusual for a child to — well, be a little mouthy when he first starts to school. It's his first real taste of independence and it rather goes to his head. It isn't intentional. Many times the child doesn't even realize he's being disrespectful."

"Well, he sure as th' world knows now."

"I believe a spanking is necessary on occasion, but I believe with most children it's more effective to sit down and talk to them, reason with them, tell them firmly but kindly what you expect of them. If they don't respond after several attempts, perhaps some kind of punishment might be necessary then, but a child should never be whipped in anger, Jane. It's too easy to overdo it."

"You ever had dealin's with four young'uns, all boys, an' one of them 'bout as hardheaded as a kid can get?"

"Of course you know I don't have any children of my own, but I am a teacher. I've had to learn how to handle a whole room full of young children, boys and girls."

"An' you never had to whip one of them?"

"I can only remember spanking one child, a young boy, but I did it with my hand and I waited until I was calm and in control before I did it."

"So what you're sayin' is you're better'n me, is that it?"

"No, Jane, I didn't mean that. I didn't mean that at all. It's just that — "

"I got plenty of beltin' in my day an' it didn't hurt me none."

"Perhaps not, but the belting Jimmie got this morning did hurt him — it hurt him a lot. It was much too severe, in my opinion. You're going to end up with an emotionally disturbed little boy if that kind of treatment continues."

"I think I heard enough. You may be th' teacher, but you ain't got no right to come here tellin' me how to raise these here young'uns of mine." She rose and went to the door and stood holding it open, her expression hard and grim. "You done a lot for me an' I ain't forgettin' it, but I think likely I know a little more about how to raise these boys than you do. Now I got things to do, if you don't mind."

I rose also and took a couple of steps toward her, but I couldn't leave it at that. We stood and faced one another. She was several inches taller than I and it was her house, but I stood my ground.

"I'm sorry I've offended you," I said. "That wasn't my intention, but I can't go, Jane, until I say what I came to say."

I almost held my breath, wondering if she was going to bodily throw me out. She looked so angry. But she stood silent, meeting my eyes grimly.

"The first year I taught school in St Louis," I continued, "I made friends with another teacher about my age. She had a little boy in her class, a second grader. The parents were divorced, the mother had custody of the two children, the boy and a younger girl. The mother also had to work to support them, so she had her hands full, a lot of pressure and loneliness and frustration in her life.

"Well, the little boy kept coming to school with injuries, a black eye, bruises on his arms and his cheek was quite swollen. The teacher, my friend, was concerned. She talked to the mother. The explanation was that the boy was clumsy, he fell a lot, ran into things. My friend thought there was more to it than that. She thought the mother was taking her frustrations out on the little boy by knocking him around, but she didn't have any proof, and she was afraid to make accusations without proof, so she did nothing. Then one day, he didn't come to school and we heard on the radio that night that he was dead and the mother was facing a term in prison. She had hit him in a burst of anger and knocked him down the stairs. He hit his head and died.

"My friend was devastated. She never got over the fact that she hadn't done anything to help the little boy and his mother. She never stopped blaming herself. I don't intend for that to happen to me."

"An' what are you meanin' by that?"

"Just this, Jane. I don't think Jimmie is a bad boy. I don't think he's deliberately being mouthy and rebellious. I don't think he's doing anything that you couldn't handle by talking to him. I think, because you're not feeling well and because you're alone with these four boys to raise with another one on the way, and because your husband has left you and things are so hard — "

"You ain't got no right to be judgin' me," she broke in hotly.

"I think," I continued doggedly, "that because Jimmie is more like his father than the other boys and is a little bit difficult to deal with, you're taking your frustrations out on him, and I think there's a strong possibility that you're going to end up doing him some serious permanent damage. It must not continue, Jane. I won't allow it to. Not for Jimmie's sake or for your own. I don't want — "

I don't quite know how it happened, but I was suddenly out the door and it had closed decisively behind me. I stood a moment, tempted to force my way back inside and have it out with her, but I couldn't do that. I wondered if I had done more harm than good, but it was unthinkable not to do anything at all. Somehow, I had to reach her, help her and Jimmie, too.

I squared my shoulders and walked to my car, got in, and drove away.

CHAPTER FOURTEEN

A Family Matter

"Where the dickens have you been?" Davy asked in a mildly complaining voice as I got out of the car.

"Didn't Calvin tell you?" I asked in surprise.

"Calvin didn't tell me nothin'. I ain't seen him."

"You haven't seen him! But I told him to go straight home."

"He ain't here. Ain't been here, far as I know."

"Then where on earth is he?"

"Search me. I figgered he was with you."

"No. I had to go talk to Jane, so I sent him on home. I told him to tell you where I'd gone. Have you looked in the oak tree?"

"No. Didn't see no reason to. What's goin' on, anyway?"

"Jimmie Decker is having some problems so I've spent a lot of time with him today. We had lunch together and I think maybe Calvin felt a little left out. Go see if he's up in the tree, will you?"

"That boy's gotta learn he don't own you," Davy grumbled as he turned away.

I gathered up my books, papers, and purse and went into the house, not yet overly concerned because I was still upset over my confrontation with Jane. When Davy came in through the utility room door, I glanced up to see a little frowning furrow between his eyes.

"He isn't there?" I asked sharply.

"No sign of him."

"Maybe he took Brownie for a walk." *

"Brownie's in his pen where I put him a couple hours ago."

"But where can he be? It's been over an hour."

"Prob'ly out playin' in th' woods somewhere, or maybe hidin' out there to punish you for payin' more attention to another kid than to him. I wouldn't worry about it. He'll turn up soon."

I sat down rather hard in a nearby chair and felt the tears start to my eyes. Davy came over and put his hand on my shoulder. He was looking more displeased than worried.

"I'll tan his hide for worryin' you like this," he said.

"We have to remember he was allowed to come and go as he pleased when he was with Granny," I said, wiping the tears away and trying to hide my anxiety. "It takes time to adjust to new rules, you know."

"Adjustin' to new rules an' deliberate disobedience are two different things in my book," Davy said a little grimly.

"I can't remember exactly what I said, but perhaps he didn't understand that I meant him to go straight home. I don't think he would deliberately disobey me."

"You're too soft with him."

"We have to be patient, Davy. He's not very old and Granny's rules, if she had any, were pretty flexible and seldom enforced. He'll learn."

I rose, trying not to worry, and stacked my books and papers neatly on top of the bookcase. When I turned back to Davy, he was studying me and still frowning.

"So," I said, striving for lightness, "what have you been doing with yourself today?"

"The usual."

"I'm sorry I'm so late getting home. I'll start supper. Anything in particular you'd like?"

"Yeah. I'd like a kiss for starters."

I went into his arms and lifted my lips to his, but my attention was divided, wondering where Calvin was. Davy put me away from him and held me at arms length, looking down at me.

"Are you really worried about that kid?" he asked.

"I am, a little. I can't imagine where he could be."

"Prob'ly around close somewhere. I'll have somethin' to say to that young man when he does turn up."

Davy turned and left the house and I went into the kitchen to start supper.

I kept glancing out the window as I worked, but there was no sign of Calvin. The table was set and the meal ready and still he hadn't come home. I was worried by that time.

Davy came in and went into the bathroom to wash up. I filled a plate for him and one for myself and left the rest of the food on the stove so it would stay warm.

"He ain't here yet?" Davy asked as he sat down at the table.

"No. Davy, I'm getting worried. Suppose he's had some kind of accident?"

"What kind of accident could he have between here and school? Let's eat. I'm hungry."

I sat down, too, and picked up my fork but I had no appetite.

"He could have sprained his ankle or something," I said after awhile.

"You'd of seen him when you come home, wouldn't you?"

"You'd think so, but I was pretty preoccupied, thinking about Jane. I could have missed him."

"I don't think it's likely. It's been over two hours. He'd of made his way home by now, sprained ankle or not. It ain't that far."

He continued his meal but he kept glancing up at me. "Quit worryin' and eat. I'll go look for him, soon as I've finished."

"It'll be getting dark soon."

"Not for a good hour or so yet. He'll show up when he gets hungry enough."

I said no more but I was still very concerned, not just about Calvin but also about Davy's anger. It looked as if Calvin had run away again. Davy was right. Calvin was too attached to me, too dependent.

"I'll take the car and go look for him," Davy said as he rose from the table.

"I'll go with you."

"Don't you think you oughta stay here, in case he decides to come home?"

I sat back down. "I suppose so, but Davy — "

"What?"

"Don't be too hard on him. Don't lose your temper."

His eyebrows lifted. "Am I in the habit of losin' my temper?"

"No, but sometimes when a person gets angry — "

"I'll bring him back to you in one piece," he said dryly.

I cleared the table and washed the dishes. I stirred the food in the pans on the stove and turned the burners on warm. Then I went into the living room and gathered up the books and papers I'd brought home from school, put them on the coffee table, and sat down on the sofa.

I graded a few papers but had a difficult time concentrating. It was over an hour later and dusk was deepening when I heard the car drive up at last. I jumped up and went to the door. Davy and Calvin were getting out of the car. I waited.

Calvin came slowly toward me, his small face wan. As he stepped into the light, every freckle he had stood out on his cheeks and across the bridge of his nose. His eyes looked too big for his face. I wanted to reach out and hug him, but I forced myself to stand aloof and looked sternly down at him.

"Where have you been, Calvin?"

He didn't answer, but Davy, coming in behind him, answered for him.

"I found him at Granny's. He'd found a window unlocked an' climbed in. He was asleep in a chair. Good thing I decided to walk around the house and saw that window open, otherwise we wouldn't have found him 'til mornin'."

"Calvin, why did you do it? Didn't you know how worried we'd be?"

"I'll handle this," Davy said grimly.

"Davy, I can handle it. I think I understand — "

"Not this time," Davy told me in a no-nonsense voice. He turned back to Calvin. "Now you listen to me, young'un. This is the second time you've run away since you been with us and it better be the last time. You're lucky this time, 'cause of Teacher here. Next time you won't be so lucky. You do it again and I'll tan the hide off you so you won't be settin' down for a week."

Davy was standing with his legs slightly apart, his hands on his hips, hat on the back of his head, his jaw set. Standing there before him and looking up at him, Calvin looked very small and scared. I put my hand on Davy's arm. It was rock hard.

"Davy," I began. His eyes turned to me and there was no softness there.

"You had it your way so far," he said quietly. "Now it's my turn."

I felt myself begin to bristle, but before I could say anything he turned back to Calvin.

"From now on you'll be answerin' to me," he said. "I'm layin' down the law an' you'll be obeyin' it, or else."

"You see that you come straight home from school ever' day, whether Teacher has somethin' else to do or not. You can get yourself a snack, don't expect anyone else to do it for you, you do it yourself, and if you make a mess, you clean it up. After your snack, I want you to go outside an' play for a hour or so, but don't leave this yard unless you got permission from me or Anne. After a hour, you can come in and read awhile or write, if you want to, or you can stay outside for a little while longer and play. Six o'clock is supper time. Be here. You can help clean off the table and wash the dishes, then I want you to come out with me to do the chores. After that, one hour of homework, no more. If it ain't all done in a hour, leave it."

I opened my mouth to protest but he held up his hand to silence me.

"At eight o'clock," he continued, "you get your bath an' get yourself ready for bed. Be in bed by nine, an' I mean lights out, no readin'. Set your alarm for six-thirty. When it goes off get yourself up, don't expect Anne here to do it. Make your bed as soon as you're out of it and keep your own room neat and your clothes put away an' all. Get yourself ready for school, then come in to the kitchen for breakfast." He paused. "Is that clear?" he asked then.

Calvin nodded.

"Stick to it or you'll answer to me, an' no more runnin' away when somethin' ain't to your likin'. Now go get yourself some supper and get ready for bed."

He turned and left the house, leaving silence behind him. I stood there seething, but I knew in my heart he had been fair. Nevertheless, I'd have something to say later about that rule of only one hour of homework each day. If Calvin was going to skip a grade next year as I'd planned, he'd have to do more homework than just an hour.

"Go wash your hands, Calvin," I said quietly. "I'll fix you a plate."

When Calvin was in bed, I went back to my homework. It was some time before Davy came in, so I had time to think over the events of the evening. I came to the conclusion that Davy was right to insist on a more regulated life for Calvin. I had been too soft with him, not giving him any responsibility around the house. He was old enough to need some responsibility, and it would give him a greater sense of self-worth.

However, in the matter of the amount of time Calvin spent with his homework, I felt I was a better judge of that than Davy, but I was no longer upset about it. I felt certain I could convince Davy to change his mind. He was an indulgent husband and I knew that he loved me very much. He wouldn't insist on anything that he knew I didn't like.

When he came in, I looked up and smiled, then patted the sofa beside me. "Come sit down a minute, will you?" I asked. "I want to talk to you."

"What about?" he asked with a certain amount of reserve.

"Come sit down and I'll tell you."

"Jist let me wash up first."

When he came out of the bathroom, he came and seated himself beside me. I reached for his hand and he returned the clasp warmly.

"I think the rules you gave Calvin are good rules, for the most part," I said. "I guess I have been too indulgent with him. However, I'm afraid one hour of homework just won't be enough. You see, I'm trying to get him caught up to where he would have been if he hadn't dropped out of school those two years. He's actually taking two grades this year and there's only so much extra he can do at school, so for homework, I'm assigning him basically the same work I've assigned the fifth grade class. He'll need at least two hours to get it done."

"No."

I straightened, surprised and definitely displeased. I removed my hand from his. "What do you mean, no?"

"Jist that. Two hours of homework after bein' in school for seven hours is too much, far as I'm concerned. You're pushin' him too hard."

"Davy, you don't understand. You make it sound as if I'm forcing him. I'm not. He wants to do it. We agreed."

"You an' Cal may have agreed. I didn't."

"What do you mean?" I asked after a moment's silence.

"I mean you didn't ask me. You mighta talked it over with Cal, but you didn't discuss it with me."

"But Davy," I said helplessly.

"Ain't it usual to talk to both parents and get their okay before you make a decision like that?"

"Well, yes, but — "

"You didn't ask me. If you had, I'd a said no."

"But why? Calvin is intelligent. He's perfectly capable of doing the work."

"He's plenty smart, but to my way of thinkin', he spends too much time with his nose in a book, and he spends too much time with you. It ain't good for him."

"I don't know what you mean by that. Perhaps right now he is a little too attached to me, but he'll get over that as time goes on."

"He thinks he owns you. He don't want to share you with no one else and I say it ain't good for him. He needs to be outside, runnin' an' playin' like other boys his age, and he needs to learn how to work, learn some responsibility," Davy said.

"And that's exactly what he is doing. By taking an extra grade this year, he is learning how to work, how to accept responsibility."

Davy shook his head. "He needs to learn how to work

with his hands, too. He ain't balanced. You're turnin' him into a — " He hesitated and regarded me out of the corner of his eye.

"A what?" I demanded icily.

"A mama's boy," he said.

I jumped up and walked halfway across the room, then turned back to face my husband. I was hurt and furious with him.

"I would never have believed you could be so short-sighted," I said hotly.

"And I'm thinkin' maybe you're the one that's bein' short-sighted this time," he said mildly. "You took a shine to Cal right away when you come out here, and he took a shine to you. You wanted us to have him when we found out Granny couldn't take care of him no more, and I agreed to it 'cause I knew how much it meant to you, and 'cause I didn't think Granny should have the raisin' of him either, but you're carryin' it too far. He's goin' to have to grow up to live in a man's world, and you ain't teachin' him how. You're bringin' him up in a woman's world, and I'm sayin' it ain't good. From now on, he's goin' to be feelin' my hands on the reins."

"Oh is that so? Well, I'll have you know, Davy Hilton, that I intend for him to go on to sixth grade next year. I'm not having him come this far and not finish."

"If he can do it with one hour of homework ever' day, fine, but if he can't, then I'm afraid he won't be goin' on to sixth grade."

He spoke quietly but I knew he meant it. I stood and glared at him.

"I don't think it's your business to interfere," I said, seething.

"I can see you don't."

"This is a school matter, and in this case, I think I'm a better judge of what should be done than you are."

"It ain't jist a school matter. It's a family matter 'cause it's affectin' our family."

"Your grammer is atrocious," I said irrelevantly and was immediately ashamed. "Anyhow," I hurried on, "that is not why Calvin ran away. It was because I spent so much time with Jimmie today and sent him home alone."

"He run away 'cause you spend so much time with him on this extry homework an' all, that he thinks you belong to him. He don't want to share you with no one else — not even me."

"Jealousy is a very small-minded, shallow emotion," I retorted.

"You talkin' about me or Calvin?"

"I'm talking about you."

"So I'm small-minded and ignorant and jealous, too now, am I? Okay, I admit it, the jealous part anyway. The ignorant part too, maybe, but I mean what I say, Anne. I'm not changin' my mind."

"I'm sorry I said that, but I don't know why you suddenly have to be so stubborn about this."

"I'm not the only one that is bein' stubborn," he said with a touch of humor. He rose and came toward me, holding out his hand. "Come on, little fire-eater. It's gettin' late. Let's kiss an' make up, okay?"

"Don't you touch me," I said backing away.

"Why not?"

"Because I don't want you to. You're arrogant and domineering and — and impossible, and if you think you can lay down the law to me, then you can just think again."

He stood regarding me steadily, but there was no anger in his eyes. I knew I was being unreasonable, but I steeled myself against him.

"You're not my boss, even if you are my husband," I added defiantly.

149

"We're a family, Honey. We have to work together. If you'll stand off and take a good clear look at this, I think you'll have to agree I'm right."

"I don't think it. Maybe I have kept him too close, but Calvin needs at least two hours of homework each evening if he's to catch up."

"Why does he have to catch up? What's the rush? He's little for his age. Who's gonna know or care if he's a year or two behind the other kids?"

"I care. And Calvin cares."

He shook his head. "I don't think he does. He's doin' it to please you."

"He is not!"

"Is too."

"He isn't!"

"Is too," he said, his eyes laughing at me. I turned away, refusing to be amused.

"Calvin is going on to sixth grade next year," I said doggedly.

"One hour of homework. I mean that, Anne, and Cal knows I mean it. Don't try to undermine my authority."

"Your authority?"

"My authority," he repeated, calmly but quietly.

I stood silent, my back to him. Presently I felt his hands on my shoulders. I moved out from under them.

"I'm goin' to bed," he said after a moment's silence. "Are you comin'?"

"No."

"Anne."

"I have homework to do. I suppose next you'll be ordering me to keep it to an hour, too."

He didn't answer. I sat back down behind the coffee table and drew some papers toward me. I didn't look at him.

"Don't let me keep you up," I said coolly, distantly.

"Talk about me bein' stubborn," he said.

"Goodnight."

He didn't answer for a minute, then he said goodnight and went off to the bedroom. I tried to grade a few papers but I was too upset to concentrate. Finally I flung my pencil down and curled up on the sofa, still fuming.

When I woke, it was morning and I was still curled up on the sofa. A cool breeze blew in the open window and a light blanket was thrown over me. I realized Davy must have got up during the night and covered me. I felt a small stab of guilt, but not enough to make me back down from the stand I'd taken.

I sat up, a little stiff. I heard the alarm go off in Calvin's room and I wondered for a moment if he would obey Davy and get up without me having to rouse him. I heard the alarm shut off and his feet hit the floor. Evidently he was taking Davy at his word, at least for now. I got up and went into the bedroom to get clean clothes and saw that Davy was gone and the bed was made. Generally I did that, but I supposed he felt that since he was the only one who had slept in it, he'd have to follow through and make it up. He was probably out doing the chores, though I hadn't heard him go through the house.

I took a quick bath, dressed in my bathrobe, and then went into the kitchen to start breakfast. Calvin came in as I was putting breakfast on the table. He was dressed for school, his face washed and his hair slicked down with water.

"Good morning, Calvin," I said.

"Mornin'."

"Say good morning," I instructed.

"Good morning."

"Thank you. Go ahead and sit down. Davy should be in soon. Do you want orange juice or grape juice today?"

"Grape juice."

I poured it for him and set it on the table. Davy came in and set a foaming bucket of milk on the counter. I was aware that he looked at me, but I busied myself pouring two cups of coffee.

"Mornin'," he said.

"Good morning," I replied coolly.

He went into the bathroom to wash. I strained the milk and refrigerated it, then sat down at the table just as he came and took his own chair. I took an egg and a slice of bacon and passed the platter on to him in silence. He took it and slid three eggs and some bacon on to his own plate and passed it on to Calvin. After Calvin filled his plate we began the meal in silence. After a few minutes, Davy cleared his throat.

"Get a good night's sleep?" he asked me.

"I slept very well, thank you," I replied coolly. "Calvin, would you like some more juice?"

He held out his glass. I poured the juice and went back to my meal.

"I took a look at your room, Cal," Davy said then. "It looks good."

Calvin looked up at Davy but made no reply and we finished the meal in silence. Davy helped himself to a second cup of coffee while I began to clear the table. Calvin helped me and I was touched but a little chagrined that Davy should witness it. He was getting his way too easily, I thought.

"You don't have to dry the dishes this morning, Calvin," I said. "We'll just leave them in the drainer to dry. What would you like for lunch? Will peanut butter and jelly be all right?"

He nodded, so I took down the peanut butter and fixed our lunches. Davy stood propped in the kitchen doorway watching me. Calvin went back to his room.

"Still mad?" Davy inquired softly when we were alone.

I didn't answer. I put our two lunches in paper sacks and turned to go past Davy to go to our bedroom and get dressed. He set his cup on the counter and reached out and took me by the upper arms.

"Don't I get a kiss this mornin'?" he asked.

"No."

"Then I guess I'll jist have to take one."

He bent his head and kissed me hard on the lips and let me go. I went out of the kitchen, my head high. In the bedroom, I closed the door and got dressed. Davy was lounging in the kitchen doorway again with his coffee cup in his hand when Calvin and I left for school. His "see you later" was a little sardonic. I didn't answer and neither did Calvin.

I was a few yards from the house when I stopped. I couldn't leave my husband this way, I was hurting myself more than I was hurting him. I laid my books on the grass, along with my sack lunch.

"Calvin, I forgot something," I said. "You go on. I'll catch up with you in a minute."

Davy was still there in the kitchen doorway. He looked surprised when I walked in. I went straight to him and put my arms around him and hugged him tight.

"Davy, I'm sorry," I said, my voice muffled against his chest. One of his hands held the cup of hot coffee away from me, the other came around me tight.

"I'm sorry, too," he said, his voice a little husky.

I lifted my head. "Does that mean you've changed your mind?" I asked hopefully.

A rueful look of amusement sprang up in his eyes, his lips tilted upward. "You little dickens," he said. "Is that why you come back, to try a different tactic?"

"No. I came back because, in spite of the fact that you've suddenly decided to become so dictatorial, I love you and I can't stand for us to be angry with each other."

"I wasn't mad."

"Maybe not, but I was."

"I know it."

"I'm sorry I acted the way I did and said the things I did, at least, some of the things. I didn't mean to fall asleep on the sofa either, but Davy, have you changed your mind?"

He shook his head, his tongue in his cheek.

"But you said you were sorry."

"I didn't mean I was sorry about the decision I made. I'm not. I been thinkin' a lot about it for quite awhile, and I think it's right, but I am sorry I made you mad."

I drew away from him and stamped my foot. "Why have you suddenly decided to become so unreasonable?" I demanded.

"I don't think I am."

"Well, I think you are."

"Sorry."

"You don't look sorry," I said petulantly. "Davy, if you love m — "

"You know I love you. That's why I'm not changin' my mind. Way things have been goin', it ain't — it's not good for you, or Calvin either. You're both tryin' to do too much."

"Don't you think I should be the judge of that?"

"Not this time."

I stood moodily regarding him for a long moment. This husband of mine couldn't be wound around my little finger quite as easily as I had thought. It was something of a surprise to me, I had to admit. I was half pleased, half vexed about it.

He grinned at me and took another sip of his coffee before he put the cup down and reached out for me. I went willingly enough.

"Davy, I have to go," I said after a moment. "I'll be late."

"Thanks for comin' back," he said as he released me.

"But you won't change your mind, even when you know how important this is to me?"

He shook his head. I sighed and turned away.

"See you this evenin'," he said. "

"Yes."

"Still love me?"

"I'll think about it," I said as I went out the door.

CHAPTER FIFTEEN

Babysitting

I had to hurry to catch up with Calvin. He was moving slowly up the hillside, shuffling his bare feet through the dust, his shoulders a little slumped. I put my hand on his shoulder.

"Calvin, there is something that I didn't get a chance to explain to you yesterday that I want you to try to understand. As a teacher, I have a responsibility to all the students, and when one of them has a problem I have to try to help. Right now the Decker family is going through a bad time. Their father has left them, they're very poor, and their mother is going to have a baby and she isn't feeling well. Things like that affect the children, some children more than others. The Decker's problems seem to be affecting Jimmie the most right now, so I'm trying to help. I'll have to keep on trying and that may mean I'll have to spend extra time with him, as I did yesterday. You can be a big help to me, if you will."

He glanced up at me with a question in his eyes and waited.

"At recess, you could make an effort to talk to him, maybe ask him to join you in a game or something. That way, perhaps I wouldn't have to spend so much time with him at recess, as well as in class. Will you do that for me, Calvin?"

"I'll try."

"Thank you. I would appreciate it. Also, since we generally get to school early, you might want to do a little extra homework instead of reading. That would help you keep up with the extra studies."

He looked at me with surprise and something like shock in his eyes. It made me feel as if I had suggested something underhanded or sneaky.

"Davy wasn't talking about in the mornings, Calvin," I explained quickly. "He meant in the evening you should do only one hour of homework."

I didn't know if he accepted that explanation or not, because he didn't answer, but I decided to leave well enough alone. I wasn't positive myself that that was really what Davy had meant.

When we came around the schoolhouse, Jane Decker and her four boys were sitting on the steps. She rose, her rather angular face set and grim. My heart sank.

"Why Jane," I said. "Good morning. Good morning, boys. I'm sorry I'm a little later than usual this morning."

"I was wantin' to talk to you, 'fore all th' kids get here," she replied.

"Of course," I said, unlocking the door and removing the padlock. "Come on inside."

I held the door open and she preceeded me inside. Calvin came in after me but Jane's boys stayed outside. I switched on the light and put my books on my desk while she stood aside and waited. Then I saw that Calvin had deposited his books on his desk and was ready to sit down. I spoke to him.

"Calvin, why don't you go outside and play awhile? Take a couple of the big balls out with you, if you'd like. The little boys might enjoy playing with them."

I waited until he was gone, then turned to Jane and invited her to sit down with me on the bench.

"I come to tell you how sorry I am 'bout th' way I talked to you when you come over yesterday," she said.

"That's all right, Jane. I understand. Perhaps I didn't

say what I meant in quite the right way."

"Wasn't nothin' wrong with th' way you said it. It was jist that I'd been feelin' so bad all day 'bout what I done, an' then when you started sayin' them things, I knew right away they was all true. I have been takin' my bad feelin's out on Jimmie cause he reminds me so much of his daddy."

Tears started to her eyes. I reached out and put my hand over hers.

"I been feelin' so bad," she continued, wiping her hands across her eyes, "an' ever'thing's been goin' wrong so long, jist don't hardly seem worth livin' no more. Seems like I'm able to keep it all inside for jist so long, then I jist go all to pieces an' seems like it's always Jimmie that's in th' way when I fly off th' handle like that. Seems like he's always readin' them books, always puttin' in his two cents worth, actin' like he knows more'n me no matter what I say, jist like his daddy used to do. I put up with it for jist so long then it jist goes all through me an' I let fly. It was me that give him that black eye, too. He did hit it on a doorknob, but I'm th' one knocked him into it. I did whip him harder'n I intended to with th' belt, too. Seems like when I got started, I jist couldn't make myself stop. I slapped him with th' flat of my hand many a time, but I ain't never done nothin' like that before. I'm a scarin' myself. I'm gonna end up hurtin' him real bad, jist like you said, an' he's gonna end up hatin' me. What am I gonna do?"

"You've taken the first step and maybe the most important step by recognizing the problem," I said. "Being aware of what's happening and why it's happening will perhaps help you more than anything. Part of the problem, too, is that you're alone too much."

"Beggin' your pardon, but I ain't alone enough," she said bluntly. "Ain't got a minute to myself, seems like,

'cept when th' little boys are sleepin', an' then I'm so wore
out, I lay down an' take a nap, too. Ain't got no time to set
down in peace an' study on things an' what it is I need to
be doin'."

"Yes, I see what you mean. I've been feeling a little
like that myself lately, now that I'm married and have a
child in my care. Could you perhaps arrange to get the
boys to bed a little earlier at night so you could have some
time for yourself then?"

"I'm so wore out, I'm ready for bed 'fore they are half
th' time."

"I see. But when I said you were alone too much, I
meant alone without adult companionship. Children can
be wonderful companions, but we all need a little grown-
up conversation from time to time. How often do you get
out of the house, go visiting, or maybe just go for a long
walk alone?"

"Now that Miz Proctor's moved, ain't no one close
enough to visit with, an' I don't know that many people
around here. An' how would I be goin' for a long walk by
myself with a three-year-old an' a five-year-old left home
by their selves?"

"Yes, I can see it's difficult, but it's not impossible.
We'll work something out. Things will get better, Jane.
You'll see."

She was starting to look uncomfortable because the
children were arriving and staring at us as they came into
the room. We rose together.

"I better be goin'," she said, "but I want you to know
I'm goin' to try real hard not to treat Jimmie bad no more."

"Good. How are you feeling yourself now, Jane?"

"Kinda shaky right now. Didn't get much sleep las'
night for thinkin' 'bout things."

"Do you think you'll be all right, walking all that way
home?"

"I'll be all right. You'll try to help Jimmie, won't you? Likely he's hatin' me by this time."

"I don't think so. Little children are very forgiving and they are hungry for love and approval. If you can turn things around now and let him know how much you love him, he'll eventually forget all this."

Tears were in her eyes again. She turned away.

"I have some ideas that might help," I said. "Can I come out after school today and tell you about them?"

"I'd 'preciate it. I promise I won't show you th' door this time."

I smiled. "If you do, I won't be offended. I probably won't be out until after supper, if that's all right. About seven or so."

"That'll be all right."

"Jimmie, would you like to ring the bell for us?" I asked when she was gone.

He obeyed, his face sober but not so withdrawn today. The rest of the children began to come inside and another school day had begun.

When Calvin and I arrived home from school that day, he put his books in his room and went immediately to the kitchen. I followed, and even though I was preoccupied with the suggestions I wanted to jot down for Jane, I was amused at the serious expression on his face as he prepared his own after-school snack.

He took a plate and a tall glass from the cabinet, then took out the peanut butter and a jar of honey and went to the bread box for a loaf of bread. He mixed peanut butter and honey together in a small bowl and spread it lavishly on the bread. Then he took out the half-empty bag of potato chips and carefully stuck a layer of potato chips on top of the peanut butter.

I had taken some cheese from the refrigerator for my

own snack and was slicing it when Davy came in. He looked from Calvin's sandwich to me with raised eyebrows, then reached over and helped himself to the slice of cheese I had intended for myself. I sliced another one and Calvin looked at it, hesitated, then reached out and took it and added it to his sandwich. He put the top piece of bread in place, then pushed the plate over to his place at the table. He went to the refrigerator and started to take out the crock of milk that I had strained and put there that morning.

"Let me do that, Calvin," I said quickly. "It's pretty heavy and the cream needs to be skimmed. I'll start putting some in a jar for you so it will be easier to handle."

The cream skimmed off the top, I filled his glass, then one for myself. I looked at Davy. "You want a glass?" I asked.

"Sounds good. Want to fix me a sandwich? I'm hungry, too."

I raised my eyebrows at him as I pushed the cheese and the knife toward him. "Help yourself," I said.

"Oh, I see. What's sauce for the goose is sauce for the gander, too, is that it?"

"Exactly."

He leaned over and kissed me, then took up the knife to slice the cheese.

"Have a good day?" he asked me.

"Fine," I said. "And you?"

"Okay. How about you, Cal?"

Calvin nodded, unable to speak through the peanut butter. He swallowed, then took a drink of milk, leaving a white mustache which he wiped away with the back of his hand. I handed him a paper napkin. When he took another bite of his sandwich, it crunched, making me wonder if it tasted as good as it sounded. Davy was evidently thinking the same thing.

161

"That good, Cal?" he asked as he sat down with his own sandwich.

Calvin nodded again. I joined them at the table with my slice of cheese and glass of milk, thinking how pleasant this was, just like a regular family. I drew my sheet of paper to me.

"I have to go out to Jane's after supper," I said, beginning to write.

Both Calvin and Davy paused to look at me.

"Again?" Davy asked.

"Yes. I'm sorry, but I'll try not to be too long."

"Trouble?"

"Jane's having a problem dealing with all the responsibility she has on her own. I have some ideas I think might be helpful to her. You two will be all right on your own for an hour or two, won't you?"

"We'll be fine. We'll clean up after supper so you can get out there a little earlier."

"Thank you. That would be nice."

Calvin finished his snack and put his plate and glass in the sink. He put the peanut butter and honey and potato chips away then went outside. I looked after him, feeling a little chagrined. He was following Davy's rules to the letter.

I went back to the list I was making, aware that Davy's eyes were on me in sardonic amusement. I ignored it as long as I could.

"Well?" I challenged finally, raising my head and meeting his eyes.

"Well?" he returned innocently.

"Think you're smart, don't you?"

"Who, me? Why I ain't nothin' but a ignorant, backwoods hillbilly who jist happened to catch th' eye of th' sweetest, prettiest little schoolteacher that ever come to this neck of th' woods."

162

"Don't try any of your sweet talk on me. It won't work."

"Worked before, didn't it?"

"That was before I knew better."

He leaned over and kissed me and my hand went up to his cheek. His eyes smiled down into mine.

"I'm glad you're not mad anymore," he said softly.

"I'm not mad, but I'm not ready to concede victory either. I still think Calvin wants to go on to sixth grade next year, and not just because I've been pushing him. If I'm right, he'll get the extra studying done somehow, even if he has to do it in the mornings before school."

Davy shook his head. "Don't you ever back down?"

"Not unless I'm proven wrong, and I haven't been proven wrong yet. Only time will tell. Meanwhile, I'm willing to let it ride. Maybe you're right, and then again maybe you aren't."

"And if I am?"

"Then I'll give in gracefully. At least, as gracefully as I can," I added ruefully.

He laughed, then rose and pushed his chair back under the table.

"Davy, wait just a minute, will you? I have a proposition to put to you."

"Sounds promisin'. What is it?"

"Well, you know I need to go into town to try to find a dress for the wedding, so I thought I might go ahead and do that this Saturday."

"Okay."

"And," I added, "I thought I might ask Jane if she would like to go with me."

"What for?"

"Because she needs to get out of that house and get completely away from her normal routine for awhile, do something different."

"Don't look to me like she'd be the one to help you pick out a dress, but if you want to take her, it's okay by me, jist don't expect me to go along. What about the boys?"

"That's what I wanted to talk to you about. I wondered if you'd be willing to watch them while we're gone."

"Me!"

"Yes. I can't think of anyone else. Sue's got the baby and Ellen's got her own five. Besides she's been helping the Horton's and I don't want to impose on your mother. That leaves only you."

"What makes you think I could corral them four boys, five countin' Calvin? I ain't had any experience handlin' a bunch of little kids like that on my own."

"You'll have them in subjection in a matter of minutes. Look how you've got Calvin obeying you."

"You tryin' to get even with me?"

"No, Davy, I'm not. Really. I wouldn't ask you to do it if I didn't feel it was vital for Jane to have this outing. She must do something to break the monotony of her life, and she must do it soon."

"You make it sound like it's almost a matter of life and death."

"If not that, at least very near it. Please, will you think about it? It would only be for four hours or at the most, five."

"Would I have to go there and watch them?"

"No, I don't think so. I haven't talked to Jane about it yet, but I'm sure she wouldn't mind them coming here. I ought to take Calvin in to stay with Granny when I go to town, but I think I'd rather leave him here. He can help you entertain the boys."

"I still think you're tryin' to get even with me."

I laughed. He went out shaking his head and I rose

and put my papers aside and started supper.

"I've made a list," I told Jane, seated on the sofa beside me. She had sent the boys outside to play. The room was bare and hot, and smelled of cooked cabbage and onions. Jane's face was flushed and shiny with perspiration, her hair scraped back severely and twisted into a knot at the back of her head. She looked hot and tired and worn, her shoulders slumped, the picture of discouragement.

"Don't know if I got th' strength for it, but if you think it'll help, I'll try to do like you say," she said.

"You need a schedule," I said. "At least, in my own case, I find a schedule very helpful. It helps me get everything done and keeps things fairly orderly. What time do you generally get up?"

"Used to always get up at six, but lately I ain't been gettin' up that early. Ain't much point in it. Only got th' goat to milk an' th' chickens to feed an' that don't take much time."

"Do you feel better for sleeping later?"

"Can't say as I do. Always get up draggin' my tail anymore."

"What time do the boys get up?"

"Th' oldest ones have to get up 'bout seven thirty or so, but I been lettin' th' little ones sleep long as they want to."

"What time do the boys have to start to school?"

"Little after eight."

"And does that work well? I mean, does it give the boys enough time to have breakfast and get ready for school without a lot of rushing around and prodding from you?"

"No," she said, sounding resentful, "but like I told you, Jimmie took th' alarm clock apart an' couldn't get it back together again. My brother give me another clock, but it ain't got no alarm an' I'm always so tard, I don't always wake up like I used to."

"I see. And when is it that things get most frustrating for you, Jane? In the mornings, during the day, or in the evening?"

"Mornin's," she admitted almost reluctantly.

"Tell me something about your day, while the older boys are at school."

"Lately I been goin' back to bed half th' time, then when th' little ones get up, I get up too an' get them some breakfast. Then I clean up th' dishes an' do th' chores an' whatever else needs to be done. I fix a little dinner, an' sometimes lay down a little if th' boys take a nap. They don't want to take a nap though when they sleep late. Then th' boys come home an' I fix supper an' do th' chores an' go to bed."

It sounded like a very drab life to me. No wonder she was feeling discouraged and hopeless. Before I could speak, she spoke again, bristling a little and on the defensive.

"I ain't always been so lazy. I been a hard worker all my life, but I ain't been feelin' good, an' jist seems like there ain't much use even tryin' anymore. Don't seem to matter what I do or how hard I try, things ain't gettin' no better an' don't seem like they ever will."

"I understand, Jane. Please don't think I'm criticizing you, I'm not, but I'm trying to understand the situation so I can help. If I make out a schedule for you, will you try to follow it, say for at least two weeks? By that time, you should know if it's going to help or not."

She nodded.

"First of all, I think it would be good to go back to getting up at six o'clock again. I have an extra alarm clock you can have. After you get up, get dressed right away and drink a glass of water, then go outside and go for a walk, say for about half an hour. You don't have to go out of sight of the house if you don't want to, but do walk for at least half an hour."

"What's th' use of walkin' if I ain't goin' nowhere?"

"For exercise. Walking is very good exercise, especially for pregnant women. Walk briskly and breathe deeply. It'll clear your head and your lungs and invigorate your whole day. Just try it and see if I'm not right."

"Okay."

"That puts you back in the house a little after six thirty. Take a half hour for yourself then. Sit down and read the paper and have a cup of coffee or — "

"I give up coffee, can't afford it no more, an' any newspaper I got around here'd be too old to get any good out of."

"Well, then have a glass of juice or milk or even another glass of water. Look at a magazine or read some in a book."

"I ain't much of a reader."

"All right then, do something else you'd enjoy doing, or don't do anything at all. Just sit and relax if that's what you feel like doing. Brushing your hair is sometimes soothing and relaxing, too."

She nodded.

"I think it would be good to get the two older boys up at seven o'clock. That should give them time to get ready for school while you fix breakfast. We'll allow a half hour for that. You can use your own judgement here, but if I were you, I think I'd get the younger boys up then, too, so you can all have breakfast together and get it over with. By shortly after eight the boys should be ready for school and you'll be ready for whatever needs to be done for the remainder of the day. How do you think that sounds? Do you think it will work for you?"

"Might."

"Try it at least. If, after two weeks, you find it isn't working for you, we can try something different. I do think a personal schedule is important for all of us. Without it, life can get pretty hectic. Now how about the evenings? Does that go pretty smoothly or do you think we need to work something out there, too?"

"Don't do nothin' much, 'cept do th' chores, get supper an' go to bed."

"Do the boys have some time for play when they get home from school?"

"Johnny goes outside, but Jimmie's jist been settin' around with his nose in a book most of th' time since school started."

"That's probably my fault. He loves to read and I've been encouraging all the children to take books home. I've been making the same mistake with Calvin. My husband cracked down on us yesterday."

She looked at me with a little spark of interest. "What'd he do?" she asked.

"He said after his snack, Calvin has to go outside and play for an hour and he has to help with the chores. After that he can read. I think perhaps that might be a good thing for Jimmie to do, too."

"I always have give these boys chores to do, but lately I have to holler at Jimmie so many times when he's got his nose in a book, half th' time I jist give it up or I get mad an' end up hittin' him."

"I'm sorry. I can't help feeling responsible for that."

"It's good of you to say it, but ain't nobody's fault but mine. I oughta jist take th' book away from him an' make him do what I say, but I ain't got th' patience. I used to have. I'm thinkin' that schedule you said to go by in th' mornin's is likely to help. I knowed all along I oughta go ahead an' get up in th' mornin's, jist ain't had th' gumption to do it. I will now."

"Good. I really do think it will eliminate a big part of the problem, but of course, you won't always be able to follow it exactly. One of the boys might get sick or wake early or something, but follow it as closely as you can, at least for two weeks. Then if you have to make some adjustments, you'll know better where to make them."

"What am I gonna do about th' damage I already done to Jimmie?"

"I think you'll have to talk to him, explain to him how you've been feeling and why you've lost your temper with him the times you have. Explain to him what you're going to do to correct it and ask for his help. Make him see that he has a few things he needs to work on, too. I think he'll understand and be willing to cooperate."

"You think he'll get over it?"

"I think he will. Tell him you love him and you're sorry you've hurt him and you'll try never to do it again. He'll understand."

"I ain't been in th' habit of talkin' to them boys like that. They're jist kids."

"In my opinion, Jane, that's the main problem between parents and their children, even between husbands and wives. We don't talk to each other enough. We don't communicate. Anyhow, you try it and see if it doesn't work. Now I think you need some kind of general schedule for after school. Let's see. How about an hour of play when they get home, all four of them, and I mean lots of running and yelling and climbing trees, something to get rid of all that excess energy that kids have. Tell Jimmie absolutely no reading until later. Then maybe after supper and the chores are done, including helping you with the supper dishes and all, and after their homework is done, you could all sit down as a family and let Jimmie and Johnny take turns reading to the rest of you. You might like to start on a book and read a chapter a night, like we do at school. Jimmie would certainly enjoy that and probably Johnny would, too, and it would be good for the little ones. Even though you say you're not a reader, Jane, I think you would enjoy it, too."

"Jesse used to always read to us in th' evenin's. I liked it all right."

"Will it bother you to have the boys do that?"

"No. Jesse's gone, an' far as I'm concerned, he can stay gone. I'm thankin' you for goin' to all this trouble. I feel some better, like things is not completely hopeless, at least." She paused and looked at me, her color heightened. "Have you told anyone?"

"Told anyone?" I repeated puzzled.

"About what I done?"

"Oh. No, Jane, I haven't told anyone, and I won't. That is," I added almost against my better judgment, "not if it doesn't happen again."

"It won't."

"Good. Now there's one more thing I wanted to ask you. You've probably heard that my sister is marrying Jim Baker the last weekend in October, and she has asked me to stand up with her. Would you like to go into town with me Saturday and help me pick out a dress?"

Her mouth fell open in surprise. "You want me — "

"Yes, if you would. We went in last weekend, but with two men in tow, I didn't get much chance to look at dresses. I don't much like to go alone, so I thought maybe you would go with me."

"I'm thankin' you for askin' but I ain't got nothin' to wear. You'd be 'shamed to be seen with me."

"No, I wouldn't. I thought it would be a nice break for both of us. We could have lunch at a restaurant and perhaps go to an afternoon movie."

"But I ain't got nobody to keep these boys."

"Davy will watch them. I've already asked him and he

said they could come to our house for part of the day."

She looked more surprised than ever. "Your man would be willin' to do that?" She asked almost in awe.

"Yes. He likes kids. He'll take good care of them and it will do him good to see what mothers and teachers go through. His mother is right next door, you know, and I'll alert her to keep an eye out, if he seems to be having trouble. Then there's Calvin. He's twelve now. He can help watch them."

She considered it, then reluctantly shook her head. "I ain't got nothin' to wear to town. Only decent dress I got I can't get in to anymore an' I give all my hatchin' dresses away when I left Jesse. Didn't figger on needin' them no more."

"Well, wear the dress you have on now if it's all you've got and maybe we can shop around for some clothes for you, too. You'll be needing some soon."

"I ain't got th' money, an' I couldn't go to town in this ol' dress, could I? Wouldn't you be 'shamed to be seen with me?"

"The only way I'd be ashamed to be seen with you, Jane, would be if you were dirty, and you're never that." I rose and looked down at her. "You think about it anyhow. Send a note to school by the boys and let me know. I really would like for you to go with me."

"And," I added, turning back at the door, "I would just love to see how my husband copes with five lively youngsters for several hours."

It won a laugh from her and I left feeling much better about her and Jimmie.

"Jane is coming with me tomorrow," I told Davy when I got home from school that Friday. "She sent a message by the boys. Sue has given her a maternity dress, and since you've said you'll watch the boys, she's decided there's no reason she can't go. I'm going to pick them up about ten. We'll drop the boys off here and go on."

I glanced up at my husband and had to suppress a smile. He still wasn't resigned to the role of babysitter for Jane's boys. "I thought it would be better to go in the morning, that way the two little ones won't get fussy from missing their nap."

"Am I gonna have to feed them, too?"

"I'll fix something before I leave, sandwiches and cookies and Kool-aid, probably. All you'll have to do is serve it, and I suggest you serve it outside. You can spread an old blanket on the ground and let them sit on it, that way you won't have to worry about spills."

"I believe you're enjoyin' th' idea of leavin' me alone with them boys more'n you're enjoyin' the idea of goin' in to town," he said accusingly.

I laughed. "Well, I just thought before we start our own family, I really should find out what kind of father material you are. Don't you agree?"

"Don't usually start with five at a time."

"True, but you just never can tell. It's been known to happen."

He looked at me under lowered brows as he went out the door. I laughed to myself after he was gone.

The next morning Calvin decided to ride along with me when I went to pick up the Decker family. He ran ahead of me out to car and I paused in the doorway and looked back at Davy.

"Remember the boys' names?" I asked. "Oldest to youngest, it's Johnny, Jimmie, Jerry, and Josh. Got it?"

He nodded.

"Jane says Jerry is the mama's boy. He may cry when she leaves, but I'm sure he won't cry long."

He just gave me a sardonic look and said nothing. I turned away, then hesitated.

"Davy?"

"Hmm-m?"

"Be extra kind to Jimmie, will you? He's been having a rather hard time of it lately and may be a little difficult. Be patient with him, will you?"

"I wasn't plannin' on beatin' up on none of them," he said a bit dryly.

"I know, but — "

"But what?"

"Nothing. Just be kind."

"I'm kind. I'm the kindest guy in the world. Truth is, I'm thinkin' I've gone soft in the head, agreein' to somethin' like this."

"You'll do fine. We'll be back in a little while."

When Calvin and I got to the Decker's house, everyone was ready. The boys' faces were scrubbed and shining, their hair slicked back with water, their expressions varying from expectant to anxious. I greeted them with a reassuring smile.

I felt a pang of dismay as I looked at Jane. She wore Sue's second best maternity dress, a dress I remembered well. On Sue it had looked pretty and feminine, but on Jane it looked totally incongruous. Her hair was drawn back and twisted into its usual tight knot at the back of her head, her narrow face was devoid of even a hint of makeup. On her legs she wore brown knit stockings, and on her feet, the same pair of old fashioned black-laced oxfords that she always wore. The dress was short on her, striking her right at the knees, making her legs and feet stand out like sign posts. I preferred that she had worn one of the faded cotton house dresses that I was used to seeing her wear. I was afraid that in town we were going to attract unwanted attention.

For just a minute I toyed with the idea of taking her inside when we got to my house and suggesting a few changes. Her hair could be loosened and put up in a more attractive way. Some of my foundation cream would brighten her somewhat sallow complexion, a touch of lipstick would moisten and soften her dry lips. The shoes and stockings would have to be discarded completely, at least with that dress. I could loan her a pair of hose and I had a pair of white sandals with adjustable straps that she could probably wear. In this guise, she would be much more attractive and far less conspicuous, but I had to discard the idea almost immediately. Jane was proud. If she got even a hint that I disapproved of how she was dressed, she would be hurt and would probably refuse to go with me.

"Miz Proctor come over an' give me this dress. She said you give her some clothes when she was a needin' some, so she wanted to pass th' favor on. Ain't it jist th' prettiest thing?" she said almost shyly.

"It is. Very pretty. That was nice of Sue."

"Yes. She stayed to visit pert near a hour an' it jist made my day. Guess you was right about all of us needin' some grown-up company from time to time. Well, we're ready. Your man ain't backed out on watchin' these young'uns of mine, has he?" she ended a bit anxiously.

"No, not at all. He's at home waiting for us."

"I hope they don't give him no trouble. I feel awful funny askin' him to do this."

"You didn't ask him, Jane, I did. He's looking forward to it."

"Now that's stretchin' th' truth jist a mite too far," she said with dry humor as we went out to the car.

"Perhaps," I conceded with a little laugh. "But he will do fine. Let's just you and I relax and forget our men folks for a few hours today, shall we? The change will be good for both of us."

We dropped the boys off and had our day in town, and

both of us enjoyed it. I resolutely shut out the stares we received and ignored the few stifled giggles I heard and set my mind to the task of showing Jane a good time. She had put off her somberness, totally unaware of the incongruous picture she presented, and was pleased with the dress she was wearing. Several times I saw her stroke the material lingeringly with her work-worn hand and wondered how long it had been since she'd had a new dress.

We looked in a few dress shops, but I couldn't find a dress in the peach color my sister wanted me to wear. We did some browsing and I bought a few school supplies I was in need of and we picked out a small toy to take home to each of the boys, plus a sack of candy to divide. At noon, I treated Jane to lunch at a nice restaurant, and then there was just time to go to a matinee at the movie theater, which we both enjoyed. By that time it was three o'clock and I was beginning to be concerned about how Davy was getting along with the boys. We made a short stop at the grocery store, then started for home.

When we drove up into the yard, Davy was chopping wood at the woodpile, Josh was curled up on a blanket, sound asleep, and the four older boys were belly down in the dirt, like spokes in a wheel, their heads together. When we approached them, I saw that they were shooting marbles.

"Well, they all seem to be in one piece, at least," I told Jane. "A bit dirtier than usual, but unharmed."

"Mine ain't no dirtier'n usual," Jane said. "It's amazin' how dirty them boys of mine can get in no time a-tall. Wonder how your man is feelin'?"

"I'll go ask him," I said, handing her the sack with the toys and the candy in it. The boys had risen and were looking expectantly at us.

"You can go ahead and give them their toy, if you'd

like, and perhaps one piece of candy. I'll be right back."

Davy stuck the ax in the chopping block when he saw me approach and wiped his sleeve across his face. "How did it go?" I asked him.

"We managed."

"Any trouble?"

"Nothin' I couldn't handle."

"Good for you. I knew you could do it."

"How 'bout you? Have a good time?" he asked with a little grin, glancing over at Jane.

"We had a ball," I answered lightly.

"Find your dress?"

"No. I have to confess we didn't look too hard. We went out to lunch and to a movie instead. Davy, I'd like to ask Jane and the boys to stay for a light supper with us before I take them home. Do you have any objection?"

"No, but I'm afraid I can't join you. I got things to do."

"Davy," I chided.

"What?"

"Are you sure it isn't something that you can't put off?"

"Could, I guess, but I ain't been outta sight of the house all day and I need to check on some fencin' in that back pasture. You go ahead and eat without me. I'll have somethin' later."

I smiled at him a little skeptically and he grinned back and bent and kissed me swiftly on the cheek.

"Well, all right," I said with a sigh. "But at least come over and speak to Jane. She'll be getting the idea you don't like her or something."

"Have I got to?"

"Please, Davy."

"Okay, if you want me to."

"You're sweet, Davy. Thank you for keeping the boys."

I took his hand and we went to where Jane was standing with the boys around her. She lifted her eyes to Davy almost shyly.

"I hope they didn't give you no trouble," she said.

"No trouble at all," Davy returned easily.

"It was mighty good of you to take care of them."

Davy didn't immediately reply, so I spoke up to fill the little silence. "Davy has to go check on some fencing, but I would like for you and the boys to stay and have supper with me and Calvin before I take you home. Will you do that?"

"It's mighty nice of you, but I et so much dinner, I ain't a bit hungry yet."

"I'm not either, but I'll bet the boys are. We'll just have something light and I promise to get you home in time to do your chores."

"If you're sure it ain't too much trouble."

"It isn't."

I looked up at Davy. "Thanks again for watching all the boys. What time do you think you'll be back?"

"'Bout dark, I guess."

"All right. I'll save you some supper."

"I'm thankin' you for what you an' your wife done for us," Jane said almost gruffly as Davy turned away.

"S'all right," Davy answered. His long stride took him rapidly away. Both Jane and I stood for a moment looking after him.

"You got yourself a good man there," she said.

"Yes. I wish every woman was as fortunate."

"Awful good lookin', too."

I smiled. "I think so."

"He's crazy 'bout you, ain't he?"

"We're crazy about each other."

She heaved a big sigh. "Well, it's good to know there's a few good marriages in this world. You plannin' on havin' a family of your own one of these days?"

"Yes. One of these days."

"He'll make a good daddy. Ain't too many men that are willin' to help out."

"Yes. Davy likes children. Well, shall we go into the house and see what's for supper? Boys, will you go to the car and bring in those bags of groceries?"

"I better wake Josh up," she said. "He sleeps any longer, he won't be wantin' to sleep tonight."

She knelt on the blanket beside the little boy while I went on into the house. I seldom bought meat, but today I had bought ground beef and buns. We'd have hamburgers and chips and milk for supper, and store-bought cookies, which were a real treat for the children here. I cooked the hamburgers while Jane supervised the washing up of the boys out at the pump. The meal went well, then after the table was cleared, I gave Calvin the sack of candy to divide evenly. He made quite a production of it, making five piles on the table while the Decker boys stood and watched, making sure he didn't short anyone.

I gave each boy a small plastic bag to put his candy in and added an orange, then Calvin and I drove them home. Jane and I hadn't discussed the situation with Jimmie and whether the schedule was making a difference or not, but I felt good about the day. I was sure it was just the kind of break she needed.

When Davy came in, it was nine o'clock and he was ravenously hungry. I made him two large hamburgers, put what remained of the sack of chips on the table, poured him a large glass of milk and sat down across from him while he ate. Calvin had gone to bed, evidently worn out from his active day.

"So tell me how you got along with the boys," I said.

"We done — did all right. At first, they jist kinda stood around and stared at me like they wasn't too sure I could be trusted or somethin', but then they got to runnin' around and playin', an' after that it was all right."

"How did lunch go?"

"Okay. I give it to them outside like you said. Jimmie spilled his Kool-aid down his shirt, so I took it off and washed it out and hung it on the line. He run around without a shirt 'til it was dry." He cocked an eyebrow at me. "Did you know he's got black an' blue stripes all across his back and shoulders?"

"Yes, I knew it."

"Who's been beatin' up on him?"

"I can't say, Davy."

He nodded. "That why you been spendin' so much time with her?"

"Davy, I'm not supposed — "

"Okay. I won't ask questions, but I figger it's got to be her. His daddy's not come back that I heard about, and there ain't anyone else woulda done it, less it'd be the teacher, and I know better'n that."

"Davy, she's had a really hard time of it, so poor and trying to raise those four boys alone, and not hardly knowing anyone here. I think she's down on herself, too, for allowing her husband to come back just long enough to get her pregnant and take everything of value she had. Then, too, she hasn't been feeling well and Jimmie is a rather difficult child."

"Thought he was a pretty special kid, way you talked there at the beginnin' of school."

"He is. He's very interested in reading, in learning. I don't find him difficult, at least I didn't before all this started, but Jane does. I'm afraid he reminds her too much of his father."

"This jist happen lately?"

"From what I've been able to figure out, just since school started. She says Jimmie has become mouthy and argumentative, and that he always has his nose in a book. I know I'm partly responsible for that."

"Ever think Jane might not be able to read?"

I sat and stared at my husband, surprised into speechlessness. "No," I said finally. "It hadn't occurred to me. Why do you say that, Davy?"

He shrugged. "Wouldn't be all that unusual. She told you her family moved around a lot when she was a kid, didn't she, hoein' and pickin' cotton an' all. Lots of times, folks like that keep their kids out of school to help, or they're movin' around so much they jist don't bother to start the kids into a new school 'cause they know they won't be there long. Jist occurred to me, if she can't read herself, might make her feel bad, havin' a kid wantin' to set around and read all the time."

"I wonder if you're right. I never even thought of that, but now that I do think about it, she didn't write me that note as I asked her to. She sent a message by the boys. But she must have read the message I sent by the boys."

"Coulda had one of the boys read it to her."

"That's true. I wonder if you don't have something there, Davy. She may be able to read some, but not well, and if that's true, Jimmie's attitude might well make her feel inferior so that she gets angry and lashes out at him. I wonder how I could go about — "

Davy put his hand over mine. "Ain't we had enough of the Deckers for one day? School's out for the weekend, Teacher. It's time you spared a little thought for your poor, neglected husband."

"Poor old Davy. Are you a neglected husband?"

"Ain't hardly seen you all week, and now you're gone half the weekend, too. Then when you get home, all you can talk about is the Deckers."

"I'm sorry. I didn't forget you, though."

I rose and went to the cabinet and took out a sack of

chocolate mint drops I had bought and laid them before him. "See? I bought you some of your favorite candy and I didn't let anyone else have any either. Does that make you feel better?"

He put one of the chocolate drops in his mouth, then reached for me and drew me down on his lap. "Don't think you're gettin' by that easy," he said. "You owe me, Woman!"

CHAPTER SIXTEEN

A Black Eye

"Calvin, it's almost a full hour before school starts. If you get started right away on that extra homework, you could — " I looked up and stopped in mid-sentence. His books were there on his desk, but Calvin was nowhere to be seen. I glanced around the room then went to a window.

He was walking toward the basketball goal, bouncing the basketball as he went. As I stood and watched he paused before the goal, shot a basket and missed. He caught the ball, dribbled away then turned quickly and shot again and this time made it. Slowly I turned and went back to my desk. It looked as if Davy had been right again. Calvin wasn't that interested in the extra schoolwork. He had been doing it to please me. I was disappointed.

Soon the other children began to arrive. Some of the older boys joined Calvin at the basketball goal and the sound of the ball hitting against the backboard was a constant accompaniment to my thoughts as I sat at my desk grading a few papers and greeting the children as they arrived.

I must have been aware of extra commotion in the schoolyard, but I was so intent on finishing what I was doing that it didn't consciously register until one of the little girls came panting in to tell me there was a fight. I flew up out of my chair and rushed out into the yard. On the ground near the basketball goal there was a melee of flailing arms and legs and tumbling bodies.

"Boys!" I cried, grabbing at the nearest arm. "Stop it!"

It took some time to quell them and I received a sharp kick to the shin that almost brought tears to my eyes before they were finally subdued. Three grubby, dust-covered bodies slowly rose and stood panting before me. One of them was Calvin, one was Jimmie Decker and the other was Alan Ray Sutton.

I was shocked that Calvin was involved, and at the same time had to suppress an impulse to rush to him and see how badly he was hurt. One eye was reddened and beginning to swell. He was blinking as if it hurt, his mouth open as he gasped for air. A trickle of blood was running from Alan Ray's nose. Jimmie was as dusty as the other two but seemed to be unharmed. I stood there regarding them with my hands on my hips.

"You should be ashamed of yourselves, all three of you," I said severely. "Fighting never solves anything. If there was a problem, you should have come to me with it and we could have worked it out."

Alan Ray wiped the blood from his nose with the back of his hand. All the rest of the children were clustered around us. No one said anything. I turned to Ruth, who was standing nearby.

"Will you ring the bell, Ruth? The rest of you get ready to go inside, it's almost nine o'clock." I turned back to the combatants. "Brush yourselves off," I instructed, "then come over to the pump."

I watched as they brushed themselves down, resisting the inclination to go help Calvin. Apparently the injuries were only superficial, but Alan Ray was a lot bigger and heavier than the other two. Jimmie was more sturdily built than Calvin but he was younger and shorter. However, he appeared to be unharmed. I went and stood by the pump with my hand on the handle. Most of the other children had gone inside.

"You first, Jimmie," I said as I began to pump.

He stooped and washed his hands and arms and splashed water over his face, then dried himself on the tail of his shirt.

"All right, Calvin, you're next."

He came and bent to the stream of water, not looking at me. The eye was now a mere slit. It looked quite painful and I couldn't help being a little worried about it, but I refrained from saying so. His light hair was full of dust.

"You'd better let me have a look at that eye," I said. He lifted his head and stood quietly before me as I lifted the lid to look at his eye. He winced but remained silent. I was relieved to see that the eye itself looked all right.

"If you'll wet your handkerchief and hold it over that eye for a few minutes, perhaps that will take the swelling down," I said as I stepped back. "All right, Alan Ray, your turn."

I felt Alan Ray was the culprit here, but I made an effort to reserve judgement until I could find out what happened. I was not overly fond of either of the Sutton boys, and it wasn't entirely because of my dislike of their sister. They were cloddish and dull children, barely getting by in their schoolwork and often sullen in their attitude. I hadn't met either of the parents and knew very little about their background so I had to reserve judgement, but it was was difficult balancing the role of teacher and parent. Although I didn't think Calvin was badly injured, I found myself having to repress the urge to grab Alan Ray and box his ears.

"Do you have a handkerchief?" I asked him when he was unable to staunch the thin flow of blood from his nose. When he shook his head, I reached into my pocket and brought out a clean white handkerchief and gave it to him. "Wet it and fold it and press it against the side of

184

your nose until the bleeding stops," I told him. "All right, let's go inside and there's to be no more fighting. Do you understand?"

Calvin and Jimmie both nodded. Alan Ray was holding the handkerchief to his nose and made no response.

"Do you understand?" I asked him sternly.

"He jumped on me first," he responded, sounding sullen.

"Who did?"

"Him," he said, indicating Calvin.

"Why did he jump on you?"

He shrugged and didn't answer. The others stood silent.

"We'll discuss it later. Let's go inside now. Your nosebleed seems to have stopped, Alan Ray, but you may keep the handkerchief in case it starts again. Calvin, wet your handkerchief again and keep it over that eye for awhile. Are you hurt anywhere, Jimmie?" He shook his head.

"And you, Alan Ray? Are you hurt anywhere else?"

A negative shake of the head, eyes averted.

"And you, Calvin?"

He also shook his head and I followed the three of them into the schoolhouse. They went to their seats while I took up my position behind my desk and called the children to order.

When I dismissed the other children for first recess, I kept the three boys in their seats. Alan Ray looked his normal self except for a little extra dirt, but I was afraid Calvin was going to end up with a very black eye. However, the swelling had gone down some.

"Which one of you would like to tell me why you were fighting this morning?" I asked, walking down the aisle between their seats.

There was no answer.

"Alan Ray, you said Calvin jumped on you first. Do you want to tell me why?"

Evidently he didn't. His head was down, his expression a little belligerent.

"Calvin, do you want to tell me?"

No answer, though he looked at me with such appeal in his eyes that I had difficulty suppressing the urge to comfort him.

"Jimmie, how did you come to be involved?"

"He's bigger'n Calvin an' he had him down on th' ground an' I was afraid he was hurtin' him."

"So you went to Calvin's aid, but you were not actually involved in the original fight? Were you there when it started?"

"No."

"So you don't really know what it was about?"

"Alan Ray was hoggin' th' ball."

"Do you think that was why they were fighting?"

He shrugged. "I dunno, but Alan Ray's always pushin' th' little kids around."

"I see. All right, Jimmie, I'm going to let you go outside now because I think you were only trying to help a friend, but the next time, come tell me. It's my responsibility to put a stop to fighting, not yours. Go on outside now and play." I motioned toward the door with my hand.

He obeyed, and since it appeared that the other two had nothing to say, I gave my standard lecture on the futility of fighting and the superior way of handling difficulties and problems by discussion, knowing all the while that it was not necessarily true. With some people, discussion was useless and there were times when a person must defend himself. However, it appeared in this case that Calvin had been the aggressor. It was strangely unlike him and I felt certain Alan Ray had given him strong provocation.

I made them write fifty times each "I will not fight at school." By that time, recess was almost over. I knew they would both need to go outside for a few minutes, but I hesitated to dismiss them together, feeling there was sure to be trouble, perhaps out at the toilet, out of sight of me.

"Calvin," I said. "You may go outside to get a drink and go to the toilet, but come straight back inside when you've finished."

He obeyed, and when he came back I gave Alan Ray the same instructions. Then it was time to ring the bell and resume classes.

At noon I stayed outside the whole time to prevent more trouble developing. I organized the older children in a volleyball game with Calvin and Alan Ray on opposite sides. Just before the lunch hour was over, little Lori Proctor came sidling up to me.

"I know why they were fighting," she said barely above a whisper.

"Alan Ray called Calvin an awful bad name."

"All right, Lori. Thank you for telling me."

I didn't mention the matter to the boys again and I decided against sending a note home to Alan Ray's parents. Hopefully, it would be an isolated incident that would not occur again.

"Calvin," I said gently when we were on our way home. "Is your eye hurting a lot?"

"It aches a little."

"I'm sorry. When we get home, we'll put some ice on it and maybe that will help. He didn't hurt you anywhere else?"

He shook his head.

"One of the girls told me you fought because he called you a bad name. I know that upset you and made you angry, but Calvin, we can't solve that kind of problem by fighting. We are what we make of ourselves, and someone else's opinion, no matter how spiteful or hateful or low, is not really that important. People who know you are not going to think less of you because of what someone like Alan Ray might say."

I paused, but he made no comment. I put my arm across his shoulders and hugged him.

"Next time, Sweetheart, just ignore it. The very best thing to do is just turn and walk away. No matter what he says, I don't want you fighting with him again, okay? Partly because I don't approve of fighting and partly because he's a lot bigger than you."

"He ain't so tough," Calvin said, his voice scornful. "I coulda handled him by myself."

"Perhaps, but I'd rather you didn't put it to the test. Of course I'm not saying you shouldn't defend yourself if you are attacked and in danger of being hurt, but most of the time fights can be avoided. It takes a bigger man to walk away from a fight than to stay and slug it out. You remember that, will you?"

He nodded and we walked on down the hill together, silent, my arm still across his shoulders. When we reached home, I fixed an ice bag for his eye. He held it in place for awhile, then losing interest, he had his snack and went outside to check on the dog and the rabbit. I picked up the discarded ice bag and held it against my bruised and aching shin. Davy came in and stopped short.

"What happened to you?" he asked.

"There was a fight at school and when I was breaking it up, I got kicked in the shin. I think the bone is broken."

"Let me see." He bent down and I removed the ice bag. He touched the purple bruise with gentle fingers, but it still hurt.

"Ouch!" I said, pulling away.

"Sorry. I know it hurts, but nothin's broke." He rose to his feet and I replaced the ice bag.

"Who was fightin'?"

"Calvin and Alan Ray Sutton."

He whistled and a small grin appeared on his face. "Our Cal was fightin' Alan Ray Sutton? He's a lot bigger'n Cal, if he's the one I'm thinkin' of. What was they fightin' over?"

"They wouldn't tell me. Alan Ray said Calvin jumped on him first, then Jimmie Decker joined the fight to help Calvin. It was his opinion that they were fighting because Alan Ray was hogging the basketball. Lori Proctor told me later it was because Alan Ray called Calvin a bad name."

"Oh." The grin disappeared from his face. "Any other injuries?" he asked then.

"Jimmie came off unharmed, but Calvin has a black eye and Alan Ray had a nosebleed."

"Cal musta got in one good punch then."

"Davy," I chided.

"Well doggone it, I'm proud of him, takin' on a kid that size. You hafta admit, he's got spunk."

"He has plenty of spunk, but I've already told him fighting is not the way to solve problems. This is something I'm afraid he'll have to face all his life, Davy. I don't know what name Alan Ray called him, but I can guess, and I'm sure it will happen again, and probably again. He can't go around fighting everyone who does it. I've told him the very best way to handle it is just to turn and walk away."

"I guess you're right, but it sure goes against the grain."

"Of course it does. I had all I could do today to keep my hands off Alan Ray, and that was before I found out why they were fighting, but it's a lesson Calvin has to learn, Davy, and we've got to teach him, set the example for him. People who learn to fight at the drop of a hat are not happy people. I don't want Calvin to grow up to be one of them."

"No. He ain't got the build for it, for one thing."

"That's not the main reason though, Davy."

"Still, might not be a bad idea to teach him how to defend hisself."

"I don't want him taught to be a fighter," I said.

"Okay. Which one of them kicked you?"

"It had to be Alan Ray. He was the only one with shoes on."

"You think he did it on purpose?"

"No. It was an accident."

"You think you got it settled then?"

"I don't know. I'll have to make my presence felt a little more at recess, I guess. I wouldn't put it past Alan Ray to be lying in wait for Calvin somewhere, though Calvin says he's not so tough as he thinks he is."

Davy grinned again. "Where is Cal? I gotta see that black eye."

"He's in the backyard. You behave yourself, Davy, and just remember that you are a responsible adult, able, I hope, to see things objectively and in proper perspective, and able to impress that on a young boy."

He raised his brows at me. "Yes, Teacher. Anything else?"

"As a matter of fact, there is. Evidently you were right about Calvin's lack of interest in the extra schoolwork. He went out to play basketball this morning instead of doing extra homework."

"Umm-huh," was all he said.

"So I guess I'll just forget it, too. There's no use my trying to push it if the two of you are not going to cooperate."

He grinned at me, his eyes amused. "You ain't gonna

be a sore loser, are you?"

"Just don't get too inflated an opinion of yourself," I retorted. "If he'd been inside doing the extra schoolwork this morning instead of going outside to play basketball, there wouldn't have been a fight."

"Maybe not this mornin', but it prob'ly would've happened sooner or later, and for myself, I'm glad to see him behavin' more like a regular kid. Better keep that ice on that bruise a little longer or it's gonna be awful sore tomorrow."

He went out and I went through to the utility room to look out the window as he approached Calvin. I saw him put his hand under Calvin's chin and lift his face to scrutinize the black eye. After awhile, Davy's hand dropped to Calvin's shoulder and they stood talking for a few minutes. They turned then and walked away together, going toward Davy's workshop. I smiled and turned back to the kitchen, pleased at the closer bond between my husband and Calvin.

CHAPTER SEVENTEEN

Hillbilly Husband

*T*he weather was still warm at the end of September. As Calvin and I walked home from school on Friday, I was preoccupied with thoughts of my sister's wedding, which was just a month away. So far, nothing concrete had been done in preparation, at least not as far as I knew. I hadn't seen or heard from my sister or Jim for a couple of weeks, but perhaps she would be down this weekend. Since the wedding was to be at our house, I felt it was time I knew how she wanted things handled, so I could begin preparations. When we reached home, the truck was parked in front of the house and Davy was arranging some things in the back. I stopped beside the truck and Davy jumped down to stand beside me.

"Are you going somewhere?" I asked him.

"We are," he replied.

"<u>We</u> are?"

"Yes. At least, I hope so."

"What do you mean?"

"Shoulda talked to you about it first, I know, but jist thought about it today myself and I didn't think you'd be wantin' me to be botherin' you at school. Thought we'd go back in the woods and camp out for the weekend."

"Camp out! But why?"

"Always do it a couple times durin' the summer. Didn't get around to it this year 'cause there's been so much goin' on. Figgered if we're goin' we better go now while the weather holds, and before you start gettin' busy

192

with the weddin' plans."

"But Davy, I don't think I can. Liz and Jim will probably come this weekend, and as you said, there are wedding plans to be made. I have a lot of schoolwork to do, too, and there's the laundry and ironing and the extra housework I always have to do on weekends."

"I done the washin'."

"You did?"

"Most of it anyway. Mom helped me. Got it all folded and put away. Didn't wash your good clothes, though. Thought you'd prob'ly rather do them yourself."

"That's awfully good of you, Davy, but still — "

"I cleaned up the house a little, too. Washed the dishes up and run the dust mop over the floor. It looks all right."

I felt dismay. This was something he evidently wanted very much to do, but I just didn't have the time or inclination. I'd made very different plans for my weekend.

"We'll get back early enough Sunday for you to do the rest of your washin' and get the ironin' and other stuff done. Me an' Cal can help you."

"But Davy, why do you want to go? It seems an awfully lot of unnecessary work — " I stopped. He was looking at me, his eyes sober.

"I want to go for the peace an' quiet of it," he said. "Been so much goin' on, and so many people comin' an' goin', we haven't had very much time to ourselves. I want us to get away from it all for a couple days. I thought about takin' Cal in to Granny, but I figgered you'd be worryin' about him if we left him, so I'm willin' for him to go, too, but I'm in the mood for a little peace an' quiet and I think you need some time to get rested up from all you been doin'."

"I appreciate that, Davy, but — " I stopped, about to say that I couldn't think of anything that sounded more unrestful. I also thought about suggesting he go ahead without me, but I couldn't do it. I knew he would be hurt and disappointed if I did, and probably he would end up not going at all. After all, he was a very accommodating husband. Now it was my turn to be accommodating. I smiled and reached up to touch his cheek. He bent and kissed me briefly.

"All right, Davy, but I'm afraid I won't be much help to you. I've never been camping before."

"You won't have to do anything but rest. I'll do it all. I got ever'thing pretty well packed up, I think. I told Mom where we're goin' and when we'll be back. Dad will do the chores."

"We're leaving right now?"

"Yep. Soon as you've changed your clothes."

"But I'll have to have some time to pack my things."

"I already done it."

"But how do you know what I'll want?"

"Don't need more'n one change of clothes when you're only campin' two days."

"What about toothbrushes and towels and — "

"Got 'em."

I stood regarding him in slight exasperation. He bent and gave me another quick kiss.

"Get a move on, will you? Gotta get out there early enough to set up camp and get ever'thing organized 'fore it gets dark."

I started toward the house, then paused and almost turned back, but I stifled the impulse to ask him about snakes and bobcats and who knows what else back there in the deep woods at night. I didn't even know if he had a tent. I could imagine him sleeping out in the open under the stars, but surely he wouldn't expect that of me.

However uncertain I was of what awaited me, I trusted my husband and knew he would take care of me. I was afraid, though, if one of the reasons he was doing this was to give me a rest, the project was doomed to failure. I was sure I wouldn't be able to sleep a wink.

Calvin was in the kitchen. I stuck my head in and told him we were going camping and saw his eyes light up with excitement. Two against one, I thought with wry amusement, so I'd be a good sport and go along with them. I put my books away, hesitating a moment over the test papers I had to grade, then resolutely left it all and went to change into jeans and blouse and tennis shoes.

"Ready?" Davy asked when I went out to join them at the truck.

"You've got clothes for all of us?"

"Yep."

"Underwear? Sweaters if it turns off chilly? Blankets?"

"Yep."

"Food? Or are we going to live off the land?"

"A little of both. I got ever'thing. You don't need to bring anything but yourself."

"You've got my makeup?"

"You don't need makeup where we're goin'. B'sides, you're pretty enough without it."

"This ought to be interesting," I said dryly as he opened the door on the driver's side and stood aside for me to get in.

"Hop in, Cal," he said.

"Can I ride in th' back?"

"Can if you want to, but set up close to the cab and keep your head down when we get into the woods. Ain't nothin' but a wagon track where we're goin', so you'll have to hang on."

Calvin climbed in the back and I got in the front. Davy got in beside me and we were off.

We traveled a familiar dirt road for some distance, then we left the road and entered the woods. There was, as

Davy had said, only a wagon track here, and it was narrow and winding and rough. We went up hills and down and I had to hang on to prevent myself being thrown around in the cab of the truck, though Davy drove slowly and had to shift gears frequently. I kept turning to look out the back window at Calvin, but he seemed to be doing fine, his eyes darting here and there with eager interest.

"I can almost imagine that we're going west in a covered wagon," I said after a long silence.

"We are goin' west," Davy said, grinning at me.

I looked at the trees surrounding us. The foliage was so thick overhead that we traveled in deep shade. It was cooler here and the air was rich with the smell of decaying leaves and other scents that I could not identify. I could see now why Davy had wanted to get an early start. It wouldn't be long before darkness set in out here in the deep woods. I shivered.

"I can almost imagine an Indian skulking behind every tree," I said.

"Don't think so. Lots of birds an' squirrels an' rabbits, foxes an' skunks, things like that, even deers and wild turkeys, but no Indians."

"What about bobcats and panthers?"

"Yep. Few of them, too."

"Snakes?"

"Yep."

I swallowed. "You aren't afraid to camp out with — "

"Nothin' to be afraid of," he said comfortably. "Cats don't hunt people, and no self-respectin' snake stays around a campsite. A snake's philosophy is live an' let live. Only time they'll strike is if you run up on one unexpected or you get 'em cornered so they can't get away. Same with a bobcat."

I wasn't completely reassured, but I decided to keep

my fears to myself. He knew much more about such things than I did.

"You're a girl that likes adventure, ain't you?" he asked me with another grin.

"Yes, but — "

"Jist another experience to tell your gran'kids." He changed gears to negotiate a sharp turn, then glanced in his rearview mirror at Calvin. "Wonder what adventure he's dreamin' up," he said dryly.

I glanced back. Calvin sat cross-legged, his expression dreamy and far away. I had to smile.

"Probably covered wagons and Indians, too," I said.

Finally Davy pulled the truck off the barely discernible track and came to a stop. "Far as we go with the truck," he said.

"We're camping here?" I asked in alarm.

"Nope, but the trail goes off to the left and we want to go to the right. We'll leave the truck here and pack the stuff in on our backs," he added with a little quirk of a grin at me. I swallowed.

"Through that?" I asked, indicating the dense woods.

"Yep."

"My goodness. When you decide to get away from it all, you really get away from it all, don't you?"

"That's the whole idea, ain't it? Hop out. We got a ways to go yet. It'll give you a fair idea of what things was like when Mom an' Dad first come out here."

We got out and Davy got up in the back of the truck and began tossing things toward the tailgate. Then he jumped down and took up a bundle of blankets tied together with a thin rope.

"Turn around," he said to me. When I obeyed, he brought the rope around my waist and up over my shoulders and secured the bundle of blankets on my back. He did the same with three pillows tied together on

Calvin's back. He set two suitcases on the ground and two small cardboard boxes tied with the thin rope. Then he took up a backpack himself, shouldered a bundle of canvas that I assumed was a tent, and with his rifle over his other shoulder and bent slightly turned to the west.

"Grab one of them suitcases in one hand and a box in the other," he instructed me and Calvin, "and follow me."

I told Calvin to go first and I fell in behind. All was silent except for the twitter of birds overhead and the crunch of twigs and fallen leaves under our feet. Davy twisted and turned, dodging low limbs. Calvin followed close behind him and I followed Calvin, resisting the impulse to keep looking over my shoulder to see what might be following me.

Calvin was bent almost to a crouch, though I knew his load really wasn't that heavy. His steps grew longer, he began to swagger from side to side, the suitcase swinging from one hand, the box from the other. I smiled, wondering what prey he was stalking in his imagination. Watching him, I almost forgot my apprehension of the deep woods.

Calvin pushed a low hanging branch aside and went under it, but he let go too soon and it whipped back and caught the upper part of the pillows strapped to his back. The next thing I knew, he was lying sprawled out before me, legs and arms flung out wide.

"Davy! Wait!" I cried, afraid we would be left behind.

Davy stopped and turned to look back. "What happened?"

I started to laugh. Calvin was unhurt, the pillows had cushioned his fall, but he had been jerked so abruptly out of his daydream that it was evidently taking him a minute to adjust to reality. He lay there blinking owlishly up at the leaves above him, the one eye still a little yellow where it had formerly been black.

"A panther sprang on him from the trees," I said, still laughing. "Calvin, you're not hurt?"

He struggled to a sitting position and I pushed the branch aside and helped him to his feet. He brushed himself off and took up the box and the suitcase again. Davy forged ahead and we fell in behind him.

It was just a short while then until we broke out of the trees and into bright sunlight. We were in a flat grassy area on the bank of a rushing, gurgling stream of water that glistened in the sunlight and widened out into a small lake just a few yards downstream. On the other side of the water, tree-covered hills rose up, green and rolling. Davy had stopped and dropped the roll of canvas and was taking off his backpack. I stood just outside the woods, rooted to the spot and enthralled.

"It's gorgeous," I said. "Why, it's the same place where we came earlier in the summer and had the picnic!"

"You liked it so much then, I thought maybe you'd enjoy comin' back again," Davy said.

"I'd almost forgotten how beautiful it is."

"Plenty of time to admire it later. Right now we got to go back and get the rest of the stuff from the truck. It'll be gettin' dark soon in them woods."

"We have to go back again?" I asked in dismay.

"If you want to eat tonight we do. When I come by myself, I can make it in one trip, but I had to lay on extry provisions for women and children, you know. Are you up to it?"

"Of course, but let's hurry."

"Jist drop them things where you are and let's go."

When we came back from the second trip, it was growing dusky before we broke out of the trees, but at the campsite all was brightness and sunshine. However, now I had another problem besides worrying what might be in the woods.

"Where's the bathroom?" I asked Davy.

"Tub's right there," he answered, pointing to the little lake. "Toilet's right there," he waved toward the woods.

"Complete with snakes and bobcats and poison ivy, too, I suppose."

"Gotta go, or can you wait 'til I get the tent up?"

"I can't wait too long. I should have gone before we left the house, but you were rushing me so," I ended a bit accusingly.

"Toilet facilities comin' up," he said, letting the tent fall back to the ground. He went off a short distance into the woods and I stood waiting.

"Come on," he said when he reappeared a few minutes later. "Toilet's all ready."

Reluctantly, I went to him and he took me by the hand and led me into the woods.

"I've tramped around so I know there's no snakes here. No poison ivy either, and no bobcats. Yet. If you have to come out here durin' the night, better let me come with you, though."

"That's all I need, an audience," I said dryly.

He grinned and left me. When I went back to the campsite a while later, Davy and Calvin were putting up the tent. It was not large, but it had a floor and a zipper closing which I was profoundly glad to see.

"What do you want me to do?" I asked.

"Nothin'. Soon as the tent's up, I'll fix supper. If you're hungry, I brought along some cheese and crackers."

"What are we having for supper?"

"Steak an' sweet corn on the cob an' tomatoes."

"And you're cooking it?"

"Sure am."

"Then I'll wait. Is that Willow Creek?"

"Yep."

"Is the water drinkable?"

"Prob'ly 'bout as pure an' fresh an' cold as any you'll get anywhere. There's a bucket there and a dipper, if you want to go get some."

I took the bucket and made my way down to the stream, taking my time and looking around. It certainly was a beautiful and peaceful spot. I no longer regretted Davy almost making me come. Perhaps I would get a lot more rest and relaxation here than I had supposed.

Davy gathered up some wood and made a fire between two big rocks he'd picked up down by the creek. When the fire died down and the coals were red-hot and glowing, he placed a heavy metal rack across the two rocks. On this he laid six large ears of corn, still in their husks but with the silk removed.

Calvin and I sat cross-legged on the ground near the campfire and watched. The sun had gone down in a blaze of glory and now it was growing dusky and pleasantly cool. I had a strangely unreal peaceful feeling as I sat there with the dark woods and the hills enclosing us on all sides. To the west, the narrow creek rushed and gurgled over the rocks down to the small lake. Gradually, over the noise of the creek, a multitude of other sounds began to swell up around us, frogs, crickets, locusts, and off in the distance, another sound that made a shiver go down my spine.

"What's that?" I asked Davy, my voice hushed.

"Coyotes," he answered. "They're harmless."

"Oh."

He put the corn to the side of the grill and laid the steaks over the hot coals. Soon the delicious smell of sizzling meat filled the air. I was suddenly aware that I was ravenously hungry.

The meal was the most delicious I had ever eaten. We finished every bite and sat back, replete.

"Why didn't you tell me you could cook like that?" I asked.

"Nothin' to it."

"It was wonderful. Any time you want to take over the job, just let me know."

"Don't throw that bone away. If we leave scraps layin' around it'll draw ever' animal in the area to our camp, and you wouldn't want that, would you?" He looked at me with a grin.

"What will we do with them?"

"Bury them. I'll do it, soon as me an' Cal take these dishes down to the creek and wash them. You sit still."

I sat still, though I wasn't too comfortable there alone. However, since Davy and Calvin were within sight, I wasn't too uneasy. Darkness was closing in fast now that the sun had gone down. Davy and Calvin came back with the clean dishes and a fresh bucket of water. Davy brought out an old battered coffeepot and made coffee. Then he put it on the grate and stirred the coals so that a small fire sprang up again. He lit a lantern and took it and hung it up in the tent. He stayed there for awhile, arranging the bedding, I supposed. Beside me, Calvin yawned widely. The coffee was perking, filling the air with a delicious aroma.

"Bed, Cal," Davy said quietly behind us.

Calvin's head was drooping, but at Davy's words he jerked it upright. I imagined he looked apprehensive. Perhaps he was afraid to go to the tent alone.

"I think I'm getting a little sleepy myself," I said.

"Stay and have a cup of coffee with me, then you can go to bed, too. Come on, Cal. I'll show you where you're gonna sleep."

"Goodnight, Calvin," I said as he rose to his feet and followed Davy rather reluctantly to the tent.

"I left the lantern lit for him," Davy said, coming back with two tin cups in his hand. "Think maybe he was a little nervous, but he'll be asleep in two minutes."

"That coffee smells so good, but if I drink it I'll be awake all night. You don't normally drink coffee in the evening either, Davy. Aren't you afraid it'll keep you awake?"

"Don't seem to, when I'm camping. Maybe it's the fresh air or somethin', but I always sleep like a baby when I'm campin'. You ain't really lived 'til you've set around a campfire at night drinkin' hot coffee out of a tin cup and listenin' to the night sounds."

"Then I suppose it's time I lived a little. You didn't happen to bring any cream, did you?"

"Right here," he said, holding up a small can. He squatted by the fire and poured out two cups of coffee. He added cream to one of them and set it down on the ground beside me.

"Careful," he said. "The cup gets awful hot."

He replaced the coffeepot on the grate and sat down beside me and put his arm around me. "Glad you come?" he asked.

"Very glad," I said, leaning against him. "I had no idea it would be so pleasant and peaceful. Look at that moon. Did you ever see it so bright? And those stars. I've never seen so many."

"When I'm out here, I get to thinkin' this is the way people was meant to live," he said softly against my hair.

"You may be right. I really didn't want to come, but I'm so glad now that I did. Everything seems somehow larger than life and so extraordinary."

"It's extry special 'cause I got you here with me this time." I tilted my face up to look at him.

"Is it, Davy? Thank you. It's nice of you to say so. You're a very good husband, did you know that?"

"I'm glad if you think so, at least."

"It's really quite a surprise to me," I said almost to myself.

"You wasn't expectin' me to be a good husband?" he queried, sounding a little piqued.

"I didn't mean that. It's just that I remember being warned when I was younger by my mother and my older sister that when a woman has been married for a short time, she can't expect her husband to continue giving her compliments or telling her he loves her because men just take it for granted that their wives know they are loved. It seems to be a common complaint that wives have. I guess I'm just surprised that you — "

"You didn't expect a hillbilly husband to know how to pay his wife a compliment?"

"I'm just saying it's an unexpected bonus, Davy," I said, reaching up to touch his cheek.

"Who taught you how to be such an excellent husband? Your mother?"

He didn't answer immediately, but reached for his cup and took a sip of coffee. Then his eyes came back to me, dark in the flickering firelight. "You taught me," he said then.

"I did?" I asked in surprise. "How did I do that?"

"When a man finds hisself with somethin' in his possession that is so precious that no price can be put on it, well then, he tries to take care of it the best way he knows how, 'cause he don't ever want to risk losin' it."

Tears came to my eyes and I turned away so that wouldn't see. A tear rolled down my cheek and surreptitiously I wiped it away.

"You cryin'?" he asked, startled. He put his hand on my wet cheek and I turned my face into his shoulder. He put his cup down and put both arms around me and held me close. "What's wrong?" he asked against my hair.

"Nothing," I said, my voice husky. "It's just that that's the most beautiful thing you've ever said to me, and I don't think I deserve it."

"Why not?"

"Don't you remember what happened last week?"

"Sure I remember."

"But I got mad at you and I called you names."

"So you got a right to your feelin's. Some men might like to have a puppet for a wife, but I ain't one of them. Can't expect to go through life always agreein' on ever'thing, but one of the sweetest things about you is when you find out you're wrong about somethin', you ain't afraid to admit it. Takes a pretty special person to be able to do that."

"Thank you, Davy. I think you're pretty special, too, and I'm so glad I married you."

I put my arms around his neck and lifted my lips for his kiss. An owl hooted softly some distance into the woods. A cool breeze sprang up and Davy released me to put another stick of wood on the fire. We took up our coffee cups and sat there leaning against each other and looking into the fire, silent for some length of time.

"Who says marriage is the end of romance?" I said softly then. "Here we are, an old married couple sitting together before a campfire in the woods, and I defy anyone to find a more romantic scene. Let's do this again sometime, Davy."

"We will," Davy said softly, deeply. "But next time I think we'll leave Calvin home."

I had two cups of coffee before Davy and I finally went to bed, and with that and the strange night sounds and the hard bed on a blanket on the ground, I got very little sleep. However, I felt secure enough, with Davy on one side of me and Calvin snoring gently on the other side. I lay there with my eyes wide open, my thoughts occupied for some time with my husband.

I had come to understand, from the talk of other

married women, that disillusionment and marriage went hand in hand, that once the honeymoon was over, and a couple got down to the daily business of living, everything changed. Husbands became tyrants, or boorish slobs, or indifferent and uncaring. It was one of the reasons I had not been anxious to get married at the age that most girls were thinking of marriage and babies. I loved teaching and was content to remain single until I met Davy. He had rushed me into marriage, there was no doubt of that. Since my father's visit just before the start of school I had found myself a few times feeling somewhat resentful toward my husband because of that. It had resulted in the alienation of my father, and indirectly of my mother, too. To no avail I reminded myself that Davy had not forced me — I had allowed myself to be persuaded. Still, the nagging thought kept reoccurring, that if he had not been so persistent, we might have waited and I would have remained on good terms with my father. They would have come to visit me and I could have freely visited them, whereas now that was not possible.

I had not allowed my mind to focus on my father's visit, his accusations and his feelings. Now I deliberately recalled them. As I visualized each scene, each accusation, I found they had lost all power to wound. My father was wrong, that was all there was to it, and I was wrong to let what he had said make me begin to resent the fact that Davy had rushed me into marriage. If he hadn't, perhaps I would not have married him at all as he had feared, and as I had told Liz earlier, that would have been the biggest mistake of my life. I was learning to love my husband more all the time and I knew I was well-loved in return. I was happier than I had ever been in my life and I felt sure that my happiness could only grow as time went on. The disappointment and disillusionment that seemed to come so often with marriage was not for me.

I snuggled closer to Davy and in his sleep he put his arm around me. I was filled with content, my mind free of any doubts that had been stirred up by my father's visit. I thought about the time of Davy's proposal and had to smile. He had told me that if I would agree to marry him immediately and live there in the hills with him, I could have everything else the way I wanted it. He was certainly an easy-going and indulgent husband, but I hadn't always had it all my own way, as the little incident about the extra homework for Calvin had proven. Mine was no henpecked husband, and I found I was glad to have it that way. He would not give in to me when he was convinced that I was wrong, just to keep the peace.

I was beginning to feel sleepy and I fell into a light doze just as daylight came creeping into the tent. I was aware of it when Davy woke and sat up, and after giving me a light kiss on the forehead, carefully eased himself away from me and left the tent. I turned on my side in the less confined space and finally slept soundly. I woke to the smell of frying bacon and perking coffee. Since we had all gone to bed in our clothes, there was nothing to do but rise from the blankets, put my shoes on, duck my head and step through the door of the tent into the fresh morning sunshine. The morning was cool and still, and the sunlight glinting off the water of the narrow rushing creek was so bright I had to look away. My eyes came to rest on my husband and Calvin, squatting by the campfire cooking breakfast. I stretched and yawned and made my way over to them.

"Mornin', Sleepyhead," Davy said, squinting up at me.

"Good morning, Davy. Calvin."

Davy poured a cup of coffee, added cream and handed it up to me. I took it and sipped it, looking around and enjoying the beauty and the peace and quiet of the spot.

"Get some sleep?" Davy asked me.

"Enough."

"Hungry?"

"Starving."

"Bacon an' eggs comin' up, but after this we live off the land."

"How do we do that?"

"I'll show you."

"Did you pack my brush, or do I use a twig on my hair this morning?" I asked lightly, not really caring one way or the other.

"I packed it, but forget your hair right now. Let's eat."

He reached into the bucket of water that was setting on the ground nearby, squeezed out a washcloth and handed it to me. It was cold, and when I had passed it over my face and hands I felt wonderfully refreshed and ready for my breakfast.

The three of us had a wonderful day together. After breakfast we just sat around the fire and relaxed. We talked little and were silent a lot. There was no hurry to get the dishes done, no need to get up and rush off somewhere. We had no one to please but ourselves and we did just that.

Since we had eaten a late breakfast we decided two meals would be enough that day. Fruit and crackers were available if anyone got hungry. Instead of lunch, we went swimming in the lake.

Davy had brought shorts for each of us and we donned these for swimming and went shivering into the water. The lake was cold, but not quite as cold as the creek water. We played and splashed and swam until we were chilled, then we climbed out on the bank and lay on the grass in the sun until we were baked, then went into the lake again.

Later in the afternoon I stayed at the campsite by myself while Davy and Calvin went off into the woods with the gun. I was feeling heavy-eyed and sleepy after all the swimming and my sleepless night, so I crawled into the tent and took a nap. When I woke Davy had built up the fire again and had a dressed and skinned young rabbit threaded onto a stick and suspended above the glowing coals. Calvin crouched nearby, turning the stick occasionally.

We had a supper of roast rabbit and large Irish potatoes baked under the hot coals and hoe cake baked in an iron skillet placed on the grate, which Davy served dripping with butter. Supper was absolutely wonderful. Davy and I sat around the campfire again that night long after Calvin had gone to bed, but I refused to drink any coffee so I slept soundly when we did go to bed. It was barely daylight when Davy roused both me and Calvin with a finger on his lips to insure silence.

"Somethin' I want you to see," he whispered.

"What is it?"

"Sh-h-h. Jist step outside real quiet an' you'll see."

We did, and stood looking where he pointed and saw three large deer drinking at the far edge of the lake. We watched until they lifted their heads and turned, their short tails flicking as they trotted off into the woods.

"They're beautiful," I said. "I've never seen wild deer before. I wonder how many other animals came here to drink during the night."

"Prob'ly quite a few, but I thought you'd like to see the deers."

"Yes, thank you. Oh, what a gorgeous morning! I'm glad you got us up early. I'm going to hate to leave all this. When are we leaving, Davy?"

"I thought 'bout noon, unless you think we ought to leave earlier."

"No. Noon will be fine."

"Thought I might try fishin' for our breakfast this mornin'. Want to come along?"

209

"But you didn't bring a fishing pole, did you?"

"Got a hook and a line, that's all I need. Comin'?"

"I'll come and watch. Are you going to fish in the lake?"

"There's a little place further down, jist a kinda deep hole in the creek bed. Always been able to catch a fish or two there, ever' time I've tried."

"All right. Let's go."

There was a fine stand of tall cane in one of the low places. Davy took out his pocket knife and cut one, then he looked at Calvin and cut another one.

"Sure you don't want to try it?" he asked me.

"Not this time. I'll just watch."

With their cane poles in hand, we made our way down to the place Davy had in mind. We had to climb over a few boulders and wade through tall grass, but it wasn't too far. The creek was wider and deeper here, the water not nearly so swift, but still clean and clear.

Davy's fishing line was a ball of baling twine that he took out of his pocket. He cut two pieces about six feet long and attached small hooks that he took out of a small box in his other pocket and tied the other end to the cane poles. Then he rolled an old dead log over and stooped to gather up a couple of white grubs and put them on the hooks. I shuddered and averted my eyes at this part of the procedure.

We seated ourselves side by side on some big overhanging rocks and Calvin and Davy let their baited hooks down in to the water.

Very soon a ripple appeared and we could see the fish swimming straight for Calvin's bait. Without hesitation, the fish's mouth opened wide and he swallowed the grub.

"Hang on to the pole," Davy instructed. "He's hooked good. Pull him on in."

Calvin stood up and pulled the fish out of the water

and landed him on the grass behind us. Davy thrust his pole into my hands and went to help him.

"Davy!" I shrieked a minute later. There was a fish on his line now, and it was twice as big as Calvin's, though Calvin's was a good foot long. The fish was thrashing around and I was afraid it was going to get away or pull me into the water with it. My perch on the rocks was none too secure.

Davy rushed back and took the pole from me and landed his own fish, then we stood over the two fish on the grass and looked at each other.

"That was too easy," Davy said, nearly disgusted.

"Can we try again?" Calvin asked, excited.

Davy shook his head. "This is all we'll be able to eat and more. Ain't right to go killin' anything if you ain't gonna use it, even a fish."

"We could take some home."

"We could, but we got enough to pack as it is. 'Sides, we ain't got any way of keepin' it fresh that long."

Calvin looked disappointed but Davy reached out and ruffled his hair and grinned at him. "We'll go fishin' again some other time. There's a pretty good fishin' hole not more'n a mile or so from the house. Not as good a place as this, maybe, but there's more sport to it."

He cut a branch into a fork and threaded the two fish on it and handed it to Calvin. Then he cut the string from the poles, rolled the hooks and lines into a ball, tossed the poles aside, took the fish from Calvin, and we made our way back to camp.

Davy built up the fire, put the coffee on, then took Calvin with him down to the creek to clean the fish. When he came back he put the skillet over the fire, added bacon grease, dipped the pieces of fish in corn meal and put them in the skillet to fry. We had coffee while we waited. When the fish was done, he removed it and wiped the skillet out with some paper towels, added more bacon grease and sliced the two leftover baked potatoes into the skillet. A few minutes later he handed breakfast to Calvin and me. Breakfast was served on the tin piepans Davy had brought for plates.

"Watch out for the bones," he said.

Fried fish, potatoes, cold corn bread, and hot coffee made a satisfactory breakfast, I discovered. Even Calvin, who didn't care much for fish, ate his share. I sighed and sat back, replete.

"That was wonderful. If I'd known you could cook like that, I'd have let you take over the cooking at home a long time ago," I told Davy.

"Only kind of cookin' I know how to do, I'm afraid. Learned how to do it when I went campin' all them times by myself, 'fore I had a wife to take care of me."

"I haven't done any taking care of you on this trip. You've done it all. It's been wonderful, but I feel so lazy, not an ounce of ambition in my whole body. I think I could stay here forever."

"And forget about teachin'?"

"And forget about teaching, forget about laundry and ironing and housework, and getting ready for Liz and Jim's wedding, forget about everything. But I suppose all this would get old after awhile."

"I never have got tired of it."

"When you camped alone those times, did you stay very long at a time?"

"Stayed a week once."

"And lived off the land?"

"Yep."

"Did you grow a beard?"

"Didn't shave the whole time, but don't know that you coulda called it much of a beard. Not like ol' man Miller's, at least."

I laughed. Mr. Miller had a long flowing beard that came halfway down to his waist. After two days without shaving, Davy's chin was dark with stubble. I reached out and ran my hand over his cheek. It felt like sandpaper.

"I think you'd grow a fine beard, Davy. I wonder if I would like you in one. I think I would."

"Always wanted a beard, but ain't never been quite brave enough to do it. Mom don't like beards. Thinks men grow beards 'cause they got somethin' to hide."

I laughed again then sat up and looked around for Calvin. He had disappeared.

"Where's Calvin?" I asked sharply.

"Down by the lake, lookin' for frogs, prob'ly."

I looked and saw him and relaxed again. "He's had so much fun. How can you even think of leaving him behind next time we come?" I asked, looking provocatively up at him through my eyelashes.

"Easy," he said.

"But he'll be heartbroken."

"Wouldn't have to tell him where we was goin'."

"Selfish," I teased.

"Un-huh."

I sighed and looked around me. "It would be a wonderful spot for a second honeymoon, wouldn't it?" I murmured.

"That's what I thought, but I was afraid you wouldn't come if we had to leave Cal. Next time though, we will."

"When will that be?"

"Want to come again in a couple weeks? The leaves will be startin' to turn by then, and by the end of October it's a sight to see. If you think it's pretty now, oughta see it then, with all the reds an' oranges an' yellows mixed in with the green. With that hill there and the lake in front of it, it makes a picture."

"I'll bet it does, and I would love to come, but I don't

think there will be time, Davy. We have to start planning for the wedding, you know. It's only four weeks away and there's still a lot to do."

"If the weather holds, we might be able to come the weekend after the weddin'."

"But your mother is planning her yearly family get-together then, isn't she?"

"Forgot about that. Next year then."

"Yes, next year for sure. Perhaps we'll be able to come several times during the summer. I love it here, Davy. Thank you so much for bringing us."

CHAPTER EIGHTEEN

The Secret

The next week passed quickly and without incident. I spent more time outside with the children at recess, because I was afraid the Sutton boys might try to pick on Calvin or Jimmie. I didn't obviously watch over them, but I knew my presence would deter any mischief that they might be planning.

The Decker boys seemed to be doing all right, too. I hadn't had time to visit with Jane again, but I had talked with Sue Proctor about her. Though I didn't mention the abuse of Jimmie, I pointed out how difficult her position was and how lonely. Sue was sympathetic and agreed to help. Her husband Lewis was supposed to take a load of firewood to Jane soon, so when he went Sue would go along and spend some time visiting with Jane again, and perhaps invite her over to her own house. I felt confident that Sue's befriending Jane would perhaps be of more help than anything else I could suggest.

The weekend turned off cold and blustery. Sporadic rain dashed against the windows and a chill crept into the house. Davy wanted to put the woodstove up in the living room, but I convinced him to wait until after the wedding as it would give us less room. I decided to do some baking, something I didn't have as much time for now as I had had during the summer, and the heat from the oven helped to warm the house. I baked cookies, bread and a couple of pies, and the house was filled with the delicious baking smell.

We had a quiet evening at home that Saturday. Calvin and I sat at either end of the sofa, and each of us was wrapped in a blanket. He read a book and I wrote the letter to my father that I hadn't had time to write before then. Davy, wearing a heavy flannel shirt, sat in one of the rockers and read the newspaper.

Once I paused in my writing and sat studying Davy, trying to put into words the quality of this man I had married. He glanced up and met my eyes and we exchanged a smile. My heart was full of tenderness for him.

"Writin' your folks?"

"Actually, I'm writing just to Daddy," I said.

"Givin' him a personal invitation to the weddin'?"

"Yes."

"Think he'll come?"

"I don't know, but at least he'll know he's welcome. Did I tell you Liz and Mama are planning on coming a couple of days early to get things ready? You won't mind them being here, will you?"

"No, I won't mind. I like your mama and your sister. Will your other sister and her husband be stayin' here?"

"I don't know. Liz wasn't sure of their plans, just that Mary wrote and said they were coming."

"You say her husband's a pilot?"

"Yes, and Mary's a nurse. They've been in Alaska for about three years now and they don't get home too often. I haven't seen her since I came out here. I'm so glad they can come."

"Is she anything like you and Liz?"

"I suppose so. She's the oldest, six years older than I am."

"They don't have any kids?"

"No. They are both pretty involved with their careers."

Davy looked puzzled, as if he couldn't quite comprehend that kind of attitude. Here in the hills, if a married couple didn't have children, it was only because they couldn't. Rumors about Davy and me had been rife, probably still were.

"Liz will no doubt provide the first grandchild," I said. "She told me that she and Jim are hoping for a baby right away."

Davy nodded. "Jim's always been lonesome, long as I've known him. Always said when he got married he wanted to have a big family."

He went back to his newspaper, but I sat looking at him and wondered if he felt deprived. I knew he wanted children, too, and if the decision had been left to him, we would probably be having a baby of our own right about now. I wondered if he would mind Jim and Liz being first. I went back to my letter, but my mind was preoccupied.

Another week passed, and although the weather turned pleasant again there was a feel of autumn in the air. The days were warm but the nights were cool and breezy. The leaves started to change and some of them began drifting to the ground.

Liz and Jim came. She had found a dress for me that fit her specifications. It was of palest peach, street-length, and she had brought along a spray of artificial flowers in the same color for me to wear in my hair. My own white strap heels would complete the ensemble. When I tried the dress on, it was a perfect fit.

"It's really lovely, Liz," I said. "And I think street-length is best for a simple wedding. Your own dress is street-length, too, isn't it?"

"Yes. It's white lace, very simple with a short white veil. I'll carry a bouquet of flowers the color of your dress and the men will be in navy blue. My wedding may be simple, but there's no reason why it can't be beautiful, too.

Let's go into the living room room and show the guys."

"Oh, but Liz — "

She opened the bedroom door and gave me a push so that I had no choice but to go on into the living room. Jim, Calvin, and Davy were there and they all turned to look at me. Jim whistled.

"You'll be almost as pretty as the bride," he said. I looked at Davy. He said nothing, but he smiled and his eyes were full of warmth.

"Go stand over there beside Davy," Liz told me. "We have to decide where we're all going to stand and where the guests will sit and all."

"Let me change this dress first, Liz," I said, feeling a little self-conscious. "I don't want to get it dirty or perhaps snag it. I'll be right back."

When I got back to the living room, Liz had arranged our kitchen chairs with their backs to our bedroom door, three on each side with a short aisle between them.

"We'll need four more chairs," she said. "The Carters are coming and we've invited Sue and Lewis and their kids. They were over at Jim's this morning and it seemed only right to invite them since they'll be our nearest neighbors."

"That's nice, Liz. I'm glad you did. You'll like them."

"The Carters and Sue and Lewis and the girls can sit on this side," Liz continued. "Sue will have to hold the baby, of course. I hope he doesn't cry. If Daddy comes, he and Mama and Kevin can sit on the sofa. Can we move it just a little more toward this end of the room? Then, your mom and dad can sit on this side, Davy, along with Calvin and the photographer."

"I don't think — " I began impulsively, but I caught Davy's warning look and stopped. It wouldn't do to advertise Davy's father's attitude toward Calvin.

"What?" Liz asked. "It's just possible that Davy's

218

father won't come," I said. "He isn't too keen on social functions."

"Well, if he doesn't want to come, that's all right, but Jim wanted to invite them, since they've more or less been a second family to him. Clemmy will come, won't she?"

"I'm sure she will."

"We'll have to move the two rockers to make more room. Then we'll fix up a sort of altar at this end of the room, a small table will do, and I want it covered with flowers. The minister will wait behind it. Jim, you will stand here and you will stand on the other side of him, Davy. Anne, you'll stand on this side, about here. Mary will be seated at the piano. She'll play through one piece, I don't know which yet, maybe she'll have some ideas, then she'll play the wedding march and I'll come in from your bedroom. I'll have to use it to dress in and all. You won't mind, Davy?"

"No."

"I'll come up the aisle, such as it is. I wish it was longer, but that can't be helped. You'll take a step forward to meet me and take my hand, Jim, then the four of us will turn to face the minister. Mary will stop playing and the ceremony will begin. It will last only about fifteen minutes, then we'll turn to face the room, the minister will introduce us as man and wife and that's it. The photographer will take pictures, cake and punch will be served in the kitchen, and Jim and I will be off on our honeymoon. How does that sound?"

We all looked at each other and nodded.

"It sounds like you have it planned out quite well," I said. "You're not going to invite any of your friends from St. Louis?"

"No. It's really too far to expect them to come. My friend Amy said something about having a reception for us in St. Louis in a couple of weeks to introduce Jim to everyone, but no definite plans have been made as far as I know."

"Is there anything in particular you want me to do in preparation — other than make sure the house is clean?" I asked.

"No. Mom and I are planning on coming Wednesday. That will give us enough time to get everything done. Mom is going to bake and decorate the cake. She'll probably do that on Friday. Jim and I are going into town this afternoon to order the flowers and make sure of the arrangements for the minister. We've already had our blood tests and we'll get the license next week. We'll have to get four chairs from somewhere, but other than that, I think everything is pretty well taken care of."

"Sure appreciate your lettin' us have th' weddin' here," Jim said. "Hope it won't be too much trouble."

"It's no trouble. I just wish I could take some time off to be here and help with the preparations, but I'm afraid I can't." I said.

"That's all right," Liz said. "Mom and I will manage."

"Guess we better be runnin' along, now that we got all th' particulars figgered out. See you at th' weddin', if I don't see you before," Jim said.

"Well," I said when they were gone. "They've made their plans pretty well. It certainly won't be an elaborate wedding, but it sounds like it will be nice. What do you think of all this, Davy? Do you think it will be all right?"

"The weddin', you mean, or the marriage?"

"Both, I guess. I will admit I'm still a little troubled about it."

"Their minds are made up, so there ain't no use frettin' about it. They're both adults, even though your sister does seem awful young sometimes. Ain't nothin' you can do, 'cept help both of them as much as you can."

"You're right. I wonder if Daddy will come to the

wedding. Liz says he won't say, one way or the other. It doesn't seem to be bothering her too much, though."

"Does it bother you?"

"No, not that much. I'd like for him to come, of course, but that's up to him. It doesn't do to try to make someone's decisions for them. Or be their conscience. One of these days, that's a lesson my father is going to have to learn."

The week of the wedding was beautiful with temperatures in the mid-seventies. The trees were a riot of color, running the range from green to yellow to orange to red to brown. I had never experienced such a beautiful autumn. I was proud of our home in the hills and couldn't wait for my family to see it.

I went around in a glow of happiness all that week. I had a small secret hope growing inside of me that I hadn't told anyone about, not even Davy, because it was much too soon to be sure of anything.

I had known all along how much Davy wanted a child, but I hadn't known until now that I very much wanted children also. I was having difficulty focusing on anything else and I was surprised that no one else seemed to notice my state of mind. If it turned out not to be true I was going to be terribly disappointed, but no point in disappointing Davy, too. I would wait at least a few more days to be more sure before I told him.

Mama and Liz came on Wednesday as planned. When Calvin and I came home from school they were there and already established in Calvin's room. The evening before we had moved the things he would need into the utility room, where he would be sleeping on a cot Clemmy had provided.

Jim stopped by after work and carried Liz off. Davy and Calvin went to the shop after supper so Mama and I were able to spend some time alone together.

We didn't talk about Daddy or about Liz and her wedding. Mostly Mama wanted to know about my home and my work and I enjoyed telling her about it, but I had difficulty suppressing the desire to let her in on my secret, knowing I would hurt my husband if I told her before I told him. Anyhow, this was Liz's moment to shine and I had no desire to detract attention from her to myself. My news would wait, if indeed it was news. I had to keep reminding myself not to count my chickens before they hatched, as my mother-in-law was fond of saying.

Mama asked me if she could come to school the next day to visit and observe my method of teaching at a one-room rural school. It would be her only opportunity, because she would be busy all day Friday with the baking and decorating of the cake. I told her she was welcome and that the best time to come would probably be right after lunch.

Davy came and joined Mama and me in the living room after the chores were done and we sat and talked while I checked a few school papers. Calvin went on to bed. Liz had not come in by the time Mama and Davy and I went to bed.

The next morning, Mama got up and had breakfast with us, but Liz was still in bed when Calvin and I left for school. However, when Mama came to school that afternoon, Liz was with her. They were both so attractive, I was proud to be able to introduce them to my students.

"Liz will soon be your neighbor," I told the children. "She is going to marry Jim Baker this Saturday, and they will be making their home here so you will have a chance to get better acquainted with her. I'm hoping also that my mother will be coming to visit more often, so perhaps you'll get a chance to get to know her, too."

I directed Mama and Liz to a couple of empty seats

then and got on with my regular routine. When I dismissed the children for last recess and Mama and Liz came up to join me at the front of the room, some of the children began to gather around, too. They were shy, their eyes downcast, but their curiosity was stronger than their shyness. I introduced a few of them, mostly the girls who had ventured the closest.

All the children knew Jim Baker, so they were naturally inclined to stare rather fixedly at Liz. She was so pretty. It embarrassed her some, but she took it quite well and was friendly and smiling. Mama had always been good with children, so we were soon surrounded.

In the general hubbub, Becky Proctor proclaimed rather loudly that her family had been invited to the wedding because they were going to be next-door neighbors. There was a moment of silence while all the children turned and looked with envy and jealousy at Becky and Lori.

"If you get to go, I don't see why th' rest of us can't go too," one of the other girls said with petulance.

Liz looked at me rather helplessly, then back at the girl who had spoken. "I'm sorry," she said. "I would love to invite all of you, but it's going to be a small wedding. There isn't enough room to invite many people. It's mostly just family."

"You're goin' to be married at Teacher's house?" Ruth asked Liz in her shy voice, and it served to bridge the awkward moment.

"Yes. That's why we can't invite as many people as we would like to," Liz explained.

"I bet it'll be a awful pretty weddin'. Teacher's house is so nice."

"Yes."

Ruth turned to me. "Are you an' Uncle Davy goin' to be in th' weddin'?"

"Yes," I answered. "We will stand up with them."

"I bet your dress is pretty."

"Why yes, it is. Liz bought it in St. Louis. It is a soft peach color with a slightly full skirt, quite plain but very pretty. I have a spray of peach-colored flowers to wear in my hair," I told her, aware that the children here had a hunger for color and beauty.

"I wish I could see it," she said wistfully. "Could you maybe wear it to school tomorrow?"

"I'm afraid not, Ruth. I'd be afraid of tearing it or getting it dirty. All right, children, outside now, there's only ten minutes left of recess," I instructed.

"They don't get much opportunity to go places or see pretty clothes," I explained to Liz and Mama after the children were gone. "A wedding probably sounds very exciting to them. I doubt if many of them have ever been to one."

"I'd like to invite them all, but I don't see how I can," Liz said a bit defensively.

"No, of course not. There would be no place to put them."

I rang the bell a few minutes later and the children filed in. I asked Mama to help young Timmy Hilton with his reading, since he was not one of my better students, and Liz helped Carl Baxter with his arithmetic. School was finally dismissed for the day and most of the children lingered to say goodbye to Mama and Liz.

"You've made a hit," I told them after class was dismissed for the day. "They'll have something new and exciting to tell their parents when they get home. Their lives have a lot of sameness about them. Don't worry about not being able to invite them to the wedding, Liz. I'll tell them all about it on Monday, and Mama, if you can make the cake big enough, I'll bring each of them a small piece for a treat. They'd love that."

224

"I'll make it big enough. They're darling children, Anne, so quaint and old-fashioned and — and earthy."

I laughed. "Are you sure you don't mean dirty, Mama?" I asked.

"Well, that little boy I was helping — "

"I know. That was Davy's sister's little boy. She's my age and is expecting her fifth child quite soon, and hasn't been feeling well all through this pregnancy. I'm afraid the children have been doing a lot of fending for themselves. The oldest is only seven so — " It was a rather lame explanation, I thought. I knew the neglect of the children couldn't entirely be blamed on their mother's pregnancy. Maggie was a rather indifferent homemaker. "Many of the people here are very poor, Mama. They make do with what they have. Of course, there's no real excuse for filth, but there are extenuating circumstances. I've learned to love them all, and to make allowances. Hopefully I'll be able to make a difference to their future. I have a regular session on personal hygiene and nutrition and that sort of thing. I'd like to have a sort of home economics class, but so far I haven't been able to fit it in."

"But should you allow them to come to school without shoes?" Liz asked. "Even Calvin was barefooted. I would never have gotten away with that when I went to school."

"Very few of them wear shoes when the weather is warm. Most of them don't even own a pair of summer shoes. The parents can't afford them and consider them an unnecessary luxury. Winter boots or shoes are all they buy. As for Calvin, he considers shoes in the summer the worst kind of torture."

"Wouldn't you get in trouble if the school authorities knew?"

"They know. Mr. Hooper, the school superintendent, used to teach out here."

"Oh. Well, if they know."

225

"Well, shall we go?" I asked, gathering up my books. "Calvin is probably waiting for us outside. What have the two of you been up to today? Get all the things done that you had planned?"

"There wasn't a whole lot we could do today. Tomorrow is when we'll be busy."

We went outside and Calvin left the swings and ran ahead of us down the path toward home. Mama, Liz, and I fell into step.

"I had a long talk with your husband this morning before Liz got up," Mama said. "He's a fine young man. I can see why you married him, and there's no question about what his feelings are for you."

"We're very happy," I said softly.

"I can see that you are. It takes a load off my mind. I just wish your Dad would give himself a chance to get to know Davy better."

"Perhaps he will someday, Mama. He'll need time, I suppose, to adjust to the idea that I'm happily married in spite of the fact that I didn't marry the man of his choice. The very best thing I could hope for you, Liz, is that you and Jim be half as happy."

"I intend to be a lot more than just half as happy," Liz returned with a slight toss of her head. "You don't have the monopoly on happiness, you know. My goodness, to hear you talk, you'd think you and Davy had been married for years. It hasn't even been a year yet. Wait until the newness wears off before you go bragging about how happy you are."

"Liz," Mama chided.

"Well, it's true. I'm tired of hearing about her wonderful husband and her wonderful marriage, as if mine doesn't have a chance of being as happy."

"I didn't mean for it to sound that way, Liz," I said.

"I'm going to catch up to Calvin, then you two can

gossip about my marriage as much as you like." She started running and we saw her come alongside Calvin and slow to match her steps to his. Mama and I looked at each other. Mama sighed.

"I'm worried about her," she said. "She's still on the defensive and I don't know why. I'm so afraid she'll go right up to the moment of the marriage and then back out."

"I certainly hope not," I said. "I don't want her to make a mistake, but that would just about destroy Jim, I'm afraid."

"It wouldn't be too good for her either, but what can we do? When I try to talk about it, she just turns away and declares she knows what she's doing. I hope she's right."

"I do, too, Mama. I guess all we can do is wait and see."

CHAPTER NINETEEN

Wedding Bells

Wedding day dawned bright and clear. We were all up early and there was a stir of excitement in the air. We had a light stand-up breakfast because the cake Mama had baked and decorated the day before sat in the middle of the table, resting on a snowy lace tablecloth. It was beautiful. Mama had always had a flair for cake decorating and often did it for friends and neighbors in St. Louis.

Davy left the house after his offer to help was refused. Liz went in to take her bath and wash her hair. The rest of us had taken our own baths the night before. While I washed the breakfast dishes, Mama arranged the rest of the table. She set the punch bowl and the crystal glasses at one end of the table and filled small paper cups with nuts and mints and put them at the other end. She carefully arranged the paper napkins beside the small paper plates while Calvin stood nearby and watched. I smiled as I saw her give Calvin one of the cups of mints and nuts when my back was half-turned, as if they were conspirators. He took it and disappeared through the door.

When the kitchen was ready, Mama and I moved into the living room. We put the two rockers in the utility room, then dusted and ran the dust mop over the already highly-polished floor. I set the small round table Davy had made especially for the occasion at the end of the room, near the kitchen door, and covered it with another white lace tablecloth that reached almost to the floor. This was for the minister to stand behind. Liz would decorate it later with the flowers that Jim was to bring from town.

"I'll take Calvin and go get those chairs Clemmy promised us," Mama said.

I was preoccupied with my own thoughts and what she said didn't register until some minutes later. Suddenly I gasped and rushed to the door just in time to see my mother and Calvin disappear into Clemmy's house. I stood there not knowing what I should do. Mama didn't realize, of course, that Calvin had never been welcome in my father-in-law's house. If he was there, it might cause trouble.

I was just about to walk up to the house myself when they came out, and wonder of wonders, it was Mr. Hilton who was handing the chairs out to them. As I watched, Davy came out of his shop and stood talking to his dad for a minute before he took the last two chairs in either hand and strode forward to join Mama and Calvin, each carrying a chair. I stood at the door, ready to hold it open for them. I scanned their faces, but no one looked the least bit perturbed, so evidently Mr. Hilton had made no objection to Calvin going into his house. I was relieved.

At ten o'clock, Jim came with the flowers. Liz, dressed in blue jeans and a loose shirt, her hair up in rollers, her face devoid of makeup, met him at the door and proceeded to arrange the flowers to her satisfaction. I thought Liz looked like a child, but I had to smile a little at the look on Jim's face as he stood back and watched her.

Jim left then and after that everything seemed to accelerate. The wedding was scheduled for two o'clock. We had an early light lunch of sandwiches that Mama had made the night before, then it was time for us to start getting dressed. Davy went in with Calvin, and Mama, Liz, and I went into the other bedroom. Mama had only to slip her dress on and she was ready. She was helping me zip my dress and Liz was sitting before the mirror in her slip applying her makeup when I heard the clip-clop of horses' hooves and the jingle of a harness. We all paused and looked at each other.

"What is that?" Liz asked.

"It's a team and wagon," I answered. "Someone is coming."

"Who could it be?"

"I don't know," I answered, beginning to feel a foreboding. "It might be Lewis and Sue, I suppose."

"But it's so early!"

"Don't worry about it, Liz. Davy can just ask them to wait outside."

I went to the door in my stocking feet and opened it just as Davy came out of the other bedroom, dressed except for his jacket and tie. We exchanged a puzzled look. Unless I was much mistaken, there were two wagons arriving, one behind the other.

"It's your brothers," I said, looking out the window. "And they've got their families with them."

"What in tarnation — "

"They're all dressed up, Davy. They've come for the wedding," I said despairingly. "And they're not the only ones. There comes someone else."

Davy and I stood and looked at each other. Outside we heard the wagons stop and the men call to each other and the laughter and chatter of the women and children.

"What do you want me to do?" Davy asked me quietly.

"I don't know. I don't think there's anything you can do. You can't send them away without offending them and prejudicing them against Liz. Just — just don't let them come in, Davy. Tell them we're not dressed or something. I'll try to talk Liz into having the wedding outside."

He went out the front door and I went back into the

bedroom. Mama and Liz were standing there looking at me expectantly.

"It's Davy's brothers," I said flatly. "They've brought their families and I'm afraid they've come to the wedding."

"But they can't!" Liz cried. "There's no room and they weren't invited. I don't care if they are Davy's brothers."

"They aren't all Davy's brothers. Several more wagon-loads are coming. They are Jim's friends, Liz, and I'm afraid out here people don't always wait for an invitation, they just come."

"But there's no room!"

"They're Jim's friends," I repeated. "And they'll be your neighbors, Liz. I'm afraid it would be a bad mistake to send them away."

"But what am I going to do?"

"Put your bathrobe on and come with me. I have a suggestion."

She obeyed and I led the way to the living room window. There were four wagons and an old truck drawn up in the yard now and about twenty people were milling around.

"Why those two men are dressed in overalls!" Liz exclaimed indignantly.

"It's all some of the older men ever wear around here, no matter what the occasion."

"But why are they bringing out all those baskets?"

"It's food," I said flatly.

"Food! I wasn't going to serve food, just the cake and punch and coffee. They're trying to turn my wedding into a picnic!"

"It's the custom, Liz. They always bring food. It's a — a form of hospitality, a way to welcome you, to give you and Jim a good send off."

Liz's shoulders slumped, her pretty mouth petulant.

231

"Seems to me I ought to be able to say what goes on at my own wedding."

"They're Jim's friends. Don't humiliate him in front of his friends, Liz. Sally did a lot of that."

Her eyelashes flew up. She looked at me, startled, and I looked steadily back. Out in the yard there were more arrivals. Liz drew the curtain back and looked out the window again.

"What was your suggestion?" she asked then, her voice small and frozen.

"See that big yellow maple tree? The colors are just gorgeous. Don't you think it would make a good background for an outdoor wedding?"

She looked where I indicated, studied it for a few minutes, then looked back at the people in the yard. Davy was directing them to park their vehicles off to the left, a little away from the front of the house.

"It's a beautiful day," I continued. "It's so bright and sunny and warm, not a cloud in the sky, so no threat of rain. There's not even a breeze, or only a very small one, not enough to mess up your hair. You wanted a longer aisle to walk down, well there you have one, only it's more of a path than an aisle, but it could serve the same purpose. You wouldn't even have to worry about seating your guests. They can stand since the ceremony is a short one. What do you think, Mama?"

"I think it's a wonderful idea. It wouldn't require that much change either. We could do it."

Liz was looking thoughtful. Her eyes fell to the piano and flew up again in alarm.

"Can Mary play the piano loud enough to be heard out there?"

"I suppose she could, but it would be difficult for her to time it right since she wouldn't be able to see what's going on outside."

"But I have to have music!"

"Perhaps the radio — " Mama suggested tentatively.

"But you never know what's going to come on the radio and I will not walk down the aisle to a commercial!" Liz cried, on the verge of hysteria.

"No. No, of course not, Dear. That was a very poor suggestion. I'm sorry."

"Besides, I had my heart set on the wedding march." She was near tears as she turned back to the window. Mama and I looked helplessly at each other.

"Perhaps Mary can play and someone can stand beside her and look through the window and tell her what's happening," I began when Liz interrupted, her voice indignant.

"There's Jim and he's shaking hands with everyone and grinning! I'll kill him!"

"Remember Jim is an orphan," Mama reminded quietly. "He had no family of his own to invite. It must be very gratifying to him to have his friends and neighbors rally around him like this."

She was silent a moment, her brow wrinkled in thought, then she spoke rather shortly. "Tell Jim I want to see him," she said to me.

I went toward the door. "Tell Davy to come in, too," she added, so I opened the door and called to the two men, then stood silent and waited. Davy was looking a little wary, but Jim's face was flushed and his eyes bright. He was dressed in a navy blue suit with a white shirt and matching tie. His sandy hair was ruffled and he couldn't hide the little grin that quirked at the corners of his mouth. I found my own lips curling a little in sympathy.

"I'm sorry, Honey," he said to Liz with a shrug and widespread hands. "They're my friends, so I guess they figgered they was welcome to come to my weddin'."

"Did you invite them?" Liz asked quietly.

"I swear I never did. I mentioned I was gettin' married, a course."

Liz's eyes went from him to Davy and back again. We all more or less held our breath. Jim took a step forward and reached for her hands.

"I'll try sendin' them away if you want me to, but — "

"No, I don't think you can do that, but I might — "

"You might what?" Jim asked apprehensively.

"I might just decide to call the whole thing off."

"Ah, Sweetheart!"

Liz looked at him and relented. "Everything else can be changed, I suppose, and we can have the wedding outside, but there's no music and I won't have my wedding with no music."

Her voice broke on a sob and Jim stepped closer and put his arm around her. She leaned her head against him and wiped her eyes.

"Ol' man Miller's out there," he said, a note of suppressed excitement in his voice. "He's got his fiddle in his wagon. I know 'cause he told me if I felt like dancin' a jig after th' weddin', he'd play his fiddle for me."

"A fiddle at a wedding!"

"Violins are often used in wedding music, Liz," Mama said.

"Ol' man Miller plays th' sweetest fiddle you ever did hear, don't he Davy?"

Davy nodded and we all stood watching Liz and waiting.

"Well, why not?" she said a little wildly. "This whole thing is turning into a three-ring circus anyhow. What difference is a little thing like the music going to matter?"

"Liz dear," Mama chided.

"He can play jist about anything he wants to," Davy said quietly.

"All right. Call him in if you want to. I don't suppose

he can possibly play the wedding march but — "

"Wait a minute, Jim," I said. "Perhaps we ought to settle the other details first, then I'll talk to Mr. Miller about the music while you go ahead and get dressed, Liz. Have you thought how you'd like to have the actual wedding handled?"

"Well, since we've got the longer aisle, or path, and we've got music, hopefully, we might as well go ahead and have a regular wedding, I suppose," Liz said in a calmer voice.

"Jist tell us what you want done, Honey, an' we'll do it," Jim said.

"The table will have to be taken outside and set up again for the minister to use. Put it this side of the maple tree, Davy, not right under it, and will you arrange the flowers again, Mama? I can't very well do it."

"I'll take care of it," Mama said.

"I guess that's all the accessories we'll need. When it's time — Oh good heavens, it's one o'clock and I'm not even dressed, and where is the minister and the photographer and Mary and Kevin and Daddy?"

"They'll be here," I said soothingly, in an attempt to stem the rising panic in her voice.

"There's a station wagon jist drove up," Davy said quietly.

"It's Daddy," I said, "and Mary and Kevin are with him. We can go ahead and make plans. I'm sure the photographer and the minister will be here soon. It's still an hour."

Mama and I met Daddy and my sister and her husband at the door and there was the confusion of everyone talking at once. I managed to introduce my sister, Mary, to Davy and Jim, but that was all the introductions I was able to make. I noticed that Davy shook hands with my father and introduced himself to my brother-in-law. Jim had his hands full trying to calm Liz.

"I thought this was going to be a small private wedding," Mary said calmly, her eyes glinting with amusement.

"We thought so, too, but the plans have been changed," I said. "It's so good to see you, Mary."

"It's good to be here. We stopped by the Carter's for a minute. They are on their way. They had to go pick up the photographer. Well, can anyone tell us what's going on? Who are all those people?"

"Neighbors, friends, relatives," I said.

"In fact, the whole countryside?"

"Just about."

"Will everybody please be quiet?" Liz cried. "I have less than an hour to revise all my plans and get into my wedding dress and — and everything. You can all visit after the wedding."

"Yes, of course," I agreed quickly. "Liz and Jim have decided to have the wedding outside. Liz was just going to tell us how she wants it handled."

There was quiet at last. Everyone else looked at Liz and Jim, but I looked at my father. His eyes were on them, too, but his face was devoid of any expression. I couldn't tell what he was thinking, but at least he was here and he had been civil enough to Davy. I was encouraged to hope that the wedding would go off without any further hindrance.

"Everything has to be changed," Liz said. "There won't be any piano music, Mary. One of Jim's friends is going to play the — the violin. I'm sorry."

"No problem."

"He'll wait outside and the wedding party will wait inside. When the minister steps outside, he'll pause a minute, and that will be the signal for the music to start.

You'll tell him, Anne? The minister will walk down the aisle, I mean path, to the table that Davy will set up and Mom will decorate. He'll stand and wait behind it, facing the house. Then Davy and Jim will walk down the path together."

There was a little murmur from someone and Liz turned with flashing eyes. "Well, what are they supposed to do, hide behind the tree?" she demanded. "There's no vestibule to wait in, you know."

No answer. Jim hid a little grin behind his hand and Davy said in a soft voice to me, "Sounds like someone else I know."

Liz continued. "When they get to where the minister is, stop in front of him and to the right, Jim on the inside, and turn and also face the house. Have you got that?"

Both Davy and Jim nodded.

"Then I want you to come next, Mama. You can come down the path on Kevin's arm, no, on Calvin's." She glanced around, "Where is Calvin?"

"Oh good grief, no telling," I groaned. "Never mind, Liz. Go on. I'll find him and instruct him."

"Mama, you and Calvin walk almost to where Jim and Davy are waiting, then step off to the right, and also turn to face the house. I want all the other guests to stay on the other side of the path."

"I'll see to it," Davy said.

"Then Mary, I want you and Kevin to walk down the aisle," she paused and shook her head and corrected herself, "down the path to where Calvin and Mama are and wait with them."

They nodded.

"Then Anne, you walk down alone and stop before the minister and turn, but on the left hand side of him. Then the music will change to the wedding march." She turned to Jim. "Can he play the wedding march?"

"I don't know."

"Well, if he can, good, if he can't, he'll just have to play something else, but I want the music to change here. I'll walk down with Daddy. We'll stop in front of the minister. Jim, you will step forward, Daddy will hand me over and step back to join Mama and the others. The four of us, you Anne, and Davy, Jim and I, will turn and face the minister. The music will stop, the ceremony will begin and when it's over, more music. Jim and I will walk back to the house together, Anne and Davy will follow, then Mary and Kevin, then Mama and Daddy and Calvin. We'll take the rest of the pictures, then go back outside for the reception, or picnic or circus or whatever it turns out to be, and that's all. Okay? Does everybody understand what they're to do?"

She looked around at all of us. Heads were nodding. It seemed simple enough. Then the bride bowed her head in her hands and burst into tears.

Mama and Jim and I rushed to Liz, but it was Mary who disentangled her and led her off to the bedroom.

"I'll take care of the bride. You take care of the rest of it," she told me.

Jim took an anxious step forward, but Mama put a restraining hand on his arm. "She'll be all right with Mary," she said. "It isn't at all unusual for a bride to cry on her wedding day."

My eyes met Davy's. "Will you take the table out, please?" I asked him. "And maybe you could ask your brothers to set up another table off to the side for the food. And find Calvin and send him in to me, will you?" I turned to Jim. "Mary will look after Liz and see that she's ready on time. Will you go out and ask Mr. Miller to step inside with his fiddle? Then I think perhaps you ought to go look for the minister and the photographer and tell them about the change in plans."

"I'm here," said a woman with a camera over her shoulder. "I'm the photographer. Don't worry about me. I know what to do. I'll just slip out and get a few pictures of the guests. It's a most fascinating crowd."

She slipped out and I was left alone with Daddy and my brother-in-law, Kevin. "I'm sorry for all the confusion, but I'm so glad both of you came," I said.

"Anything I can do?" Kevin asked.

"I don't know of anything. There's coffee in the kitchen if you'd like to have some. Excuse me, I have to talk to this man about some music."

Mr. Miller was at the door. I went to let him in as Daddy and Kevin went into the kitchen, looking over their shoulders in surprise. I couldn't blame them.

"Come in, Mr. Miller," I said and he stepped in and halted just inside the door, his fiddle in one hand and his bow in the other.

He was probably in his sixties, his face round and red, his eyes blue and merry. His bushy hair was white as snow and so was the full beard that reached to the top of the bib of his overalls. He reached up now and stroked his beard with the hand that held the bow, his eyes steady on mine, waiting.

"Jim says you will play for the wedding," I said smiling. I had met Mr. Miller before and knew him slightly. "It's very nice of you on such short notice."

He nodded. "I'll be right happy to if you'll tell me what to play," he said.

"I'm not sure myself. Do you know, oh let's say, "Always" or "Oh Promise Me"?"

He shook his head. "Don't reckon I ever heard either one of them songs, but if you'd want to hum them for me, I can pick up most songs after I hear them a time or two."

I dismissed that thought. I didn't quite believe him and there wasn't enough time.

239

"Do you know the wedding march?"

Again he shook his head.

"Which songs do you know, Mr. Miller?"

He put the fiddle under his chin, lifted the bow and broke into a lively rendition of "Turkey in the Straw." When the music stopped I heard a little wail of anguish from behind the bedroom door. I spoke up hurriedly to cover it.

"That's very pretty, but we need something slower for a wedding procession. Do you know any slow songs that you think might be appropriate?"

"I know "Down By Th' Ol' Mill Stream" an' "When You An' I Was Young Maggie Blues" an' I know "Let Me Call You Sweetheart"."

"That last one might work. May I hear you play it?"

He played it, his eyes half closed. His fiddle sang, his body swayed and his foot kept time with the music. I was impressed.

"That will be perfect, but do you suppose you could play it just a little slower? We don't want to have to walk down the path too fast."

He played it and I was satisfied and thought Liz would be, too, but she did have her heart set on the wedding march.

"Are you sure you don't know the wedding march? It's been around a long time. It goes something like this."

I hummed a few bars, then went to the piano and lifted the lid and played through the wedding march. When I finished, he asked me to play it again and stood with his head cocked a little to one side, listening attentively. Then he lifted the fiddle and repeated it exactly. I was amazed and delighted.

"That's wonderful, but don't try to tell me you've never heard that song before. You played it perfectly."

"Mighta heard it a time or two when I was younger," he admitted.

"Do you think you can remember how it goes?"

"Nothin' to it."

"That's wonderful. Now here's what my sister wants you to do."

I went over the plans with him very carefully. He nodded and went back outside. Davy came in with a slightly bedraggled Calvin. He was dressed in his suit, but his knees were dusty, his collar was up on one side, and his tie was under one ear. I was surprised to see that he still wore his shoes.

"Look at you," I scolded like any mother. "What in the world have you been doing?"

He evidently didn't think my question deserved an answer. He stood passively while I brushed him down and straightened his collar and tie.

"How is it going out there?" I asked, lifting my eyes to Davy.

"Okay. I think ever'thing is about ready. How's Liz?"

"I don't know. Go finish dressing, Davy. Is the minister here?"

"Jist got here. Jim's fillin' him in."

Davy went into the bedroom and closed the door. I told Calvin that he was to have a part in the wedding.

"Hold your arm like this, Calvin," I said, showing him. "My mother will put her hand on your arm like this and you'll walk down the path together. Walk slow. There's nothing to be nervous about. Mama will tell you what to do if you forget. Now sit here in this chair, and don't move until I tell you to and don't you dare take off your shoes."

I rushed into the bedroom. Liz was finally dressed in her wedding gown and she looked lovely, but somewhat detached and remote. I stepped into my shoes, at the same time grabbing a brush to run through my hair. Mary came and took the brush from me and pushed me unceremoniously into a chair. I smiled up at her.

"Thank goodness you're here," I said gratefully.

"You'd have managed" she said calmly.

I looked over at Liz. "You look lovely, Liz," I said. "It's going to be all right. Everything is ready. The minister is here and Jim is filling him in on the changes. Just be careful in those high heels. The ground may be a little uneven."

Mary fastened the spray of artificial flowers in my hair. I applied lipstick and powder and was ready.

"Where's Mama?" I asked.

"Here I am," she said breathlessly as she entered the room. "Just let me powder my nose. It's warm out there. It's an absolutley beautiful day, just perfect for an outdoor wedding, and the people are so interested and friendly. They all seem to think the world of you, Anne, and they're looking forward to getting to know Liz."

She turned and surveyed the three of us. Mary was putting the crown of white roses with the short veil on Liz's head.

"And here are my three beautiful daughters, all together for a change, and my baby, all grown up and — " She stopped, choked, and went to Liz. They hugged, both a little teary, and Mama gave a shaken laugh. "We'd better go before I get maudlin. The men are waiting. Be happy, Darling."

The wedding went off as smoothly as if weeks had gone into its planning instead of less than an hour. Mr. Miller, in his bib overalls, stood just outside the front door with his fiddle under his chin, waiting as instructed for the minister to appear. The group of people behind him stopped milling around and waited expectantly. I was standing by the window out of sight behind the curtain, watching with my heart in my throat.

"Ready?" the minister asked me softly. I nodded and he opened the door and stepped through it and paused a moment on the steps. Mr. Miller's bow came softly down on the strings of his fiddle and the strains of "Let Me Call You Sweetheart" filled the air. It might not be the most conventional of music, but then nothing about this wedding was turning out to be conventional. Unique was the word, I thought, but the music was so hauntingly beautiful that it almost brought tears to my eyes.

"All right, Jim," I said. "He's arrived. It's your turn now, and Davy's."

Jim took Liz's face in both his hands and kissed her tenderly on the lips, then he and Davy went out the door.

"Come and look, Liz," I said. "It's going to be a beautiful wedding."

She came and stood beside me and we watched Davy and Jim walking side by side down the path. I saw that some of the men in the crowd were grinning and whispering to one another, and it wouldn't have surprised me at all if one of them had called out some ribald comment to the two men, but they held their tongues. I let my breath out in a sigh of relief.

"Are you ready, Mama?" I asked. "Calvin, hold your arm the way I showed you and remember to walk slowly."

Mama kissed Liz on the cheek, then took Calvin's arm and they went out the door. Next it was Mary and Kevin's turn, and then mine. As I started slowly toward where Davy and Jim and the minister waited, I was aware of a small murmur that went through the crowd. I imagined it came from my students, a good many of them seemed to be there, and I allowed myself a small smile in their direction.

I was proud of the way Davy looked, standing there in his suit and tie. Jim looked nice, too. When I arrived before them and before I turned and took my place to their right, Davy surprised me by holding out his hand, his eyes holding mine. My hand came up to meet his, and as if compelled, I smiled back at him, then I drew my hand away and took my position.

The music changed to the wedding march and I almost held my breath, afraid Mr. Miller might make a muddle of it, but he played it faultlessly. Liz came down the path on Daddy's arm, beautiful and smiling and ethereal. Daddy's face looked stiff and sober, but perhaps the people would attribute that to the fact that he was losing his last and youngest daughter. Jim stepped forward, and Liz dropped Daddy's arm and took his. Daddy seemed to hesitate a moment before he stepped back to join Mama and the rest of the family where they waited. We turned to face the minister and the ceremony began.

They spoke their vows flawlessly, and when the minister pronounced them man and wife and Jim kissed his bride, a loud cheer went up from the crowd. They turned, Jim grinning and Liz blushing, the minister presented them as Mr. and Mrs. James Baker, then they started back to the house together. I took Davy's arm and we fell in behind them.

"Almost forgot there for a minute that you wasn't the bride," Davy said, low-voiced to me.

"I noticed."

"If we'd waited 'til spring to get married like you wanted to, we could prob'ly have had a weddin' like this one. Are you sorry we didn't?"

"No, not in the least, Davy. This is very nice, but I liked our own wedding just fine."

"You sure?"

"I'm sure. Davy, there's something I've been wanting to tell you."

"What is it?"

"I can't tell you right now, but later, after the guests

leave and we have some time alone — "

"Somethin' wrong?"

"No, nothing is wrong. At least, I don't think so, and I don't think you will either." I smiled at Mr. Miller as we passed him and went on into the house.

I went to Liz and hugged her and congratulated her, then gave Jim a kiss on the cheek which he solemnly returned. Davy gripped Jim's hand, and then the rest of the family was there and there was a babble of voices as everyone crowded around them. Only my father stood aloof. I went over to him and linked my arm through his.

"It was a beautiful wedding, wasn't it?" I said, then hurried on before he could answer. "I'm so glad the whole family could come. You and Mama and Kevin and Mary will stay the night with us, won't you?"

"I'm afraid not," Daddy said. "Their plane leaves at eleven in the morning. I'm afraid if we don't get back tonight we won't get them to the airport in time."

"Oh. I'm disappointed, there's so little time to visit today, but you and Mama will come down and visit us some weekend, won't you?"

"Maybe," he said with reserve.

"Good. I would love to have you, and so would Davy." I kissed him on the cheek and then the photographer was grouping us together for pictures and there was no further opportunity to talk, which I thought was probably just as well. I knew from experience that my father would have to come around in his own way and in his own time.

When the pictures were all taken except the ones of the bride and groom alone, the rest of us went out to join the guests who waited. The long table made of boards and sawhorses was loaded down with food, and a smaller table held wedding gifts. Few of the gifts were wrapped, and I saw that there were doilies and embroidered pillowcases and scarves, and a stack of hemmed dish cloths made of flour sacking. There were two rag rugs and a beautiful patchwork quilt that I guessed would be from Clemmy. The gifts represented hours of work and I was touched that they had gone to so much trouble. Perhaps they were things that they made up ahead of time and held ready for just such an occasion. I wondered what Liz's reaction to them would be, and I hoped she would not be dismayed. She already had so many elegant things stored away in her hope chest at home.

"Oh," Mama said. "They've brought gifts, too. We'll have to go in and brings ours out — "

"I think it might be best if we left them inside, Mama," I said quietly. "Liz can open them later."

"Oh. Yes, of course, Dear. I wasn't thinking. How kind everyone is being. I won't worry so much now about Liz living away off out here, especially with you being so close, too."

"The people here are wonderfully hospitable, for the most part. If Liz can just learn to take them as she finds them, she'll be all right."

Liz and Jim came out and were immediately surrounded. There was no formal reception line, but the men and children gathered around them to offer best wishes, with some questionable jesting and teasing from a few of the men. The women hung back, some of them getting the food ready to serve. Liz was beginning to look flustered, so I whispered to Davy that it might be a good idea to suggest to the minister that he say a blessing so the feasting could begin, and to set the proper tone for the occasion.

Davy raised his hand and his voice and asked for silence. The minister bowed his head and prayed, then Jim and Liz were escorted to the table and each given a plate. Everyone insisted that the wedding party be fed next, so I took a plate and got in line, realizing suddenly that I was hungry. None of us had had much to eat that day.

We ate, standing around in little groups. Daddy didn't come to the table, but stood apart and only accepted a plate of food when Mary handed it to him. The Carters, our friends from town, joined him with their plates and I was glad he wasn't left there alone, though I couldn't help thinking it wouldn't have hurt him to make himself a little more agreeable to the other guests.

About fifty people were present, and I found myself hailed which ever way I turned, so I hadn't much time to worry about Daddy. My students surrounded me and touched my dress with curious, caressing fingers, some of them none too clean. I suppressed the impulse to warn them not to get my dress dirty and smiled down at them and let them touch it as much as they wanted. The dress could be sent to the cleaners. It was not important enough to make an issue of.

Many of the parents offered rather shy congratulations to me on my sister's wedding, and said how nice it would be for me to have her so close. Some of them wanted to talk to me about their children and school, so I had little opportunity to spend time with my own family.

"Anne, Dear," Mama said, appearing at my side. "I want to bring the cake out here and serve it, since most of the people are finished eating. If I cut the pieces small enough, I think there will be enough for everyone. Liz and Jim are agreeable. What do you think?"

"I think it's a good idea, Mama. Maybe you can get Davy and Kevin to carry it out for you."

"What about the coffee and punch? I'm afraid there won't be nearly enough of that to go around."

"I think we'll have to forget about the coffee, but I have several packages of Kool-aid I could make up and add to the punch. No one will notice, or if they do, they won't mind." I smiled at the woman who was standing beside me. "Excuse me," I said. "I'll be back in a few minutes."

"The only thing is," I said to Mama as we started to the house, "I don't have a container large enough to hold enough to serve everyone."

"Do you suppose Clemmy might have something?"

"Possibly. I'll go ask her and I'll find Davy and Kevin and send them in to you."

Davy and Kevin carried the cake out and Clemmy unearthed a big crock that held five gallons. She washed it, then had one of her grandsons carry it to the table for me, and then carry several buckets of water so I could mix the Kool-aid there at the table. I added what ice I had and the punch was ready. My sister-in-law Ellen came and volunteered to serve it. I put Clemmy's water dipper in her hand and stepped aside. Mama was taking the top layer off the cake to save for Jim and Liz, then she began to cut the rich cake into small pieces and serve it to the children who gathered around. My sister Mary came over to join me.

"This is quite a place you have here," she said. "Country living must be agreeing with you. I've never seen you looking better. Or is it marriage that's agreeing with you?"

"Both, I guess," I answered.

"I like the appearance of your husband." Her eyes left Davy where he was standing talking with another man and met mine with a glint of amusement. "Your hillbilly husband," she amended.

"And I know exactly who described him to you that way," I said dryly.

She laughed. "Poor old Daddy. I don't think he's having a very good time."

"No, I'm afraid not, but I know what it must have cost

him to come here today and I appreciate it. I just wish the four of you could stay longer and get better acquainted with Davy. Daddy says you have to leave this evening."

"Yes. I suppose it's best, although — But anyhow, next summer I'm coming home for my vacation and spending the whole time with my family. All right if Mama and I decide to get away from it all and come out to spend a week or so with you here?"

"We'd love to have you, but just you and Mama? Daddy may not be ready to come yet, but don't you think Kevin would enjoy it?"

"He's quite involved with his job and we're not always able to get our vacations at the same time," she said, and I thought she sounded evasive. I felt a touch of concern. "Well," she said, changing the subject, "this has turned out to be quite some wedding, hasn't it?"

"Yes, it's a wonderful beginning for Jim and Liz, all the neighbors rallying around like this. It means a lot to Jim, I know."

Mary raised her eyebrows at me. "You think they came because of Jim?"

"Why of course. They don't know Liz, at least most of them don't, but they've known Jim most of his life. He grew up out here, you know."

"So I understand, but I've been mingling and I've been listening and observing, and I've come to the conclusion that most of these people are here because of you."

"Because of me?" I asked blankly.

"Yes. According to what I've been hearing, the kids just love 'teacher' and they begged so hard to come to the wedding so they could see you in your pretty dress that their parents gave in and brought them. You seem to be very popular around here."

"But — "

"Oh they like Jim and wish him well, and they were

curious about the girl he was going to marry, but I doubt if that would have been enough to bring them. They came because of you. Of course, I wouldn't dream of telling Liz that."

"Oh no! Please don't. I'm afraid she wouldn't like it."

"I won't. Our little sister has some growing up to do yet, I'm afraid. Here comes your husband. I must say I'm impressed. I would never have recognized him from Daddy's description. Or Jim either," she added with a mischievous look at me.

Davy came and put his arm along my shoulders and smiled tentatively at my sister. "I was jist talkin' to your daddy," he said. "He says you can't stay."

"We can stay awhile, but not long, I'm afraid," she said. "I was telling Anne that I may come back in the summer and I'd like to visit you then. I love your house and its setting. You must be an artist at heart. Anne says you planned it and built it yourself."

"Anne helped me draw up the plans, and I had help buildin' it," he said. "You're welcome to come and visit us any time."

"Thank you. I'm going to take you up on that." She looked from Davy to me with understanding in her eyes. Davy seemed upset, and she evidently detected it and decided to leave the two of us alone. "I see they're starting to open the gifts," she said. "Excuse me, I must get a better look at that quilt."

"What is it, Davy?" I asked when she was gone.

"Nothin'. It's just that your Daddy more or less let me know he wasn't stayin' in no house of mine any longer than he had to."

"I'm sorry. My father is — well, he's having a hard time accepting both mine and Liz's marriage, I'm afraid. Give him time. He'll come around."

"He thinks I'm not good enough for you, don't he?"

"You're just not the man of his choice, that's all. Now let's forget it and go look at the gifts. My father is his own worst enemy at times. Don't let it bother you."

"I won't, if you're not lettin' it bother you."

"I've known for some time of my father's attitude toward you and I've come to grips with it. I promise you, Davy, that it doesn't bother me."

His arm tightened a moment and he looked less troubled. "What was it you was wantin' to tell me earlier?" he asked.

"Something — perhaps — very nice. Something you'll like, I'm sure, but I can't tell you now. It will have to wait until we're alone."

He raised his brows inquiringly, but I just smiled at him and took his hand and we went to join the rest of the people who were gathered around Jim and Liz.

Liz was holding up a long flannel nightgown amid laughter and ribald comment. The bottom was tied firmly together with string. Liz blushed and quickly stuffed the gown back into its paper sack. Jim was laughing along with the rest of the men.

"I'm proud of my little sister," I told Davy, low-voiced. "She seems to have taken all of this in her stride. I just hope she isn't totally exhausted by it all. It's been an eventful day."

Sue Proctor touched me on the arm. "I'm so sorry to interrupt you, Anne," she said, "but Jane says she has to talk to you. She seems pretty upset."

"I didn't even know she was here," I said, looking around. "Where is she?"

"She's over there on the other side of the wagons."

"All right, Sue, thanks. I'd better go, Davy."

I went around the wagons and Jane was there, her boys waiting nearby. They were a glum group in contrast to the other guests.

"Why Jane, why aren't you with the other guests?" I asked in surprise. "Have you eaten yet?"

"I didn't come for th' weddin'," she said. "Forgot all about it an' I didn't know I was invited."

"Most of the people weren't invited, they just came. Is something wrong?"

"I come to ask you if you an' your man would take these boys of mine an' raise them. I ain't no fittin' mama to have th' raisin' of anyone," she said in flat despair.

My heart fell. I looked quickly at Jimmie but he appeared to be all right. I looked back at Jane.

"What has happened?" I asked quietly.

Tears came to her eyes. She wiped them away with the back of her hand. "I thought ever'thin' was gonna be all right. I been followin' that schedule like you said for me to an' seemed like things was gettin' better, but this mornin' I wasn't feelin' good, so I didn't get up soon as I should've. When I did get up, them boys had made such a mess of th' house, it jist made me feel like there wasn't no use in even tryin' no more 'cause I jist can't keep up with it. Then Jimmie comes up to me an' says somethin', can't even 'member what it was, but my hand seemed to jist fly out all by itself an' I knocked him clean across th' room. Pert near hit his head on the corner of th' heatin' stove, so I decided wasn't nothin' for me to do but to bring them all in to you."

"Jane," I said gently. "I can't take your boys. I teach school all day. Who would look after the two little ones?"

"Figgered maybe your man could."

"Jane, you don't mean this. You're upset, that's all. You'll feel differently when you've had time to think it over."

"Will you take jist Jimmie then? Seems like he's th' only one I keep knockin' around."

"No, I can't do that. Jimmie is your son. Think how

he'd feel if his mother just up and gave him away. Besides, you love him, I know you do."

"But I'm gonna end up hurtin' him real bad."

"Was he hurt this morning?"

"No, but he coulda been, jist like that little boy you told me about in St. Louis."

"At least you're aware of the problem and you're working on it. You can't expect everything to straighten itself out immediately. Things are improving, you said so yourself. There's bound to be a few setbacks. The thing is, you have to learn from your mistakes, from the things that happen, so you can avoid them happening again. I don't think Jimmie was hurt this time, so all is not lost. I tell you what, why don't you come with me now, you and the boys, and get yourselves a plate."

"I couldn't do that. I didn't bring nothin'."

"But there's plenty of food. It will just go to waste. Come on, Jane. Please."

"I couldn't. It wouldn't be right. 'Sides, we ain't dressed for no party."

"You look fine. If you don't want to eat, then at least come and have some cake and punch. My mother made the cake and I made the punch and it's for everyone, whether they brought anything or not. Besides, I promised all the children at school I'd give them a piece of wedding cake and I can't leave your boys out. That wouldn't be right."

She hesitated. I raised my voice to the boys who were standing a few feet away. "Come on, boys. Let's go have some cake and punch. Anyhow, this is what you need, a chance to get away from the usual routine and be around other people," I said, urging her forward with a hand on her arm. "I won't take your boys, but I'll do everything in my power to help you, but let's forget all that now. We'll talk about it later."

I served Jane and her boys the punch and cake myself. I saw Sue looking our way, so I beckoned her to come join us, her baby in her arms.

"More cake, Sue?" I asked.

"I don't think so. It was very good, but I'm full."

"How is little David? May I hold him?"

She gave the baby to me and I took him and snuggled my face into his soft, warm little neck, and thought how wonderful it would be to have one of my own. I lifted my head to see Davy's eyes on me. I smiled at him and gave the baby back to Sue.

"Jane, I think my sister is getting ready to go change so they can leave for their honeymoon," I said. "I want to go with her and see her off. Are you going to be all right until we can sit down and talk again?"

"I'm all right."

"Good. Why don't you stay and let Sue introduce you to some more of the neighbors and let the boys play with the other children for awhile? Then perhaps Sue and Lewis can give you a ride home. Can you do that, Sue?"

"Yes, of course."

"Sorry I come here like this, botherin' you — " Jane began a little gruffly.

"It was no bother, and you're always welcome. Excuse me now and I'll see you later."

Mary and Mama and I all went in with Liz when she went in to change out of her wedding dress. I promised I'd pack up the wedding gifts and keep them for her until she returned. She decided to wait to open the gifts we had given her, it was past time that she and Jim were gone, she said. They had some distance to go.

She went back out dressed in a flowered cotton dress and looking very pretty. She and Jim thanked everyone for coming and for the food and the gifts, then they were driving away in Liz's car amid waves and shouted goodbyes. None of us knew their destination.

The guests began to gather up their things and leave also. Ellen and Tom and their family stayed to help clean up, and with their help and Clemmy's and that of my own family, everything was soon back to normal. When only my own family was left, I invited them inside for a cup of coffee before they started home.

CHAPTER TWENTY

Of These Contented Hills

My family stayed about an hour, but it was obvious to everyone that Daddy was uncomfortable and anxious to leave. I didn't try to detain them when he rose and said it was time to be on their way. I knew it would serve no good purpose to upset him.

We said our goodbyes and I kissed Daddy just as warmly as I kissed my mother and my sister. Kevin stood holding my hand for a long time as if he wanted to say something, but he ended up just giving my hand an extra pat and releasing it to shake hands with Davy. Daddy shook Davy's hand just briefly when Davy held it out to him and then he went on to the car.

"Come again, all of you!" I called after them as they drove away.

"It's been quite a day," I sighed when they were out of sight.

"Yes. Are you tired?"

"Exhausted. Aren't you?"

"I'm beat. Guess I better get at the chores. Calvin don't have to come this time. I sent him in to change his clothes. He was playin' marbles earlier with the Decker boys. That suit won't never be the same, I'm afraid."

"No, probably not, but he looked so cute in it, and so did you, Davy. I was proud of my men folks."

"I'm glad if you was — were proud of me, but I'm not so sure I like bein' called cute," he protested.

"Handsome then. I'm going to go in and lie down."

"Don't fix any supper for me. I couldn't eat a bite."

"I won't," I answered. "I don't intend to do a thing for the rest of the evening."

He took the milk bucket and went out to do the chores. I went to lie down on the sofa. Calvin was reclaiming his room, carrying his things from the utility room. I didn't get up to help him. I was tired and there was a lot to think about.

I fell into a light doze, and when I roused, Calvin was saying goodnight, and Davy was reading his newspaper, sitting in his favorite rocker. I yawned and stretched, but didn't get up.

"Why don't you go on to bed?" Davy asked me.

"I'm too lazy," I said.

He laid his paper aside and came over and sat down on the sofa beside me, brushing my hair back from my forehead with a gentle hand.

"Want me to carry you to bed?" he asked.

"No, I'm too comfortable where I am. Thank you for being so nice to my family, Davy. Liz was a beautiful bride, wasn't she?"

"Yes, but I had most of the people I talked to kept tellin' me how pretty you was lookin'. I agree with them."

"Thank you, Davy. It's sweet of you to say so. Jim was happy, wasn't he, and he acted so proud of Liz. I do hope they'll be happy together. Do you think they will?"

"Don't know why not. Seemed to me the knot was tied 'bout as tight as it could be tied, with what the preacher said, and with them promisin' to cleave together for better or for worse, in sickness and in health, in front of all them people. I'd sure be afraid to go back on a promise made like that."

"Would you, Davy?"

"Course I would. Wouldn't you?"

"Yes. It makes marriage seem a very solemn and

sacred thing."

"Brought back a few memories, didn't it?"

"Yes. It was a good reminder for those who have been married for awhile," I mused.

"You talkin' 'bout us?"

"What? Oh no, of course not. We haven't been married that long, only a little more than ten months. I guess I was thinking about Mary and Kevin. I'm a little worried about them. Something just didn't seem quite right."

"They been married very long?"

"Ten years."

"I liked your sister. I liked her husband, too, but he was pretty quiet, didn't have much to say."

"That's what I mean, Davy. It isn't like him."

"Maybe they jist had a little spat or somethin'. They tell me married folks do that sometimes."

I smiled and lifted my hand to his cheek. "So I've heard," I said.

"Well, maybe it's nothing, as you say. It won't do any good to worry about it."

"No. What about your friend Jane? Somethin' worryin' her?"

I smiled again. "She wanted to give her boys to us," I said.

"What?"

"She lost her temper again and decided she wasn't a fit mother. How would you like to have four more boys, Davy?"

"Great day in the mornin'! I hope you told her no."

"I did, but then she asked if we could at least take Jimmie. How does one extra boy sound to you?"

"She can't jist go around givin' her boys away. You'll have to tell her we ain't got no room for any more kids."

"Not even for one more?"

"I hope you don't mean that."

"But I do, Davy. How about just a little tiny one, about this big?" I asked, measuring about a foot and a half with my hands.

He looked down at me, puzzled and watchful. "What are you talkin' about?" he asked.

"What I've been trying to get a chance to tell you all day. In fact, for several days. Davy, there's a possibility, just a possibility, you understand, that we're going to have a baby."

He didn't say anything, just sat looking down at me, his expression almost stunned. Then, the gladness growing in his eyes, he gathered me up in his arms and put his face against me.

"A baby?" he asked, his voice muffled.

"Yes."

"Are you sure?" He lifted his head and looked at me, but his arms still held me.

"No, Davy, I'm not sure, it's much too soon," I said, feeling almost contrite. "I just noticed it myself a few days ago. We've been so busy and there's been so much going on — I probably shouldn't have said anything to you yet."

"I'm glad you did. I'd feel bad if you didn't tell me. You think it might be?"

I hesitated then nodded. "Yes. I think so. I hope so."

"You're not upset?"

"No, I'm thrilled! If I find out it's not true, I'm afraid I'm going to be terribly disappointed. I'm afraid you will be, too, won't you? I didn't realize before how much I wanted us to have a baby of our own."

"Well, if it turns out it ain't true, we'll jist have to make sure it becomes true one of these days soon. 'Specially now that we both know it's what we want."

"Yes."

"What about school? It's sooner than we'd planned."

"If I've figured right and if it's true, the baby won't be due until the middle of July, perhaps a bit earlier. That's close to two months after school is out. I think it will be all right."

"And if it's not?"

I shrugged. "What can we do?"

"Nothin' now."

"In the city, I've known women to continue teaching when they're pregnant. Surely it won't be any different out here. After all, I'm respectably married to one of the local fellers," I teased.

"And what's more, you got lots of friends out here. I found that out today when I was visitin' with some of the people. I think half of them come today as much to see you as they did to see the weddin'. I'm awful proud of my little wife, and couldn't nothin' have made me happier today than what you jist told me."

"It's too soon to be really sure, Davy," I warned again.

"But I can tell you think it is, and I think so, too. Have you told anyone else?"

"No, no one, and I'd rather we didn't for awhile, if you don't mind. I'd rather it would be just our secret."

"It's okay by me. Will you want to keep on teachin', after the baby comes?"

"Not for awhile, at least. I'll miss it, but I think I'm ready to try being a homebody for a change. We'll just have to wait and see how it goes, Davy."

"Okay."

He buried his face against me again and I put my arms around him and we were silent. I thought briefly of my father and wondered if it would make a difference in how he felt about my marriage if I presented him with the first grandchild.

Well, whether it did or not could make no real difference in my life. I was happy to be a part of these contented hills. I thought of a word the minister had used in the wedding ceremony, a word I hadn't thought of for awhile but that I knew described better than any other the way my husband made me feel. The word was cherish. I was cherished, and what more could any woman ever want from her husband?

"I love you, Davy," I said softly.

"And I love you too."

"Yes," I said. "I know you do."

THE END